THE POTTS PAPERS

POTTS PAPERS

Terry Sanderson

First Published in 1996 by The Otherway Press.

This amended edition published 2021 © Terry Sanderson

otherway@dircon.co.uk

*CIP catalogue record for this title is available
from the British Library.*

*To Keith, without whose help and support
this book wouldn't have happened.*

**The following story is set in an alternative
and totally imaginary Rotherham.
All characters are fictitious
and any resemblance to any person living or dead
is purely coincidental and unintended.
All incidents described are imagined
and not based on any actual events.**

DESTINY 1

Mrs Brigitte O'Boyle was suffering from chronic catarrh. The damp weather always made it worse, loosening the mucous and causing it to flow liberally. She'd been through a whole box of Kleenex since she got up that morning and yet still the torrent poured forth. She'd tried everything — tablets, sprays, inhalers, bottles you sniffed out of, drops you squirted up. None of it worked and she continued to be a martyr to what her little grandson called her snotty nose. Yes, indeed, her interminable sniffing and constant gurgly nose-blowing tested the tolerance of all who knew her. Her husband had even moved into another bedroom in order to escape the constant attention she paid to her nasal regions during the evening and early morning.

The doctor advised her that the only option left was an operation, but she wasn't keen on that. The prospect of having a sharp implement shoved up her nostrils, even by a trained professional, made her feel queasy, and she immediately put the idea out of her head. The search for relief would have to continue elsewhere.

Now she was going down the "alternative" route. First she took a course of evil tasting herbal tea prescribed by Mr Chan at the Chinese Medicine Centre. "It will definitely clear the problem up in a week," he had said, but so far all she'd got was a nasty rash in the groin area. Thirty quid that had rushed her. A visit to Lourdes had not provided the hoped-for relief either, despite her devotion to the Catholic church. Lourdes hadn't seen a proper miracle for years, and she had come to the reluctant conclusion that Our Lady had moved on.

Then a friend suggested she visit a gifted healer, Pastor Harold Hindley of the Isaiah Knutsford Baptist Mission. He had quite a reputation, so she made an appointment.

He seemed a pleasant enough man, a widower of many years, wearing a large crucifix and with a priestly air about him. He was terribly sympathetic to her problem and, after explaining that he was a channel for the Lord's power (having been bathed in the blood of the lamb), agreed to a laying on of hands. He didn't charge anything for his ministry, he said, although donations would not be refused. She paid him twenty pounds in the hope that it might stimulate his powers.

Unfortunately, after a brief manipulation of her nostrils, he laid hands on her breasts and spent a good ten minutes massaging them and pinching her nipples. Despite her unease, she at first felt that this might be a necessary part of the procedure, and that his heavy breathing might actually be whispered prayers. "I'm trying to locate your

1

meridian lines which run from the bust area to the sinuses. If I find your pressure points you can get relief."

"What if that doesn't work, though?"

"Don't worry. I have alternatives. It could be that you are subject to demonic possession, of course. That is quite common. I could go to exorcism if the manipulation doesn't work."

"Demonic possession? Me?"

"Oh it can happen to anyone, Mrs O'Boyle. Some of the kindest people in the land are in the thrall of imps and devils. Evil spirits take many forms and cause myriad problems."

"What form of possession do you think I might be subject to?"

"Oh, you are almost certainly harbouring an incubus. They can be shocking for causing excess mucous."

"Can you get it out, then? Rid me of it, sort of thing? I'm not happy with the idea of being in thrall to the devil. The neighbours might get the wrong idea about my lifestyle if word got out that I was possessed. I'd like to have it extracted."

"I could have a go, although it often takes many attempts before the blighters give in. They're tenacious once they get a hold. It will require what we call internal ministry. Incubi tend to hide internally. I shall have to go for it with some consecrated wine."

"Consecrated wine? Have you got any?"

"Oh yes, certainly." He went to a cupboard and brought out a bottle of Martini. "The Archbishop of Canterbury himself has blessed this wine. I caught him at a garden party once and I asked him to do a quick blessing. I'd just won this on the tombola. So, given that his Grace has personally consecrated it, it should be quite potent."

"Do you think it will it work in my case? I'm a Catholic, you see, so the Archbishop of Canterbury has little or no relevance to me."

"Don't worry, it's thoroughly ecumenical. Now the procedure is quite simple. Just remove all garments from your lower regions."

"All of them? Including the panties?"

"Oh yes, particularly the panties. Don't look so worried. I am a doctor — of philosophy. This form of exorcism requires that I make the sign of the cross internally where the incubus is hiding. I shall dip my fingers in the sanctified wine before I do it. Just relax."

Hesitating to query his methods, she became suspicious when the front of his trousers developed a jerky protuberance.

"Now I might have to chase the incubus around a bit until I catch him, so don't worry, I'll try not to make it too uncomfortable for you.

Any preference as to which of the lower orifices I use? I don't mind, personally, front or back."

He poured a small amount of the Martini into a glass and dipped two long bony fingers into it.

Mrs O'Boyle gulped. Panic began to grip her. She was sniffing alarmingly as she rose from the chaise longue on which she had been reposing. "I think I've left the gas on," she shrieked and hurried out of the house as fast as she could.

"But you haven't had your twenty-quids worth," Pastor Hindley called after her.

"No but you have, you dirty old bugger," she called as she ran down the road.

Back at home she was despondent. It was clear that the Niagara of snot would require a miracle to cure. And where do you find miracles these days? It was hopeless.

And she had a little weep.

* * *

DESTINY 2

Evergreen Close was almost complete. Just a final bit of plastering to do, a bit of clearing up and then the punters could start moving in. It was a Saturday, so the builders weren't at their duties and the place was eerily quiet. Lots of pristine houses, but no people yet.

At the entrance to the Close stood a large hoarding, the sort with an optimistic picture of what it would look like when the curtains were up and the saplings matured. "Delightful individually designed houses" was the billboard's promise: shrubbery, hedges and the added allure of individual outdoor patio seating areas. Lucky would be those who took up residence in Evergreen Close, privileged would be the few. Just far enough out of the town centre to be quiet, but near enough to be handy.

Doreen Potts looked up at the sign. "Only three units still remaining," it said. She liked the look of Evergreen Close. It lay on the regular route she took between her home and Sainsbury's Superstore, so she had seen it taking shape from the very beginning. She even remembered the Salvation Army Citadel that had once stood on this site before they'd bulldozed it to make way for these desirable residences. For the eighteen months it had taken to transform that waste ground into Evergreen Close, Doreen had secretly harboured the fantasy that one day she would live there. At some point in the future, when her circumstances improved, she would be a resident.

Now that the National Lottery was here, there was always a chance that her fantasy might become reality. One Saturday night her numbers might come up, even though so far she hadn't had so much as a sniff.

"Call in and see our luxuriously appointed Show Home" the hoarding invited — and how could she resist? It would cost nothing to look, would it? She walked into the Close carrying her two bulging Sainsbury's shopping bags.

There were baby cherry trees growing at the end of each driveway, all untouched by the hooligans who blighted her own life, the little bastards who could leave no sapling unmolested or window box uprooted. Nobody who lived in Evergreen Close would have kiddies that snapped young trees in half before they got going, not like the monsters she had to live with.

The neat little gardens in front of each impressive architect-designed home were just waiting to be given the personal touch.

Oh yes, she could see herself here.

Following the signs to the show house, she opened the front door and found a little temporary office-type of affair, just inside the hallway, with a man sitting at a desk.

"Good afternoon, madam," he said, jumping up guiltily, as though he'd been surprised reading a pornographic magazine, which, in fact, he had. "How can I help you?" He discreetly closed the draw in which the magazine was secreted.

"Well, you could start by giving me a foot massage. This shopping's crippling me." Doreen plonked the groceries on to the desk in front of him. "Just kidding. Actually I was just interested in having a look at the show home. You know, seeing if it might suit."

The man, looked her up and down. "You're in the market for a luxury development like this, are you, madam?"

What was it that had given her away, she wondered? The loose sole on her shoe? The cigarette burn in her coat? The scorched texture of her hair following the disaster with the home perm kit, perhaps? Whatever it was, this man obviously had her sussed.

Unfazed, Doreen looked him straight in the eye and gave him one of her famous slow burns. This was an alarming facial expression she had perfected over the years to silence the kids when they were getting on her nerves. She had later discovered that the narrowed eyes and pursed lips also worked a treat when it came to putting men in their place. It was a look which brooked no argument, and it did not fail on this occasion.

The man looked away from her scornful gaze, replacing his own patronising expression with one of professional bonhomie. "Now, where would you like to start, madam?" he asked.

"Why don't you just give me the standard tour? You must have done it often enough."

The man nodded, smiled and indicated that she should pass through into the first room. She was impressed. Beautifully decorated, lovely furniture, plenty of space and the smell of fresh paint. She could just see herself sitting by the window or on the floral print settee, entertaining her friend Marje Bickerstaffe to tea. God, Marje would be jealous.

They went from the sitting room into what the man described as "the spacious kitchen-stroke-breakfast lounge". It made Doreen gasp. It was like something off the telly, with enough space to have a table and four chairs as well as the cooker, dishwasher, washing machine and hundreds of cupboards. Unlike her own kitchen, you could actually turn round in here without knocking over pans of scalding chip fat.

"As you can see, madam, its a dream kitchen, and for only an extra two thousand, all the fixtures and fittings for the show home will be included. You can't say fairer than that."

"And you could have your dinner in here as well," said Doreen, continuing to marvel at the space in the kitchen-stroke-breakfast lounge. (If she lived here, of course, it wouldn't be dinner, it would be lunch; and supper time would be dinner.)

"Well you could," said the man, "but there is a separate but integral dining area-cum-entertainment lounge through here."

And so there was. Another room with a table and six chairs. A candelabra in the middle and a picture of a bunch of grapes on the wall.

The bedrooms were equally impressive. One had been done out in a "feminine" style — lots of frills and pastel shades. The other was "masculine" — tartan duvet cover, darker textures. "And each double room has en-suite bathroom", said the man.

Doreen was in her seventh heaven thinking about how she'd use the place. If ever her daughter Sylvia returned home she could have her own room. Doreen imagined what it would be like to have a bathroom to herself, no longer having to share with her husband, Derek. (Why do men make such horrible smells? she wondered.) Oh yes, if she lived here, she'd have the place exactly as she wanted it.

"Now, is there anything further you require, madam?" the man was saying as they reached the hallway again. "Perhaps you'd like to take one of our full-colour brochures to study at your leisure. Discuss the prospects with your husband?"

She could see from his face that the man had decided that she was a time-waster. He had indulged her only because either he was bored or because she had intimidated him with her terrifying facial expressions.

"Thank you," said Doreen, "I'll do that. And I'll tell you something, shall I? One day I'm going to live here. And that's a promise."

The man gave a pitying smile and opened the door for her. She left the Show Home feeling better. Somehow, her prediction had comforted her almost as much as it had amused the salesman. Something told her that it wasn't as daft as it sounded.

Unfortunately it was a dream that would have to be postponed for another two years.

* * *

6

Doreen's Diary 27th December 1995

This will be my first entry in this diary, which has been kindly given to me by my husband Derek as a Christmas present. It is a big, hard-backed book, three hundred pages of blank paper without even dates printed on it, so you can write as much as you want, not just squashed up bits about the weather and when people's birthdays are and what time your appointment is at the hairdressers.

My Derek is convinced that I have what he calls verbal diarrhoea. He says I can't stop talking and most of what I say is little more than waste product. He says that if I could confide a few of my thoughts to this diary every day, it might stop me saying them out loud, which, he says, will be a great relief to him. Don't get me wrong, it isn't that he's an uncaring man. No, it's more a case of he just can't be bothered. He says it is therapeutic to write down all the things that are getting on your nerves, psychiatrists have proved it. I think he's been reading too many of my *Women's Owns*.

And I notice that he isn't rushing to write a diary of his own.

Mind you, he's not a man of many words. Communication has never been a problem for him, mainly because he doesn't bother with it.

Up to now, I've been a bugger for writing letters to people, but I'm never quite sure what they make of them. I don't get many replies, but I expect that's because letter writing is out of fashion now. It's so much easier to ring up, isn't it? But there again, I don't get many phone calls neither.

This diary is going to be quite a challenge. I don't know whether I'll get sick of it after a bit, or whether I'll enjoy it.

You never know, it might end up in future years being like that other one, The Country Diary of a Victorian Lady. The difference will be that this one won't have no pictures of fluffy bunnies and wild flowers in it like hers had. Flowers and wild creatures don't play a great part in my life (none that Rentokil aren't interested in anyway). All the same, it will be the record of how a working-class, middle-aged woman lived and survived in the North of England in the late twentieth century, and that might be of interest to austerity.

You see, I'm surprising myself already. I never knew I could write things like that down.

So, if you're reading this in many years' time, after I'm dead, it probably means you've been rooting through my drawers.

I'd better introduce myself. My name is Doreen Potts, I'm married to my husband Derek. Because of circumstances connected with the redundancy of my husband from the abattoir where he has worked since he left school, we have been forced to move from our previous family home — a lovely little terraced house in a better part of town — to our present address, Block 3, 18th Floor, Flat 13, Ralph Vaughan Williams Towers, Cankersley, near Rotherham.

The flats were built in the 1960s and must have seemed like a good idea at the time. If you look out of the window you can see sort of archaeological remains of what was once a kiddies playground, long since vandalised and covered with abandoned mattresses and used syringes. Obviously at one time they had high hopes that this sort of place would prove a God-send to the homeless, but now it has become a sort of punishment block for those daft enough to run aground with their mortgage. The building society was merciless in regards to our arrears.

This estate consists of the kind of tower blocks that you sometimes see being blown up on the news. You know the kind of thing, a large explosion, a cloud of dust and cheers from the liberated residents. However, nobody has suggested that Ralph Vaughan Williams Towers are ready for the explosive experts yet. We seem to have been forgotten by the council, except on rent day. I never thought I would end up living in such circumstances.

My husband and I have two children: one is a boy called Gary and the other is a girl called Sylvia. Gary is twenty-nine now and has recently moved away from home to live with his friend Bill in a flat in Fosdick Road. I make no bones of the fact that my son is a homosexual gay person. I have no prejudices against lesbianistically or gay-inclined persons, male or female. How they live their lives is entirely up to them, I treat them in exactly the same way as I would any other handicapped person.

It has taken me a long time to reach this state of understanding, but as I say to my son when I go round to visit: "There's nothing to be ashamed of in the lifestyle you have chosen, our Gary. I'm proud of the fact that you've decided to be open about being unnatural. Your honesty does you credit. Just keep your bedroom door closed when I'm in the flat. I'm fine about everything so long as I don't catch sight of that double bed of yours."

He's a good enough lad, and his friend Bill is OK, too, although somewhat eccentric — he's a vegetarian and does not eat meat. He also says he's a vegan, but I don't believe in astrology any more due to several let-downs in the past. The pair of them have had their hair severely cut right down to the scalp and have grown beards. They keep

8

the beards very neatly trimmed, so I don't get a chance to moan much about that. They've also took to wearing discreet ear rings. It makes me cringe to look at it, but apparently it's all the rage in the gaeity circles. I don't know what the pair of them look like, but they seem happy enough so I leave them to it, interfering only when I deem it necessary.

We've not seen my daughter Sylvia for several months now. She's twenty-four and religiously inclined. She's always been a bit on the holy side and it was no surprise to me when she went off to become a nun. Unfortunately, due to the life she has previously led, the order she approached — the Little Sisters of Poverty, Chastity and...something else — was reluctant to take her. Our Sylvia was in floods of tears when they rejected her.

Anyway, I went round to see this Mother Superior about reconsidering her decision. I said: "Can't you help her to make a fresh start? Didn't Jesus say that we had to forgive us our sins?" "Don't keep bringing Jesus into this," she says. "What Jesus said has no bearing on my decision. I'm instructed to follow the rules of the order, and they say no people of dubious character should be admitted."

I said: "Just a minute, Mother, you ought to give her a fair hearing. Reports about her previous behaviour have been exaggerated, particularly them charges of soliciting — she simply stopped a passing motorist to ask the way to the chip shop, nothing more. The police was over-enthusiastic in arresting her." (I remember being up in arms at the time. The magistrate fined her £35 and bound her over. I was that annoyed I sent off to Amnesty International to see if they could make a fuss about it, knowing their reputation for righting miscarriages of injustices. They never came back to me, though —probably putting all their energy into the case of the Cleckheaton Seven at the time.) The Mother Superior tutted, but I persisted. I kept throwing her religion in her face — they don't like that, do they, nuns? After a bit she started to have doubts. She said she was gravely troubled about our Sylvia's commitment, but would allow her in as a pestilent. "I'll be keeping a close eye on her", she says. "I'm not at all sure she's got what it takes to be a Bride of Christ."

So our Sylvia enters the convent the following Saturday.

She'd chosen that order because she liked the shape of the head-gear. But when she found out you had to get up at four o'clock every morning and say prayers, it soon wore her down. She's never been fond of getting out of bed hasn't our Sylvia. "What do they have to get up at that time for?" she said. "Prayers are just as good after twelve aren't they?" Mother Superior was annoyed. "Stop querying everything," she said to our Sylvia. "You've signed up for a life of obedience and unquestioning devotion. Now set your alarm clock and stop moaning."

"I warned you this would happen", I said to our Sylvia, "but oh no, you would insist." She thought it was going to be like The Nun's Story where Audrey Hepburn was tempted by Peter Finch in darkest Africa. Unfortunately the only temptation our Sylvia was subjected to was in the form of a seventy-four year old priest with a club foot.

Then one day she arrives home with her suitcase. I said: "What's happened to your wimple?"

"I can't take it, Mam," she said. "I didn't realise it was going to be like that. They never give over praying and singing songs in foreign languages. They haven't even got a telly or a phone you can use. It's worse than that youth detention centre I was wrongly sent to that time. I told the mother superior where she could stick it."

I said: "Well, lady, that's put me in a right fix. I've gone round telling everybody at the Housewives' Register that my daughter has took the veil. They were that impressed. And now you've chucked it up. I'm going to look a right fool in front of Marje Bickerstaffe and her cronies. Anyway, you've made your bed, now you can lie on it."

She went into what she called "a retreat" (locking herself in her bedroom) to contemplate her future. A couple of days later she was handed a leaflet by these people outside Asda and she went off to join another order — the End-Time Charismatics I think it was. I can't keep up with her, she's been through them all now — Methodists, Presbyterians, Pentecostals, Jesus's Army, Scientologists, Moonies, Daughters of Satan, you name it. These Charismatics sound a lot better than the nunnery, though, as there are more young people — lads especially — and she does get out and about collecting money for their guru.

We haven't heard nothing from her for months. I said to our Gary, "Do you think she's all right?" He said: "They'll have brain-washed her by now. She's probably involved in a gun siege in America, waiting to get blown up by the FBI."

"Well," I said, "that'll suit her better than the convent. There wasn't much excitement there. No activities to interest young people. Not even a billiard table."

Anyway, we're awaiting to hear from her as to the latest beliefs she holds.

Yes, our life here at Vaughan Williams Towers is a bit sordid. It would be lovely to be able to live somewhere where you didn't have to have barbed wire over your bathroom window. This flat is about as low as you can get short of the Sally Army doss-house, and as for the other people who live in this block — well...I spend most nights lying awake listening for someone interfering with the lock and then footsteps in the hallway. You can't trust nobody. We had the door reinforced but they still managed to get my rent money by putting a fishing rod through the letterbox and getting it off the telephone table.

Take the next door neighbours, the Duddys. I think they used to be gypsies at one bit, going round with a caravan and having petitions got up against them every time they parked.

They're not suited to living in one place, they're nomadic by nature, you see, they need to be on the move. But the council insisted that they stay put and now I think normal life has driven them round the bend.

They've turned most of the landing into a scrapyard. I know we've all got to make a living somehow, but every time you go outside there seems to be yet another knackered car all in pieces. It's a mystery to me how they get it all up here.

Mrs Duddy was fine when we first moved in. In fact she even helped us with the furniture. Carried our solid oak wardrobe right up them steps single-handed as though it was an empty cardboard box. Couldn't do enough for us at first, all laughing and joking and fetching pieces of lucky heather round, and I could have listened to her stories of life on the road for hours. I thought: thank God we've got reasonable neighbours, perhaps it's not going to be so bad living here after all.

Then one day she knocks on the door. When I opened it I saw this wild-eyed version of Mrs Duddy standing there — hair all over the place, clothing in disarray, snarling.

"Do you know anything about that necklace?" she shouts.

"Necklace, Mrs Duddy?" I said, it was frightening to see the transformation.

"That missing necklace, do you know anything about it? And another thing," she said, jabbing her finger at me, "is this a brothel? I got a message yesterday that you're running a brothel here."

"Who told you that?"

"It was transmitted through my teeth, so I know it's true."

I was confused, but glad I hadn't took the security chain off the door. Turns out she's just been discharged from St Joseph's on tablets.

She has the peripathetic psychiatric nurse come round to see her on Mondays and Thursdays to give her a top-up and check she's stable.

I stopped this nurse one day and asked her what was going off. She said everything was under control so long as Mrs Duddy kept taking her drugs. I said: "What the hell is she on? It's like living next door to Dr Jekyll and Mr Hyde."

She said: "It's nothing to worry about. If you have any problems, just remind her to go and home and take her tablets."

I've every sympathy with Mrs Duddy, of course, my heart goes out to all those who suffer with their sanity. It could happen to anybody — in fact, living round here, it's almost inevitable.

But how am I supposed to cope with her? I've had no training in looking after the nervously broken down. "Care in the community" it's called apparently, which seems to roughly translate as "let the neighbours deal with it."

And the rest of them are little better. Five lads she's got living there on and off, and not one of them looks the full shilling. God knows how she ever conceived them because her husband only seems to come out of prison when she's in St Joseph's. They must have coincided on some occasions, I suppose. They've got an enormous great dog chained up outside the front door, their Jukels. I call it "a dog" but it looks more like something that should be in a cage at the zoo with notices warning you not to put your fingers in.

And the racket they kick up in there! I'm sure they've still got their horse, the one that used to pull their caravan when they were on the road. In the flat, I mean! I'd swear I've heard whinnying and neighing sounds coming though the wall, but them lads get up to all sorts, so you never can tell. It goes on all night long — banging and hammering, dragging heavy objects across the floor and playing loud music in the small hours. We've tried wearing ear plugs but then you can't hear the smoke detector going off when them youths are putting petrol-soaked rags through the letterbox.

On the other side we've got a single mother, Angela.

She's nice enough, if something of an inadequate. Usual story: skirts up to her navel, bringing strange men home every night, always got the tally man on the doorstep — and as gormless as they come. She's no control over that kiddy of hers, their Dolph. I saw them in the supermarket the other day, the little lad was running wild with a shopping trolley.

He was knocking displays down and opening packets of biscuits. The shelf-stacker was at his wit's end. Angela didn't seem concerned, though.

In the end, Dolph rammed the trolley straight into my ankles. I was livid. I said to his mother: "Can't you keep that little bleeder under control? He's lethal with that trolley."

She says: "He can't help it, he's allergic to E-numbers. It's made him hyperactive."

I says: "Well if that's the case, should he be eating all them blue and mauve sweets?"

She was preoccupied with a tin of pilchards she'd slipped into her pocket. I think she was debating whether or not to risk it at the checkout. "I've tried everything," she says, "I just can't calm him down."

Well, I calmed him down all right: I shut the lid of the freezer cabinet on his head. That sedated him for five minutes.

I live in hopes that my Derek will get another job at some point so that we can improve our lot, but it's almost impossible. He's fifty-two now and he's got no experience at nothing, except slitting animals throats, and there's not much call for that in these days of saving the whales, is there? He's become that depressed about it all, he just sits there most of the time, staring into space and shaking his head now and then. I try to chivvy him up, but he's getting deeper and deeper into this woeful way of seeing the world. He's always been a bit of a misery, but it gets worse. Always look on the dark side of life, that's his motto.

All this has conspired against us. I never thought I would have to sink as low as this. I try to keep my dignity, but poverty and dignity don't seem to go together very well.

Still, I was determined to enjoy Christmas come hell or high water, despite the fact that it has been one of the worst years of my life, as regards wallowing in the gutter. Derek said this was our opportunity to have some time away from the Vaughan Williams and do something a bit different. I wasn't adverse to that.

Although I class myself as a traditionalist as regards religious festivals (eggs at Easter, haddock on Good Friday and a glass of light ale for the Queen's Birthday) I had to draw the line at Derek's suggestion that we spend Christmas Day with his mother in Congleton.

Don't get me wrong. I've nothing against Congleton; it's his mother I can't stomach. She's been the same ever since her husband was fatally killed several years back in an accident concerning a revolving door and a self-erect umbrella. Chance in a million the coroner said, but all the same I haven't trusted the front entrance to the municipal library since. The tragedy has turned her head and her nerves have gone haywire. Whilst I've got every sympathy with nerves — after all, I've got them myself — she definitely overdoes it. Last time we went to see her she did nothing but complain about her failing bodily functions. She was cracking on that she'd caught the sleeping sickness off a mosquito. I said: "Don't be so silly, Iris, they don't have mosquitoes in Congleton. They only have them in tropical countries, Spain and places like that."

"Oh, is that right?" she says. "And what was that flying round my bedroom light last night, then, a bloody swing-wing jet?" She can be right sarky when the mood takes her.

"If I haven't got the sleeping sickness," she says, "how do you explain the fact that after half past eleven every night I can hardly keep my eyes open? That's not normal."

What can you say? We had all on restraining her from taking a taxi to the outpatients department at the Hospital for Tropical Medicines. She'd already been there once that week seeking a second opinion in connection with her elephantiasis. I'll admit that her legs were all swollen up, but it turned out she'd been wearing her elastic stockings too tight. I'm not saying she's a hypochondriac, but she only has to get indigestion and she starts speculating about whether it'll be a wig or a hat during the chemo.

If there's one advantage to living in this midden of a flat, it's that there isn't enough room for her to move in. She can drop as many hints as she likes, she's not coming here.

I said to my Derek, when he suggested Christmas in Congleton, I said: "If you think I'm sitting listening to her reciting her operations over my chocolate log, you've got another think coming. She's already referring to her clicky hip. You go and I'll make my own arrangements."

I was thinking in terms of my friend Marje Bickerstaffe, so I rang her up to see what she was doing over the festive season.

"My daughter June has made a point of asking, so we're going to stay with her in Ashton-under-Lyne. I don't generally hold with parking yourself on relations — you only end up rowing. But they've got this spacious semi-detached town house with integral garage, so we shan't be on top of each other."

"That sounds nice," I said, although personally I can't take to their June. Talk about stuck up — she's got more toffee in her nose than Thorntons. Every time I see her she's been to Marks and Spencers. Oh yes, she'll only have groceries from Marks and Spencers will their June. She even buys her All-Bran from Marks and Spencers. I suppose she thinks it'll give her a better quality of bowel movement.

"So what'll you be doing?" Marje says, "Going to Congleton?".

"Oh, I've been invited over to our Gary and Bill's. I don't like to impose, but they fair insisted. Wouldn't take no for an answer."

"That'll be nice for you, Doreen," she says with this edge to her voice. "But if I were you I'd take my own towel and eating equipment. And some kitchen roll to put on the toilet seat. You can't be too careful. I was reading about it in the Sunday paper."

I wasn't really listening to her. The fact is, I hadn't even considered spending Christmas with our Gary and Bill, but I wasn't going to lose face in front of Marje.

Anyway, I popped over to our Gary's place that night to try to sort it out. The flat's very nice — or it will be when they get it right. They've got pictures of nude men all over at the moment. There's one with this lad shooting fizzy pop all over his stomach. Last time I went over there I said: "I hope you've only put them pictures up to cover the cracks in the plaster, because otherwise you want to get something more tasteful. Goodness knows what the man from the gas board will think if he comes round to read the meter and sees that lot. Leave it to me, I'll get a lovely picture of a little girl and boy with tears running down their cheeks. Nobody can take offence at that."

"I could take offence at it," our Gary says. "These happen to be expensive prints from some of the world's leading photographers of the male form. They cost a fortune."

"I don't know about that, but it turns my stomach over having to look at all them heaving sinews and big bums. It's like having half a pound of tripe hanging on the wall. And look at that statue," I said, pointing to this plaster statue of a nude lad. "Couldn't you have got one with clothes on?"

"Mother, that's Michelangelo's David!"

"Yes," I said, "and you're Doreen Potts's Gary, but I don't want you on the mantelpiece with all your doings on show, do I?"

Whenever I go round to the flat I always take a bottle of Harpic with me. I know what men are like as regards cleaning under the rim of the toilet bowl.

When I'd got everything spick and span, I thought I'd broach the subject of Christmas. Our Gary didn't look best pleased and Bill flopped into his chair with his head in his hands. "Oh mother, we were hoping we'd be able to enjoy our first Christmas in our new home by ourselves," our Gary was saying.

"Well, I shan't stop you enjoying yourselves. You'll hardly know I'm here," I said. "However," — I trembled my lip and went for my coat in a meaningful fashion — "if you'd prefer it I'll stay on my own with the television in that vile flat. I understand the council does meals on wheels for lonely people who don't have a loving family to look after them. And the Samaritans are always on tap."

Our Gary just sighed and nodded his head. "All right, you can come — but only on condition that you don't try to organise us. Is that clear? No organising."

"As if I would," I said and put my coat back on the hanger. "Now then," I said. "Have you got your turkey ordered?"

"We're not having turkey, mother, we're vegetarians."

"Well, them that doesn't want turkey can just have the taters and sprouts and stuffing. Or I'll do you an omelette. And you'll want to trim this place up. Shall I pop to the pound shop and get a few festoons?"

"If it's all the same to you, Mrs Potts," says Bill, "We'd prefer not to bother with all that tinsel and stuff. We don't actually believe in Christmas. We aren't Christians."

"Well, you might not be," I says, "but our Gary is. I well remember the day he was Christened — the vicar took his particulars down in the vestry. It's all there in the parish records."

"The vicar's noted for taking things down in the vestry, especially after choir practice," Bill says. "And one of these days it'll be there in the criminal records. But it doesn't have much to do with what your Gary believes now."

"Well, I'm not here to try and change your mind, that's up to the Jehovah's Witnesses. To each his own, that's my motto. If you don't want to be a Christian fair enough. Although I can still recall the day our Gary coming home from the Sunday school joy hour when he was a kiddie singing 'All things bright and beautiful'. He got a Moses colouring book for knowing all the words, despite the fact he'd just had his adenoids out. He didn't say nothing about being a heathen in them days. I expect he's had ideas put into his head by somebody." I gave Bill a severe look. "Anyway, is it all right for us to have a Christmas tree, or is that against your religion as well?"

"The tree is a pagan symbol. I have no objection to celebrating the mid-winter solstice," Bill says. "Anyway, we've asked a few friends over for Christmas dinner. We're having Darryl from Maison Tracey's and Alice from the Lesbian Joint Shop Stewards Committee."

"That'll be nice," I said. "Although I've always considered Christmas to be a family time. It's entirely up to you if you want to invite strangers in, of course. I just hope they don't start with all that mucky talk about the difference between male and female sexuality while we're eating, that's all."

They've got a right set of friends have our Gary and Bill.

'Radicals' they like to call themselves, anarchists and subversives and all that. In reality they're just kids mucking about. They couldn't subvert the vicarage tea party.

When the day dawned I waved off my Derek and wished him every success in surviving Christmas at the Congleton Cowshed and arrived at Fosdick Street with my vanity case and a bottle of Bailey's. I got the turkey in the oven and started peeling the sprouts. Bill was making a lentil bake for himself and the other guests who don't eat meat on grounds of their conscience. I can't do with faddy eaters myself. I think it's their mothers to blame.

Darryl turns up about one o'clock and Alice comes a few minutes later accompanied by her dog, Rosa. What a sight! She was rigged out in a boiler suit as though she'd come to unblock the sink. And Darryl had that much scent on he smelt like a mucky woman's boudoir. And somebody ought to tell him the truth about them blond streaks in his hair as well.

The meal itself was a shambles with everybody eating something different. The turkey was hardly touched — there was only me and the dog interested in it. Alice said it was an obscenity, although I thought it was cooked to perfection.

Then they made a mockery of tradition by laughing and saying unnecessary things during the Queen's speech. In fact, Alice was encouraging the dog to cock its leg up against the telly whilst Her Majesty was speaking from Windsor Great Park. They all thought it was hilarious. I glared at them, but they took no notice.

After we'd cleared the table I said to Alice. "Come on, love, you can help me wash the pots."

"Y'what?" says Alice. "And what are these three men going to do whilst we're working?" "Well, they'll be having a snooze in the chair."

"If they're snoozing, I'm snoozing," says Alice. She hasn't got a ladylike bone in her body. If it were my lass I'd make her pluck her eyebrows and put her knees together when she sits on the settee. She looks like a navvy smoking them roll ups.

17

"Sit down, mother," says our Gary. "Bill and I will do the dishes when we've had a bit of a relax."

"I can't rest while there's mucky pots in the sink," I said. "I'll be fidgeting till I know they're sided."

So our Gary and Bill set about the pots and I went round with this box of Black Magic I'd been given by my Derek.

Darryl helped himself to the Montelimar which happens to be my favourite, but I said nothing.

Then I put a record on. Lovely carols from the Glasgow Orpheus Choir. Darryl started singing versions with dirty words. When he started on the Three Kings and the Shepherds and their sheep I switched it off.

I began to think I'd have been better off going to Congleton after all. At least her illnesses would have made healthier conversation than all this talk about positive images and the hidden right-wing agenda of the Labour party.

I said: "Can't you leave that sort of thing alone for a while. You're supposed to be on holiday enjoying yourselves. All this fuss over nothing."

"Nothing? Nothing?" says Alice. "We're only on the verge of becoming a totalitarian state and you tell me to enjoy myself. Well, I think I will enjoy myself. I think I'll pop out and vandalise the parish church. That's a major source of our oppression."

She gets this tin of spray paint out of her rucksack. I said: "The vicar won't be best pleased if you go spraying lesbian feminist slogans on the church, my girl. He plays holy hell if folk so much as chuck confetti these days."

I don't care about the vicar. He's a hypocritical arsehole anyway."

"That's as maybe, but he still deserves our respect. And watch your language. I don't know where you girls get it from."

"I take my inspiration from Rosa Luxembourg," she says.

"Well I prefer Radio Two, they don't have so much pop music and at least they sometimes play Herb Alpert records."

She just picked up her bag and stormed out.

"You aren't exactly diplomatic are you, Mrs Potts?" says Darryl. "You want to thank your lucky stars she never had her Stanley Knife with her."

"Why? What have I said? I don't understand these lesbians. Everything you say they take offence at."

He was getting his coat on as well.

"Aren't you stopping to play Give Us a Clue?" I said.

"No, I think I'll go for a little walk in the park. There might be a bit of action there if I'm lucky."

"There'll be no action in the park on a Christmas day," I said. "Everybody will be at home in the bosom of their family if they've got any sense."

"Well, I'll be looking for those who haven't got any sense, and who aren't interested in bosoms — family or otherwise."

He was talking in riddles as far as I was concerned, but our Gary was saying something about play safely as he saw him out.

After that it was ever so quiet. All you could hear was me cracking Brazil nuts. Bill stuck his face into this book he'd bought with his book tokens. It was called The Persecution of Homosexuals in 16th Century Spain, and our Gary put his head phones on to listen to the soundtrack from La Cage aux Follies.

"This is jolly, I must say," I said after a bit. "I think I'll pop over to the community centre and see what celebrations are going on for the lonely old folk. They generally have a knees up with their afternoon tea — angina permitting."

I'll tell you something, I've never been so pleased to see my Derek as I was when he came back from Congleton. We went up to the Trade and Labour Club on Boxing Night and had a smashing time. I was sweating for one on the Bingo and got tiddly on five Babychams. My Derek was so drunk he threw a dart into his foot and it's gone septic. Well, you've got to let your hair down and have a laugh from time to time, haven't you?

I don't know what's wrong with our Gary, he seems to have lost the art of enjoying himself since he's been knocking on with that Bill. Or is it just me that doesn't understand them?

* * *

Letter from Gary Potts

Dear Terry,

Thanks for your seasonal greetings and all the best for 1996 to you. I hope you had a good holiday. Bill and I had my mother round for Christmas dinner so you've no need to enquire what kind of time we had.

The purpose of this letter is to ask if you can give us any advice about a bit of bother we're having with our landlord, Mr Hindley. Since Bill moved in with me, Hindley has been constantly stopping me at the door of the house we live in (which has been converted into flats) and asking who Bill is.

As you may know, Mr Hindley is a Pastor in the local Baptist church.

I told him that there is nothing in the terms of my tenancy that stops me sub-letting if I want to. Yes, he says, but yours is only a one-bedroomed flat. Where does your lodger sleep? I said: "What are you, the bedroom police? You've no right to ask me that."

"It's my house," he says, "and I want to know what purpose it is being used for."

I said: "It's being used for eating breakfast in and for washing the dishes in. And occasionally I sleep here. That's what purpose it's being used for. The generic word is 'home'."

"I want to know what's going on," he said.

He already knows what's going on, of course, because we picketed his church recently after he rented rooms to a group that claims to 'cure' gay people. He didn't like that and said he would be writing our names down in his book.

The thing is, he's making life very difficult for us now. He rang my mother the other day and asked her whether she was aware that Bill and I were living together in an immoral relationship. My mother was up in arms and said that she realised the Pastor was trying to cause trouble between us.

She told him that our 'semi-natural lifestyle' had her full support.

He was angry, and now he's sent us a letter saying that he intends to take advice from a solicitor as to the legality of our tenancy. It's clear that he wants us out, but I like it here and I don't want to leave. Any suggestions what our rights might be?

Anyway, hope the New Year brings you everything you want for yourself. I'm spending mine with Mam and Dad at the Towers. I'd prefer to spend it with Bill, but he's working at the hospital over the holiday. As you know, a little of my family goes a long way. Happy New Year.

Your pal, Gary.

* * *

Doreen's Diary 31st December
I suppose this is the official start for the new diary, so I'd better kick off with my New Year's resolution. It's a simple one: we're getting out

of this hole. I don't care what we have to do to get away, but we're not stopping here one second longer than we have to.

It gets worse. There was another riot over Christmas. "A disturbance" they called it on the wireless. A disturbance! Makes it sound like a passing breeze ruffling your hair. In fact, it was terrible: cars blazing, police all over, lads chucking bricks. I wouldn't mind, but I've only just had the stitches out of my head from the last time. It's them drug dealers at the back of it. I went down to the corner of the landing to where that Nat Duddy hangs about with suspicious little packets for sale. I said to him, I said: "Can't you leave off for a day or two? All we want is one night's uninterrupted sleep."

Hence the stitches.

There was that much noise going on — police kicking doors in and charging about with truncheons causing residents to jump from fifth floor windows: in the end it was hard to say who was enjoying it most, the bobbies or the hooligans.

I said to Derek: "We've got to do something. We can't go on living like this."

"There's no way out, Doreen," he says. "This is our lot and we are doomed to endure it, so you might as well make your mind up to it."

Then, to cap it all, his mother, Iris, rings up. She doesn't want to see the New Year in at the sheltered housing, she says — Congleschwitz, as she calls it. (She says it's run by an ex-war criminal who slipped out of Germany after the last war to avoid Nuremberg. I don't think that's true. Mrs MacIvor was born in Dundee so you can hardly accuse her of being a German, can you?) "I want to be with my only child and my grandchildren over Christmas," she moaned. "This might be my last Christmas in this world."

"Tell her the flats have been condemned," I said. "Tell her it won't be safe for her because of the drug barons. Tell her there's an outbreak of mad cow disease — she'd be susceptible to that."

"Yes, of course you can come round if you want to, mother," he says. "Although don't expect good cheer, because it's in short supply this year."

So, the doorbell rings about five o'clock.

"That'll be me mother," says Derek.

"She never gave the signal on the bell," I says. "She knows what it is, one long ring and two shorts. You can't go opening the door to any old bod. It might be them hooligans."

"Go and let her in, for Christ's sake," shouts Derek. "And don't be arguing with her all afternoon. Let's have a bit of peace."

"I'd feel safer if I had a wooden stake and a hammer," I says as I went into the hall.

"Who is it?" I calls through the door.

"Open up. It's me."

"Who's me?" I says. "Have you got some form of official identification?"

"You know very well who it is, Doreen Potts. Now bloody well open this door before I kick it in. I've already been semi-mugged. If I stand here much longer I shan't be answerable."

I could hear Mrs Duddy shouting up the other end of the landing: "Do you know anything about that necklace, missus? If I find out it's you that took it, I'll scar you for life."

She'd obviously forgotten her tablets that morning.

Right, I thought, let's teach Iris a lesson. If she's not happy with her bungalow, let her see what the alternative is. So I pretended I couldn't get one of the bolts to open.

"It's stuck, Iris," I was saying. "I'll just get a bit of oil."

Iris was shouting: "Keep away from me, Mrs Duddy. Don't come any nearer. And get that bloody dog under control — if it bites me I'll brain it."

I could hear their Jukel growling and making threatening noises as Mrs Duddy let it off the chain. Before I could get the door open, it had gone for Iris. There were terrible noises on the landing — the dog growling and barking, Mrs Duddy raving, and Iris yelling oaths that would have done a docker proud.

I hesitated for a few more moments — just long enough to give the dog chance to get a grip on her — then I opened the door, expecting to see Iris blood spattered and in need of plastic surgery around the face and neck.

She stood there with her hat askew, nothing more.

"Hello, Iris," I says as I let her in. "That dog's a menace to kiddies, it wants putting down. I hope it didn't savage you did it?"

"It didn't get the chance, you'll be sorry to hear," she says, taking her coat off.

"Where is it now?"

"On its way to the vet's I expect," she says, straightening her hat and wiping the blood off the blunt end of her walking stick. "What a disgusting degenerate place this is," she says.

"I know, but there's not much we can do about the neighbours."

"I'm not talking about the neighbours," she says, "I'm talking about the state of your front hall. Haven't you ever heard of Flash? The bottoms of my shoes are sticking to this lino it's that acky."

She strides into the sitting room as though she owns it.

"And look at my Derek," she shouts and runs over to where he's sitting and smothers him in kisses like he's just been released from two years on the Burma railway. "Oh love! What's she doing to you?" She turns on me: "You aren't feeding him right, Doreen. He looks that undernourished, he could model for a Lowry painting. Are you all right, son? You haven't got a terminal illness you're keeping from me have you? I never thought no son of mine would end up living in a third world block of flats, starving to death from eating junk food."

"I've just nearly crippled meself fetching stuff back from the supermarket," I says, "and you say he's starving. I can hardly get the fridge door shut we've got that much stuff. And another thing. I give Derek a properly controlled diet. Low-fat, high-fibre."

"High fibre!" she sneers.

"Yes," I said. "High fibre. You want to be here first thing in the morning and have to use the bathroom after him. Then you'd know about high fibre."

"All you're concerned about is smoking. Fags, fags, fags, from morning till night. You could smoke kippers in here, no problem."

"Sit yourself down, mother, and we'll have a cup of tea," says Derek.

"I'll make it, Gran," says our Gary, who's seeing the New Year in with us.

As soon as he'd gone into the kitchen she started again.

"And them kiddies," she was saying to Derek, although aiming it at me. "It's a wonder they haven't been took into care. Where's our Sylvia to start with? Why isn't she with us?"

"She's exploring her spirituality," I said. "You can't ask for more than that from a daughter."

"Exploring her spirituality! It's religious mania gone mad. And it's all your fault. You must have unbalanced her. You're an unfit mother if ever there was one."

"Oh give it a rest, Iris," I says. "It's supposed to be New Year's Eve. Can't we have a truce?" "A truce?" she says. "A truce! Here's me, living in a so-called old folks home that could double as a concentration camp. I'm surrounded by death and decay, abandoned by my own family and you talk about truces!"

"It's not an old folks home," says Derek, "it's sheltered bungalow-style accommodation. You've still got your independence."

"It's not independence I want, Derek. It's my own kith and kin. You don't know what it's like at Stalag Congleton. I feel persecuted. Her next door talks about me behind my back."

"How do you know she talks about you if it's behind your back," I said.

"I've heard her through the wall," says Iris.

"Oh," I says. "So you're still listening at the wall with that stethoscope you pinched from the hospital are you? It's perverted."

"I happen to need that stethoscope to monitor my heart. You've no idea what it's like living with imminent death from cardiac failure. Look what happened to Gracie Fields. I could fall down the stairs and die of a broken shoulder before anybody found me in that bungalow."

"Well, you can abandon all thoughts of coming to live here, Iris," I said. "This place isn't suitable for someone like you who's supposed to be suffering from consumption. There's too much damp. And besides which, I couldn't stand it."

Derek was exasperated "Isn't there enough warfare in the world without you two going at it hammer and tongue," he says. "Can you pack it in for just five minutes."

Then he retires behind *The Racing Post*.

But I don't care what she says or what pressure she puts on, she's not coming here to live with us. I wouldn't trust myself — she'd have a pillow over her face within a week, I'd see to that. And she's always been the same, she's hated me since the day I first went home with "her" Derek. The feeling is quite mutual, I can assure you.

She cracks on she's a fragile old lady; in reality she's one of nature's survivors. When it comes to being crafty she could put a fox to shame. She knows the social security system from back to front — she's had every benefit known to man. In fact people at the Citizens Advice sometimes ring her up for an opinion if they get a particularly tricky case.

She's got the gas board twisted round her little finger, the catalogue companies are running round in circles — and the supermarkets! They'll rue the day they ever started their no-quibble returns policy before she's done with them. Ruthless, that's what she is, ruthless. All the same, she's never short of her Bingo money.

I'll give her her due, though, she's got us out of a scrape or two since we've been financially embarrassed. She knows what it's like when you're struggling to make ends meet, and she's put her special skills at our service a time or two. For instance, a few months back we got this letter saying we was going to be had up over the fifteen hundred pounds we owed in community charge. Pay in seven days or get summonsed it said. I'd forgotten all about the community charge — and I thought the council had as well, but they'd been tracking us down all these years and they caught up with us in the end.

"This is it, Derek," I said. "How the hell are we supposed to raise fifteen hundred quid in seven days? We couldn't do it in seven years. We're going to jail."

He said: "Don't worry Doreen. Jail won't be much different to living here."

I rang Iris up and told her about it. I thought she might want to bring forward any bequeathments she was thinking of leaving us. She came straight round to the flat. "Right, Doreen," she said, "get your coat on, we're going to get some compensation for that accident you're going to have."

"Accident?" I said.

"It's all due to the council's neglect that it's going to happen." She took me by the arm and off we went, trawling through the streets. We walked for hours with her studying the ground as we went. I thought this was weird behaviour, even for her, but there's usually method in her madness, so I kept my peace.

After about half an hour we got to Upper Houghley Avenue.

"This looks OK," she says, pointing to a loose paving-stone. She gets a little ruler out of her pocket and measures how much it's sticking up. "Five centimetres," she says. "That's over the maintenance guidelines. Now then, fall over it."

"Don't be ridiculous Iris. They'll never believe it," I said.

"They don't just take your word for it. You've got to be injured, have a doctor's note. I'm not even scratched."

She picks up her walking stick and gives me one hell of a whack across the shins with it. The pain was that bad I fell to the ground shrieking. There was blood all over me legs. I looked up for help, but Iris was busy taking photographs with one of them Polaroids. When she'd used up the film she looked round.

"Hang on," she says, as this old woman comes round the corner, walking her dog. At that point, Iris went into action.

"Oh God!" she screams (and when Iris screams, you know about it). "Me daughter-in-law's had an accident! Mrs! Mrs!"

This woman comes running up and says: "Eeeh, love, whatever's happened?" I couldn't talk for the stinging sensation in my knees and the shock of all the blood.

Iris says: "She's fell over this paving stone, Mrs. You saw it didn't you? Look at the state of her legs — I think she's busted one of her varicose veins."

"That's terrible," the woman was saying. "The council ought to do summat about it. That could have been me on that pavement — I walk past here every day. If that had happened to me, I could have ended up on a drip in the hospital and developed pneumonia. It can be serious can pneumonia at my age."

"Never mind that," I squeaked, "Go and ring an ambulance?"

"An ambulance?" she says, vacant as an empty shop.

"You mean for you?"

"Yes, for me."

She turned to Iris. " Only, I was wondering if my daughter would have come back from Canada to be by my bedside, you see, as I fought for life? I'll bet she wouldn't. Selfish little cow. Do you know, she never even sent me a Christmas card this year?"

"Get some chuffing help, you dozy old bat!" I shrieked. "I'm bleeding to death here!"

"Can you send for an ambulance, love?" Iris was saying.

"And I'll want your name and address — given that you saw everything."

"Did I?" says the woman, obviously totally incapable of remembering what was happening from one minute to the next.

"Yes, you did. Don't worry, I'll tell you what to say in court. Just give me your name and address."

She wrote it down and then said: "Right, I'll be off, then. I've got something to do, but I can't quite remember what it is."

"The ambulance," Iris prompted.

"Ambulance?" this woman says, totally bewildered.

"You were going to ring an ambulance. There's a phone box round the corner. 999."

"Oh yes," she says and sets off running.

I was laid there in a rapidly expanding pool of blood, hoping that the old girl would recall who she was supposed to be ringing by the time she got to the phone box.

"I had to do it when you weren't expecting it or you wouldn't have let me do it at all," Iris says as she ripped my blouse in half to make a tourniquet. "Don't worry. I've got a certificate from the St John's ambulance. It'll all be worth it, you'll see. This'll definitely get us a doctor's note."

She was right. I did get a doctor's note — as well as six stitches in my leg. The doctor said it was one of the most dramatic varicose vein ruptures he'd ever seen. I also got a £2,000 out-of-court settlement from the council.

Apparently this is one of Iris's favourite scams. She also paid off her electricity arrears after "accidentally" sustaining a fall on the bus.

Oh yes, she knows all the tricks. That walking stick gets her all kinds of sympathy, although all she uses it for is thrashing cheeky kids. Her activities horrify me sometimes.

She has no morality as far as ethics are concerned. I mean, I've never swizzed anybody in my life till I met her. Now she's got me involved in all kinds of semi-criminal activities in order to raise funds. Redistribution of wealth, she calls it.

"I only swizz the rich, never the poor."

And she doesn't only manipulate the local economy, she's also a dab hand at twisting your emotions as well. You want to see her in action, creating family upsets and then exploiting them to her own advantage. She'll do anything to set Derek against me, trying to split us up all the time. Consequently, you can never trust anything she says. It's all part of her propaganda war, you see. Talking to her is like having a conversation with Lord Haw Haw.

I expect New Year's Eve will involve another bout of illness. She uses ill-health like murderers use blunt instruments. It's her way of getting attention. Last year she had an epileptic fit just as we kicked off with Old Langs Zine.

The only trouble is, she's not an epileptic. Doctor Mohammed was fuming when we called him out right in the middle of his Hogmanay carry on. "I've a good mind to send you to hospital for some very painful and humiliating tests," he says to her. She didn't care, she'd got what she wanted — my Derek in a state of agitation and me crying me eyes out.

God knows what it will be this year — she'll probably be struck down with leprosy on the stroke of midnight.

* * *

Doreen's Diary 1st January 1996

What a day! I can't sleep so I'm going to spend the whole night writing down the details of what's happened. I can hardly believe it, and I'm having trouble keeping my hand steady. But I'll persevere because I think there's going to be something worthwhile writing in this diary from now on! I'll keep a record because I don't think that we're going to be quite so ordinary after the events of today.

I'd better start at the beginning.

Last night passed off OK. No sudden onsets for Iris this year. I think she was planning to develop a diabetic coma but I beat her to it — I slipped a couple of vodkas into her Guinness and she passed out before Big Ben had reached the final bong. It was lovely — her slumped in the chair snoring, with just me and Derek and our Gary having a lovely time shooting party poppers and cracking open the Sainsbury's Sparkling Perry — although I must say our Gary looks a bit thoughtful. As though he's got something on his mind.

Then the phone goes about five minutes past midnight. It's our Sylvia, ringing from the commune to wish us a Happy New Year and ask how we're all keeping. When our Sylvia enquires after your health you can be sure that she's short of cash. I said to her: "Oh it is nice to hear from you, love. I hope you get everything you deserve this year."

"That's what I'm worried about, mam," she says. "Would it be all right if I came home for a few days?"

"Course it would, sweetheart. We'd love to see you, although you might find it a bit crowded here."

"I'll see you on Wednesday, then," she says. I expect we'll hear the whole story then.

When I got back from shopping, Derek was sat in front of the telly watching the racing. Our Gary was at the table playing with his lap top and Iris was knitting furiously.

I collapsed on the settee, exhausted.

"Did you put me bet on?" was all Derek was interested in.

"Yes, I put your bet on. Another ten pound towards the William Hill cigar fund."

"Oh stop moaning at him," says Iris. "It's the only bit of pleasure he gets."

"Well he's no need to think he's having racing on all afternoon," I said. "There's a Bette Davis on at half past two and we're watching that."

"Not Bette Davis, Mam. Lana Turner," our Gary says.

"That'll do fine," I said. "Something you can get involved in. I'm certainly not watching them jockey's arses bouncing up and down all afternoon. Bloody racing!" I grabbed the TV zapper and switched over to the film.

"She were lovely, Lana Turner, weren't she?"

"She couldn't hold a candle to Magda Malkovich," our Gary was saying. "I thought Magda was the best of the lot with them eyebrows halfway up her forehead. And the way she used to walk about."

He gets up and starts doing this Magda Malkovich strut around the room. Derek looked disgusted and said: "Come on Doreen, I want to see if me third horse has won. I know it won't have, but I have to be sure."

He snatches the zapper back and puts the racing on again.

"Give that back to me," I says. "He was just going to murder her."

I switched back to the film.

Derek was furious: "We might be winning a fortune for all I know. I've got an accumulator running at Doncaster and all you lot are concerned about is Bette bleeding-chuffing-bastard Davis!"

"Look," I says. "he's just taking her for a walk on the cliffs. I want to see if he shoves her off."

"Let him have the racing on," says Iris. "This film's been on umpteen times."

"Well me and our Gary haven't seen it, have we Gary?" I says. "We want to see what happens."

"They struggle at the top of the cliff and she shoves him off," says Iris.

"Well, thank you very much, Iris," I says. "That has enhanced my enjoyment no end."

Derek switched back to the racing. The commentator was saying "And as Bargain Hunter goes into the winner's enclosure, we'll get the prices."

"That's me third one up," says Derek. "Sixteen-to-one. Sixteen-to-chuffing-one."

"So what? You've got three up, what about it?"

"I've only got to get another three. I know it's highly unlikely, but you never know."

I said: "There's about as much chance of you getting another three up as there is of me winning Brain of Britain. Let's have us dinner."

We had lettuce and tomato salad (which Iris embellished with a tin of tuna which put our Gary off because it wasn't dolphin-friendly). Derek wasn't interested in nothing but the racing. When it's on he just can't rip his eyes away from the screen.

"I can't see the fascination myself," I said. "Them horses all look the same to me. Derek, come and get your salad."

"This lettuce has seen better days," Iris was saying. "You don't store your stuff properly. If I'm rushed to hospital during the night I shall hold you responsible."

I tried to break the racing spell. "Derek, your mother says I'm mistreating her. If you don't come and get your tea, I'm going to stick this fork in her eye."

"Yes, yes," he says absently. "They're under starters orders."

A few minutes later, Derek suddenly jumped out of the chair waving his arms like a maniac. "Go on Terminator! Go on! Get in there!"

"9-1," Derek says. "Terminator did it for me. They're going in like magic."

"How much?" I said, catching him by the lapels. "How much have you won?"

"Well, nothing yet. There's two more to come. St.Christopher next and Catgut in the three-thirty."

I shoved him back into the chair. "Two more to come!" I said. "I knew it."

But my interest was renewed when the next one also obliged at something called seven-to-two.

"What now?" I said.

"Let me explain in words of one syllable, Doreen. There's twenty grand riding on the next horse."

"Twenty grand?" I says, going all quivery. "You mean twenty thousand pound?"

"Yes," says Derek.

"Can't you stop now?" I said. "Can't you just go and get the twenty thousand and leave it at that? Get down the bookies and tell him you want your money now, and bugger the three thirty."

"That's the whole point," says Derek. "You've got to get the whole six up. The last one's got to go in."

"And what do we get if it does?"

"Well, it's five-to-one at the moment. If it comes in, it'll be...£100,000."

I sat down on the settee feeling quite feeble. My breathing was shallow, I was seeing stars and my head felt as though it was floating away.

"I'm going to faint," I said.

"I know the cure for that," says Iris, and with great relish she chucked a cup of hot tea in my face.

"Feeling better now?" she says with a spiteful smile.

But the worst part was the waiting. I smoked about twenty-five cigarettes in the half hour between one race and the other. It was the longest thirty minutes of my life. In the end I was that worked up Iris had to give me one of her Valiums.

They were in the parade ring.

"Which one's Catgut?" I said

"Blue chevrons," Derek said, all cool and calm. "They're at the post."

Iris was trying to knit, but she'd lost her co-ordination and was dropping stitches. "I can't stand much more of this tension," she was saying. "If that chuffing horse doesn't win, I'll personally go down there and make it into a four course dinner for next door's dog."

"What time is it now, Derek," I was saying, lighting up another Rothman's.

"Twenty-nine minutes past," he says. "Don't excite yourself, Doreen, it won't win. Nothing I do can end in success. It's just fate tormenting me with another near miss."

Then I got this sensation in my throat. Terrible it was.

"I'm choking," I said. "I've got something in my throat. Like a cricket ball."

"It's nerves," Iris says.

"I can't breathe," I says. "I'm suffocating."

"Have another ciggie," she says.

"They're off," says Derek. "Hey, he's off to a good start."

"Is he?" I says. "Is he winning?"

"Give 'em a chance — it's over three miles."

They kept jumping over these fences, some of them stumbled and one or two fell. Every time they came crashing down, I thought: this is it, he's gone. But Derek said he was jumping well. Given that he was at the back he was hardly going to trip anybody up, was he?

"They've passed halfway now," the commentator was saying, "and Catgut has hit the front. He's one...two...three lengths clear."

"He's won! He's chuffing won!" I says.

"Hang on, there's still a mile and a half to go," says Derek, his eyes fixed on the telly like a rabbit hypnotised by a snake.

"Catgut is coming back to the field now," says this man on the telly. "And he's being challenged by Cornflower, who's making progress. Cornflower takes it up from Catgut, who is beginning to fade. Now it's Cornflower from Arthur's Seat and Milli Vanilli."

"What's happened to it? Where's it gone?" I said.

31

"It's had it," says Derek, slumping back into the chair. It's shot its lot too soon."

"Aye," I said, smacking him on the head. "That sounds familiar as far as you're concerned."

"Has it lost?" says our Gary.

"As good as," I said and I went to the lav.

"Two furlongs to go," the commentator was saying. "And it's Milli Vanilli and Arthur's Seat neck and neck. These two drawing clear. A furlong and a half now — and what's this? On the outside, Catgut seems to have got a second wind. Catgut is flying on the outside. This is amazing. Catgut is going like an express train and is coming to challenge Milli Vanilli and Arthur's Seat."

I'd no sooner got my knickers down when I heard them all whooping and shrieking in the living room. I had them bloomers back up faster than you could say Jack Robinson and ran back into the room.

"This is an amazing challenge from Catgut, but Arthur's Seat isn't beaten yet. They're fighting it out neck and neck. Half a furlong to go and there's nothing in it. Milli Vanilli fades away, but the two leaders are absolutely together. It's Arthur's Seat and Catgut. Catgut and Arthur's Seat. Two hundred yards to go and Arthur's Seat has a slight lead. Arthur's Seat has his nose in front, but Catgut is pushing. Coming up to the line and there isn't so much as a whisker between them. And as they pass the post it's...it's a photo finish. Photo finish between number two Catgut and number seven Arthur's Seat."

"Photo finish?" I said. "How long does that take?"

"Well, they don't have to take the film to the chemist, do they? It's only a couple of minutes."

I had like a lead weight in my stomach. Iris was the same.

"I can't just sit here waiting, the stress is too much," she says. "I'll go and make us some tea."

She goes into the kitchen, walking a bit unsteadily. I got through three more cigs while the adverts were on.

"It must be close," says Derek, "it usually only takes a minute or two. Catgut is bound to have been pipped. That's the way my luck goes."

Iris comes into the room with a tray of tea just as the announcer says: "The result of the photo is just coming through..."

You won't believe what happened next. That silly mare tripped over the carpet and — smash! the whole chuffing tea tray goes down the back of the telly. There was this crackling sound and a little puff of smoke and the lousy telly went dead.

"You clumsy old crone," I shouts. "What are we going to do now?"

I thought quickly. "I know — Angela next door. She's got a telly. I've heard her watching it in the middle of the night when we're trying to get some sleep."

I rushed round to Angela's flat and rang the bell. "Have you got a telly, love?" I said. "Only I've some emergency viewing to do."

"The rental firm repossessed it last week," she says.

"What now?" says Iris.

"The Duddys!" I says.

"You can't go there," Iris was protesting, but I was already knocking on the door. Mrs Duddy appeared with a face like a gargoyle. She's definitely not had her medication today.

"Oh, 'tis you again!" she says. "And your brood of demons with you!"

Normally I'd have a run a mile when I saw her in that state, but I was so worked up and desperate to gain access to her telly, I just said: "I'm sorry you're not feeling well Mrs Duddy, love, but I haven't got time for all this," and pushed her aside.

She was that shocked she just stood there for a moment. Then she said: "What about my necklace?"

"Oh shut yer gob about that necklace, can't you? If this horse has won, I'll buy you ten bleeding necklaces."

She seemed to calm down when she realised I wasn't going to take any more nonsense from her. Sensing this, the others followed me in.

You've never seen such a hovel in all your life — and I'm sure I saw a heap of fresh horse manure at the bottom of the stairs. Anyway, I got the telly on just in time to hear the commentator say: "And so there's Catgut, going proudly into the winner's enclosure."

Well, we went mad. I think Mrs Duddy must have thought she was back in that locked ward at St Joseph's when we all started dancing about and shouting.

But that didn't last long.

"There's been an objection to the winner by the second and there's also a stewards' inquiry," says the man on the telly.

"What's that mean?" I said, all the colour flushing out of my face. "What's a stewards' inquiry when it's at home?" Derek was downcast. "Catgut could get disqualified if he's done owt wrong."

"Won't we have won?" I said.

"No," says Derek. "He'll be placed second." He groaned and fell back into his usual depression. "I thought it was too good to be true.

Nothing as wonderful as this could happen to me." He shook his fist towards heaven: "Why are you torturing me like this, you bastard!"

Iris made a little whimpering noise as though she were going to pass out and had to be supported by our Gary. "Ask Mrs Duddy if she's got any major tranquillisers on the premises," she was saying. "Or alternatively ring up the cardiac unit and tell them to reserve a bed."

Anyway, we spread some paper on Mrs Duddy's settee and sat down to wait for the result. I'm telling you, dear Diary, I never want to go through nothing like it again. I had to go to the lavatory to be sick at one point. Then, when I saw the state of Mrs Duddy's toilet, I was sick all over again.

Eventually the commentator gave out the news. "The result of the stewards' enquiry is that the result stands. Catgut is the winner."

There was a little silence. It was as though Mrs Duddy had gone round with her mallet and hit us all on the head, we were that stunned. We were all waiting for the next complication, but nothing happened.

"Well?" I said, after bit, and very quietly. "Has it won?"

Derek seemed to be coming out of a deep pit, but when he reached the surface he just jumped into the air and bumped his head on Mrs Duddy's light fitting.

"Yes! Yes! Yes!" he shouts. "Bugger the lottery. Who needs the chuffing lottery! We've got a hundred thousand quid coming from the bookies."

It's a funny thing what money can do to people. Not only did Iris forget herself for a moment and give me a kiss, I actually went slightly haywire and gave Mrs Duddy one as well. It was something both Iris and me later regretted and we shared a bottle of TCP disinfectant mouthwash.

Still, the very first words that came out of my mouth when I found my voice again were "Evergreen Close".

* * *

Doreen's Diary 2nd January
You should have seen that bookie's face when we went round to get the money! You could have grated cheese on his teeth, the smile was that phoney. Worst of all he'd told the local paper about our happy news, so they'd sent a reporter and photographer round to record the handing over of the cheque.

The whole world will know about our bit of luck now — including them Duddys. We won't be safe in our beds after the *Advertiser* comes out tomorrow. But then, I suppose the poor old bookie's entitled to something out of it, even if it is only a bit of a mention in the paper. However my sympathy for bookies is limited. They've been pitiless with us over the years.

Then we all went out to the Trades Club and had a celebration rave up — gallons to drink, naturally, then a disco. We did the Birdy Song, Zanadu, the lot. Iris jumped on the stage while the turn was on and snatched the mike out of his hand. She was that drunk she tried to get everyone doing a Gracie Fields singalong, but nobody was interested. In the end the club secretary shut the curtains on her.

Derek looked like something out of a toothpaste advert: he was smiling that hard that I thought he'd got facial paralysis.

It looked as though he was catching up for all the smiling he'd denied himself over the past two years.

It was straight to bed when we got home, but of course as soon as my head hit the pillow I was wide awake. I was tossing and turning, trying to work out how we were going to make that £100,000 buy a home costing £150,000. We'd have to go cap in hand to another lousy building society — a different one to the one that had relegated us to our present state. The chuffing bastards. If they'd just been a bit more patient over our arrears we'd never have ended up in Vaughan Williams Towers.

I thought it only fair that I should now share my secret fantasy with Derek, so I rolled over in bed and poked him in the ribs: "I want to talk to you about our plans for the future now that we've got that money."

"I've been thinking about that, as well," he said, and his face had returned to its usual mournful state. "I've a feeling about it. It'll bring us nothing but misery. I can't stop mithering about what happened to that woman who won the pools. Do you remember her? Ended up with a market stall and her husband in a mangled car wreck."

I opened the drawer of the bedside cabinet and took out the full-colour brochures and flung them down in front of him.

"We're popping round to Evergreen Close tomorrow to see the man in the office about reserving one of these houses. Then we'll call in at the building society to arrange the mortgage."

"Evergreen Close?" says Derek, taken aback. "That newish development in town? We can't afford to go there, Doreen. Them houses cost a damn sight more than a hundred grand. Besides, we wouldn't fit in. Only posh people live there. You'll have to lower your sights a bit. Think in terms of a modest semi and a bit in the bank for that rainy day that's just around the corner."

"Every day's a rainy day for you, Derek. I'm not lowering my sights no lower than Evergreen Close, I'm telling you. If we put down a big enough deposit they'll give us a mortgage for the rest. It's a buyer's market. And we're good enough to live anywhere. Why should posh people have all the best things in life? We're entitled to some of them, too. We may have been reduced to the underclass recently, but that has been due to circumstances beyond our control, i.e. you getting the boot from the slaughterhouse. Well, we're moving on. We're going to be middle-class soon. And Evergreen Close is the way in."

"Oh no," says Derek. "It's got all the hallmarks of a disaster has this. It's a fantasy, Doreen. No building society is going to give us a mortgage, and we don't want one. Have you forgotten what happened last time? How are we supposed to pay a mortgage when neither of us is working? We'd be inviting catastrophe."

"We'll think of something. There must be a way. I'm desperate to get one of them houses. I've got my heart set on it."

Just then the bedroom door starts opening. I reached down for the baseball bat I keep ready for such emergencies.

"It's only me," says Iris, closing the door behind her.

"Aye, aye," I said. "The bloody trapdoor's opened and the demon king's popped up. What the bloody hell are you doing, barging into our bedroom at this time of night? You were laid out dead drunk half an hour since."

"I could help you with Evergreen Close, Doreen."

Then it dawned on me: "You've been listening at the wall with that damned stethoscope, haven't you! You are definitely perverted Iris Potts, eavesdropping on private conversations in people's bedrooms. Derek, do something about her."

"Is it right, mother?" Derek says.

"Here," I says, "you weren't tuned in last night were you? I can't bear it." (You see, in the excitement of the win, Derek had had one of his rare bouts of connubial interest the previous evening, and we'd given the bed-springs a bit of a jiggle.) "It's frightening. All our most intimate secrets being spied on by a geriatric sex monster."

"Oh shut up a minute," says Iris, sitting on the bed. "I'm not interested in your tawdry sex life. The fact that you've got vaginal dryness is absolutely nothing to make a fuss about — most women of your age suffer from it. And don't you worry, either, Derek. All men have their off days. Your father was a martyr to erectile dysfunction."

Derek flushed scarlet.

"Now listen," she says. "I've got a plan to help you out with Evergreen Close."

It's a good job she said them magic words, or I would have cheerfully launched her off the landing.

"How are you going to help mother?" Derek was saying "You haven't got that sort of money."

"Listen. You want a mortgage, I can help you get one. And keep it."

"We don't want a mortgage," Derek said.

"Be quiet, Derek," I said. "Go on, Iris — how?"

"I've got contacts. It's amazing what you can do with a few nicely-printed letterheads and an accommodation address. I've got this ex-solicitor friend who's helped me out in the past with some of my compensation claims. He'll be very pleased to give you 'special assistance' with your mortgage application — for a small consideration of course."

"We'd have to tell lies. We're not doing nothing dishonest, mother," says Derek. "I don't care how badly Doreen wants to live in a big house, we're not going to end up on the wrong side of the law. We're not doing it, and I don't want to hear any more on the matter."

"Listen a minute, Derek. Hear her out." I was mesmerised at the way Iris's mind was working, it was like watching Lucretia Borgia cooking dinner. But Derek wouldn't stop mithering.

"Yes, but even if we do get the mortgage approved, how are we going to pay it?" he was saying. "It'll be repossession time again before we've even got the furniture through the door. It'll be humiliation and degradation all over again."

"I'll see to it that you get your mortgage. And as for paying it — well, you could always think about lodgers," Iris was saying.

"That's an idea," I said. "Our Sylvia wants to come and live at home again. We could get her to chip in. And we could put an advert in the papershop window for a paying guest — must be respectable, no kiddies or pets, no visitors after eleven o'clock, full use of facilities — within reason."

"You don't want strangers in the house, Doreen," says Iris. "I could rent a room from you. They're four-bedroomed houses aren't they?"

I thought there had to be a catch.

"Just a minute," I said, switching the light on. "Just a lousy minute. This dream is suddenly turning into a nightmare. Can we get one thing clear, Iris? My dream of going up in the world does not include you!

You are not moving in with us. I don't care if we get Buckingham Palace, there's no place in it for you."

"You'll never get the mortgage without me, and you'll never keep up the payments without me, neither."

That stopped me in my tracks. She was probably right. But then again, how could the quality of our lives be improved if she was going to be part of it? I was just about to abandon the whole enterprise when the Duddy's suddenly struck up their nightly cacophony. I could have sworn I heard their Jed shouting: "Giddy up, boy". I thought to myself: which is worse, life with Iris the Antichrist, or living in the asylum? It was a close run thing, but I decided to see what she had in mind. If the worst came to the worst, I could always brick her up in the airing cupboard.

"Right, Iris, let's have it. What are you proposing?"

"Well," she said (and this had obviously been running round in her scheming little brain for some time), "I think I'm losing the use of my legs."

"Y'what?" says Derek, alarmed. "How do you mean, mother?"

"Oh, it's been coming on a long time. I've felt the twinges. And the old pins are definitely getting weaker. I could well end up in a wheelchair before much longer, totally incapacitated and dependent on the state. Or alternatively on the good will of my relatives."

"What is it, some kind of wasting disease?" Derek's eyes filled up with tears and he embraced his mother, kissing her cheek.

"I've a feeling that it's the kind of condition the medical authorities aren't going to be able to diagnose," Iris says.

"One of them mystery diseases that they just can't pin down. But perfectly real to the sufferer, nonetheless."

"Mother!" says Derek, taking it all seriously, like he does, "We'll get you the best specialists money can buy. We'll set an appeal fund up in the Trades to have you sent to America — they've got all the answers there, and we can call in at Disneyworld on the way back to help you recuperate. Why did this have to happen to us? What have we done to deserve it? I've always tried my best, but it never works!"

"Oh, Derek, for God's sake, put a sock in it!" I shouted.

"And," says Iris, "If you took me into your smashing new home to look after me in my rapidly deteriorating condition, you'd need to claim a 24-hour attendance allowance, wouldn't you? Yes, there are all sorts of benefits available to selfless people who look after their ailing elderly parents. The Government doesn't want the hospitals crowded with expensive geriatrics when for a few quid they can palm them off on the relatives. You get well paid for being a martyr these days."

Derek was horrified: "You mean...you mean...fake it?"

"Don't use words like that round me, son," said his mother. "You know my medical file at the hospital is thicker and more interesting than the Encyclopaedia Brittanica. I've got more pre-existing conditions than any insurance firm ever thought of."

She suddenly went limp in his arms. "Oh yes, no doubt I'll have to go through a lot of tests, but I have a feeling they won't get to the bottom of it. It'll be another medical enigma that stumps the boffins. And the boffins don't like being stumped. They're like the Pope, see, think they're infallible — and they don't like their failures hanging about proving otherwise. They'll want me off their hands as soon as they run out of ideas. Eventually, if I complain loud enough about their incompetence, they'll tell me that it's something I've got to live with and send me to the occupational therapy to be assessed for suitable apparatus. Then they'll pack me off home with a bath mat, modified eating utensils and a wheelchair — and it's at that point that we can start getting our dues from the DHSS."

"It's scandalous what you're planning," Derek said.

"They're not fools, them doctors. You're bound to get caught. We'll all get caught. The authorities will crush us."

"All the same, Derek," I said, "you'll be at that building society first thing in the morning for an application form."

* * *

Doreen's Diary 3rd January
Derek was severely worried about his mother's proposals, but the more I thought about them the better I liked them. Two birds with one stone. Revenge on the building society bastards, and a new life in Evergreen Close.

Anyroad, we went down to the show home at the Close and the man in the office greeted us with less than overwhelming enthusiasm. "Oh hello, madam, it's you again," he says. "You do understand that these are deluxe, architect designed residences? Are you, in fact, in the market for such a home?"

I flourished that morning's *Advertiser* in his face ("Local Couple Scoop a Fortune on Horses") and suddenly he was offering cups of fresh ground coffee with a bitter chocolate to go with it.

"This way, Mr and Mrs Potts, allow me to show you round."

Even though it had been two years since I'd last seen it, it was exactly as I remembered it — except the garden wasn't quite as big, in fact it was a bit on the tiny side. This appealed to Derek because of the low maintenance involved. But it did include an outdoor patio seating area for summer-time drinks parties.

Derek whispered to me: "You'll need to lose a bit of weight before you can sit comfortably on that patio seating area. There's not enough room to swing a cat let alone hand round cocktails."

When we'd done the full tour I said to the man: "Are you, in fact, offering any special offers at the moment? Only I understand that the property market is in something of the doldrum?"

"The doldrum, Mrs Potts? What exactly are you hinting at?"

"What I'm hinting at is that this house has been on the market for nearly two years now, and you still haven't got shut of it. Are you going to knock anything off for a quick sale?"

He was taken aback. "I'm not authorised..."

"Well, get on the phone to them that is authorised," I said.

And he did, and to cut a long story short, our mortgage requirement is only £48,000 now.

Meanwhile, Iris was as good as her word. She had been to see her ex-solicitor friend (a man who had been struck off after being convicted of conspiring to defraud the council — his co-conspirator was never caught, but I have a feeling that if pushed, I could pick her out at an identity parade — oldish woman, white hair and a stick, face like a rottweiler).

On the way back from his house she suffered a terrible collapse at the number 28 bus stop. An ambulance had to be sent for and she was carted off with an oxygen mask over her face and the sirens going. She's been in hospital that many times with her various ailments that she knows the procedure backwards.

I briefed Derek before we set out. "Now make your grief look real when we get to that hospital. Your mother's doing her bit, we have to back her up and make it seem authentic."

And off we went with some flowers and a bottle of Lucozade.

I'd expected to see her laying on a trolley in the corridor, waiting for a bed to become vacant. After all, she'd only been brought in twelve hours since, so it was unlikely she'd even seen a doctor yet, but the receptionist said she was in intensive care. I thought: well, Iris, you've suppressed yourself this time, to get yourself on the life support machine.

We was shown into intensive care, or IT as they call it, and given a seat at the side of Iris's bed.

"How are you feeling, Mam?" says Derek as we sat there all done up in masks and gowns.

She lay as still as a corpse, with her eyes shut. Her skin was yellow and they had her on a ventilator with all these wires attached to her chest. I looked closely at her. Her eyes weren't flickering like they do when you're only reckoning to be asleep, they were as still as anything. That started to make me uncomfortable. There was all the signs that she wasn't putting it on. I've never actually seen a coma before, but I think she was in one.

"Derek," I said. "I'm a bit worried about her."

When the nurse was out of ear-shot I got hold of Iris's hand, trying not to dislodge the needle. I whispered into her ear. "If you can hear me Iris, give my hand a squeeze. Is this part of the plan? One squeeze for yes, two squeezes for no."

Her hand was clammy and cold, and there was no sign of movement.

"Just a little squeeze to let us know that you're only kidding. We think you're doing a grand job."

Nothing.

I looked at Derek and shook my head.

"Oh God," he starts sobbing. "I knew this would happen. It's like a punishment from above for her dishonesty. She's been struck down for being a scheming old biddy."

"Well," I said, dibbing into the grapes, "that's finally put the mockers on Evergreen Close."

"Do you think she's had a stroke or something? Do you think she's on the danger list? Do you think she'll recover?"

He broke down in another fit of sobbing. "Will I ever taste me Mam's steak and kidney pie again?"

"She might be a vegetable when she wakes up," I said. "She might need constant attendance from morning till night, having to be bathed and took to the toilet. She might be a slobbering wreck."

Derek took his mother's lifeless hand: "Don't worry, Mam. We'll see you all right. We'll look after you. You'll go short of nothing."

"Hold on a minute, Derek," I says. "Who exactly is this 'we' who is going to be doing the looking after? I hope you're not nominating me for any martyrdom. You know I can't stomach people with unpredictable bowels."

41

"You don't mean it, Doreen. We can't abandon me mother now, not in her hour of need."

"There are alternatives. After all, she wouldn't want to be a burden. You know how independent she was, she'd hate the idea of all that undignified messing about."

"What alternatives?" "What about standing on that oxygen pipe for five minutes? She could pass peacefully away, then, without pain."

Just then the nurse comes in.

"Nurse! Nurse! How is she?" Derek pleads, all tragic.

"Well, she's been unconscious for nearly twelve hours now, and that's not good news. We're not quite sure what the problem is, but they'll be running some tests tomorrow."

"Is she...is she...going to die?"

I said: "Derek — you shouldn't ask the nurse that. She's not God. Ask the doctor."

"I don't think there's going to be much change tonight. Perhaps you ought to go home," the nurse says.

"That's a good idea," I says, "my feet are killing me."

"You go home, Doreen. I'm stopping here to hold a vigil at my mother's bedside. I shan't leave here until the matter is resolved one way or the other."

"Don't forget it's the darts championship at the Trades Club tomorrow."

"Oh aye — well tell them I'll be there. I wouldn't want to let them down, and I'm sure mother wouldn't want me to either. I'll think about her while I'm trying to get double top."

When I got home, who should be sitting on the doorstep but our Sylvia. She was dressed in this shorty patent leather coat, shivering.

"Sylvia," I says. "What are you doing here?"

I'd forgotten about the story in the *Advertiser*.

"I've come home, Mam."

"Don't tell me Jesus has failed to save you again. He wants to get his finger out if you ask me."

She carried her great big suitcase in and plonked it on the kitchen floor. "I'll make us some tea," I said.

"Where's me dad?" she says.

"Oh, he's up at the hospital on a mission of mercy. Nothing to worry about, only your granny's on the critical list again. I think it might be the real thing this time."

"Oh no! Poor old gran. Three sugars in that tea, Mam, please."

"Well, what have you been up to this time?" I said. "What happened to the Charismatics. Didn't they live up to expectations?"

"Oh, Mam, you've no idea! They meddle with your mind and once they've got you, you can never be free. I had to sign this proclamation of my commitment to the Order of Prophets. It was either for life or until the end-time comes, whichever is soonest. They said only those who had signed the proclamation would be saved when the world ends on June 24th."

"June 24th? Oh dear. We'd better think about bringing that trip to Blackpool forward."

"They predicted that the world was going to end on June 24th last year, but it never happened. Typographical error, they said, but it's definitely going to happen this year. Fire and floods, apparently."

"Well, it puts things in perspective, doesn't it? Does this milk taste off to you?"

"Guru Unsworth had us collecting money from people in the shopping centre all the time. He said our names would be cursed if we came back with less than £50. It was ever so hard. I had to endure humiliation. Guru Unsworth said it purified the soul to be vilified by outsiders."

"Unsworth? That isn't Ernie Unsworth is it, used to give lessons at the School of Ballroom and Tap on Sylvester Street?"

"It's his son, Bernard. Well, actually, it isn't his son. Bernard says that Ernie is an impostor, and that his true parents are actually John the Baptist and Khali, goddess of destruction."

"Well, they've always been a bit on the unlikely side in that family. It sounds as though you're well out of it."

"Well, Mam, you see, that's the trouble. I'm not out of it."

"How do you mean, love?"

"You can't just leave once you've signed the proclamation. You're in for life. You're not allowed to mingle with the outside world as such, except to ask them for donations. When they find out I've hopped it, they'll come looking for me."

"Well, tell them straight that you've packed it up, that it wasn't suitable for your spiritual needs. I'll tell them if you like."

"No, Mam, you don't understand. Guru Unsworth is fuming that I've left the ashram, he'll not rest till they've found me."

"Don't be ridiculous, our Sylvia. They can't force you. Have the bobbies on them if they try anything."

She lowered her head and stared at her feet. I know from the past that when she does that she's not telling me the whole story.

43

I said: "Come on, Sylvia, out with it. What's going off?"

She puts her hand on the suitcase. "We weren't allowed to have material possessions as such," she says.

"So what's in the bag?"

She puts the suitcase on the table and opens it. There must have been five or six thousand quid in used notes, and a few hundred pounds worth of silver ornaments and jewellery.

"Where the hell did you get that from?" I said.

"I'm entitled to it, Mam. I collected every hour God sent for that lousy Unsworth. I made thousands for him. It's only right I should have a share."

"You've pinched it!"

"No, I'm simply taking the money I'm entitled to. That Guru Unsworth has no right keeping it all for himself. He only spends it on cars."

"No wonder they're after you, girl. Give it back to them, tell them you're sorry."

"Bugger that," says our Sylvia. "I've had to grovel in the streets asking for this, having people insult me day after day. Now I want what's due. Besides, without this money I won't be able to keep myself. I won't be able to pay you the rent you deserve for putting me up."

That clicked. "Well, if you've worked for it, and they haven't given you a wage, it's only fair you should have a golden handshake. Just let that bloody Bernard Unsworth show himself here! I'll give him guru. I'll guru him one in the cobblers if he tries anything with you. Having young girls out in the street begging for money, it's disgusting. Here, he didn't do nothing else, did he, like you hear about in these cults? Nothing of a free love nature?"

"There was an element of that, yes, but I never participated, Mam, honest. Not after the first three months, anyway. Guru Unsworth says that if he is the son of God, any woman would want to have a baby by him, because it would be suffused by the Holy Spirit. So they were queuing up to satisfy the Lord and acquire the Holy seed."

"The dirty little bugger. Sounds like Guru Unsworth is having his cake and eating it."

She was looking at her shoes again.

"Anything else, Sylvia?" "Well, you see, Mam, I was one of the chosen."

"Chosen?" My heart started beating a lot faster. "Not chosen by Bernard Unsworth?"

She nodded her head. "I couldn't stop myself mother. I was carried away in rapture. He convinced me that I was the privileged one who had been chosen to bear the next incarnation of Unsworths."

"Don't tell me. You're in the club, aren't you?"

"No, mother, not in the club as such. I am not as others. This child growing within is going to save the world from its own wickedness."

"Don't talk so bleeding barmy. If I ever get my hands on that scrawny Unsworth neck of his, I'll..." I was going red in the face. "Is he going to stick by you? Has he made arrangements to look after the kiddy when it pops out? How far gone are you?"

"Four months, Mam. He can't be held responsible. He has simply carried out the prophecy."

"Are you going to get wed?"

"Guru Unsworth cannot marry. His mission is too important. It is his destiny to bring other prophets into the world."

"You mean get other lasses up the duff. It wants stopping. You can get him to pay through that Child Support Agency. They'll sort him out. Meanwhile stick that money in the spare bedroom. You'll want that. Babbies are a dear do."

Her little eyes filled up with tears.

"Hey up, our Sylvia. Have less of that scriking. You should be happy and contented as a pregnant mother-to-be. Blubbering isn't good for the unborn. It'll end up a misery like your dad if you aren't careful. Now wipe your face."

I put me arm round her and gave her a little hug. It was lovely, just like when she was a little lass and she used to climb up on me knee and we'd have a cuddle. Except now there was two of them to cuddle.

"Come on, love. Never mind that swine Unsworth, your Mam and Dad will stick by you. We'll see you're all right."

I smiled to try and reassure her, but inside I was thinking: oh God!

* * *

Doreen's Diary 3rd January
Derek was horrified when he heard about our Sylvia. He was even further horrified when he heard who the father was.

"This can come to no good," he said. "There'll be dire consequences."

"What's the matter with you, Derek?" I chided. "Try looking on the bright side for a while — you're going to be a grandfather."

45

He just shook his head and groaned in a melancholy sort of way. "What sort of a world is this to bring children into, Doreen? Particularly children born disadvantaged."

"Come off it, Derek. Even you can't call living in Evergreen Close disadvantaged. And they've mostly done away with the atom bomb so it's not such a bad old world. So long as the kiddy knows its curb drill and keeps away from the canal, it should be OK. See it as a challenge."

He groaned again. He's convinced that the money is a curse on us. He's been reading too many stories about lottery winners who fall out with all their friends. That won't happen to us. We have very few friends to fall out with.

* * *

Doreen's Diary 10th January 1996

I'll say this much about Iris, she's thorough — especially when engaged in conning the authorities. She'd left a ten page letter with full instructions about what we was to do if a tragedy should befall her before her plan could be carried out.

She used to read the tea-leaves at one time, but I never realised that her powers of prophecy were so well-developed. We were to read the letter, memorise the essentials, and then chuck it on the fire. We were not, under no circumstances, to put it in the dustbin, where it might be retrieved and later used in evidence against us.

The letter said that if, owing to some tragic mischance, she wasn't available to do it herself, we were to go and see this shady solicitor feller and he would give us full particulars about how to fill the mortgage application form in. He knew the whole procedure backwards, he's done that many before. He knows just what the building society will check and what they'll take your word for.

By the time we'd done, there were more lies on that application form than there are on the average bobby's report sheet. And not only that, he has a contact in the bank who will ensure that through "a computer error" the building society will receive confirmation that we are quite capable of paying off the debt we have signed up for. "A good risk for the amount involved" is what the letter from the bank will say. He's going to write financial references for us from made up employers — he's got the whole thing sewn up. I'm not kidding, it makes you wonder who you can trust, doesn't it? After that, Iris said we had to go to the hospital and harass the doctors as much as possible about what was up with her.

She said we were to make their lives a misery, asking questions about what tests she was having, what treatment they were giving her, what they intended to do next.

So, I asked to see the consultant in charge of her case.

"What exactly is the matter with her, doctor Ahmed?" I said to him when I got in the office.

"Well, that's difficult to say at the moment, Mrs Potts. We're running tests and the instant we get them back we'll be in a better position to say."

"Is it like a stroke?" I suggested.

"Well, that's one possibility, although there are no indications of brain damage from what we've observed so far."

"A heart attack?"

"No, her heart seems to be particularly strong for someone of her age."

"Could it have anything to do with diabetes. A renal collapse of the kidneys, perhaps?"

"She's clear of that."

"Could it be a wasting disease?"

"I really can't say, Mrs Potts. We'll have to leave it for a few days before we can be certain."

"And then you'll start treating her?" I said.

"Well, of course, we'll do whatever we can. Although you understand that pressure for space in intensive care is very heavy. We may have to move her into a general ward quite soon."

"Well, I'll leave it in your capable hands, doctor Ahmed, I'm sure you'll do everything you can to restore her back to us. As you know, we are a very loyal family, as regards sticking together. Oh yes, we can be ferocious if we're crossed — cut one of us, we all bleed, sort of thing."

I tried to make it sound menacing without overdoing it. The poor man was already shuffling in his seat.

"Oh, by the way," I said, on the way out. "I was reading in the paper this morning about a woman suing a health authority for neglect. Her father went into hospital to have an ingrowing toe-nail removed and ended up with a leg off. You have to laugh, don't you? It wouldn't have been so bad but they took his right leg off and the bad toe was on the left. I suppose we all make mistakes from time to time."

I gave him a reassuring smile, but then, to flummox him, I suddenly went all serious: "Still, the surgeon's reputation was dragged through the mud by the papers, and the man's daughter was awarded quarter of a million. Just goes to show, doesn't it — doctors are just like the rest of us: right berks at times. Present company excepted, of course. I've got full confidence in you, doctor Ahmed. And I expect you're insured for that kind of error, aren't you?"

He coughed nervously and showed me to the door.

I'd followed Iris's suggestions to the letter and hopefully I've introduced just the right element of fear into the proceedings.

* * *

Doreen's Diary 12th February 1996

At last, a few minutes peace and quiet, and time to bring this diary up to date. I've neglected it a bit over the past month, but there has been so much happening I haven't hardly had time to breathe.

I write this entry sitting in the sitting room of my new home in Evergreen Close. Yes, we have got here at last. To our amazement, the mortgage came through. All credit to that former solicitor and his many contacts, and well done Iris.

Those last few days in the flat were a nightmare. We were all sitting there like something in an Alfred Hitchcock film, waiting for the worst to happen. There was our Sylvia, chewing her fingers and looking through the window every five minutes, convinced that the Charismatics would be knocking on the door at any time. Then there was Derek, deeply depressed over his mother and despondent at the prospect of moving into what he calls "Albatross House". He was fully expecting the bobbies to knock on the door, having uncovered what he insisted in referring to as "our embezzlement". I tried to reassure him. "Derek," I said, "we are not swindling no-one, we have every intention of paying the debt. It's just that they wouldn't make the loan in the first place if we hadn't been — what do them MPs call it? — economical with the truth."

"That's what they call it when *they* do it. They call it lying when the likes of us do it. Fraud. Deception. We're going to get had up, I know it."

"That building society will get every penny it's owed," I said, more in hope than certainty.

Then there's our Gary, being persecuted by that man who owns the flats he lives in.

And finally there's me: up every morning at six, sitting by the front door waiting for the postman to drop that mortgage confirmation through the letter box.

I am glad to say that on this occasion, my wish was first out of the bag. The building society was pleased to offer us the loan under the terms and particulars aforementioned, heretofore and thereforewith.

Within days we was preparing to do a flit. We had decided to try and slip discreetly away — leaving as much of our misfortune and accumulated debts behind us as possible. We had decided that the best time for a midnight flit was three o'clock in the morning. I started taking our stuff out on to the landing, ready for our Gary and Bill to collect. They'd hired a van for the occasion, which will save us trying to get our tackle over to Evergreen on the handcart.

While I was stacking the stuff up outside the door, Angela and their Dolph come on to the landing to see what I was doing. "Oh," says Angela, "are you having a clear out, Mrs Potts? I could do with going to the tip meself."

I looked at my worldly goods, all piled up — the sideboard and occasional table, and my collection of CDs, Engelbert Humperdink and Frank Ifield taking pride of place. "These are not going to the tip. We happen to be moving out. Improving our lot."

"I am sorry to hear that," she says. "Well, I mean, I'm not sorry, I'm very happy for you. But you know what I mean. Where are you going, as such?"

"I think it's better if you don't know, Angela, love. Then you won't be tempted to tell no-one with a clipboard who happens to come round asking where we've moved to. Especially not people who look like they're collecting debts."

She winked. "Don't you worry about that, Mrs Potts," she says. "You kept quiet about that gas meter for me, I'll say nowt to nobody about your present or future whereabouts. As far as I'm concerned, any mention of hire purchase brings on severe memory loss."

Dolph was knocking hell out of the table, trying to break it in half with a karate kick. He'd got his eye on my CDs as well.

"Can you control that little fiend," I said to Angela. "His Doc Marten's are knocking the varnish off my bedside table."

She just shrugged and dragged him away, struggling.

"Good luck in your new home, wherever it might be," she was saying, as he bit her hand.

I went in to bring the mattress out. When I came back my Herb Alperts had gone. "Oh no," I thought, "not me Tijuana Brass."

I was that furious I went to the balcony and I screamed as loud as I could: "I'll be glad to get away from this place, I will. You're nothing but lousy thieving bastards the lot of you."

It was like shouting into the Grand Canyon, but it made me feel a bit better.

As prescribed by Iris (who seemed to be directing the whole thing from beyond the grave, so to speak, because she is still in a persisting vegetable state at the hospital, despite them trying everything to revive her), I ordered some furniture, fittings and bathroom requisites from the catalogues she runs under an assumed name. These had all arrived now, so we were ready for the flit. And so it was, in the early hours of the morning, that the Vaughan Williams Towers was vacated by the Potts family.

When we got to Evergreen Close we unloaded the furniture as quietly as we could. I looked at the house, magnificent in the moonlight, and there was a little catch in my throat. I said: "This is an important moment for us, Derek. Very important. It's the first step in our journey to a better life. Open the door, love. You can carry me over the threshold if you like."

"Give us the key then," he said.

"You've got it haven't you? I put it on the mantel piece at the flat and told you the bring it with you."

"You never said no such thing," he said.

"Don't say you haven't fetched the chuffing key. Here we are, four o'clock in the bleeding morning and no way of getting in!"

"Up there, look," says our Gary. "There's a bathroom window open on the first floor."

There was as well. They must have left it open to help the paint dry. Luckily our Gary had a ladder on the roof of the van, so he got that down and put it up against the wall.

"Go on, then, get up there," I said to Derek.

"Who me? What about one of these young 'uns doing it? You go up Gary. Or you Bill."

"Mrs Potts, we've got to get home," Bill was saying. "I'm supposed to be at work at seven and I've already been up all night. I shall be dead on my feet on that ward."

"You go home, then, love, and thank you for everything you've done. It's much appreciated. We'll manage the rest."

So they drove off.

Our Sylvia was laid there on the settee in her baby doll pyjamas, fast asleep. She'd pulled her duvet over herself to keep out the frost. That girl could sleep on a clothes line.

"Go on, Derek, get through that window and get the door open. It's your lousy fault we're stuck out here." I was shouting in a whisper, trying not to disturb the neighbours.

All the same, lights were going on all over the Close.

I noticed next door's curtains were twitching as well. I thought: you'd better reassure them Doreen, they're Neighbourhood Watch mad round here, so I shouts: "Don't worry, we're putting things *into* the house, not taking them out. No need to ring the police."

Well, Derek started up the ladder. He's never been fond of heights, but I think he was that embarrassed he braced himself. He got up to the window and tried to push it all the way open. It wouldn't go any further.

"I can't get it open far enough to get in," he says.

"Can't you squeeze through?"

"It's not big enough. I'll never get my arse through here."

"Have a go."

He was reluctant, but he shoved his head in through the crack and then tried dragging the rest through after it. His shoulders went through OK, but as he'd predicted, his thighs just wouldn't fit. Too many chip sandwiches.

"Come out then," I said. "We'll have to think in terms of smashing windows."

He was wiggling and struggling. "I can't get back out," he was saying.

"Chuffing hell, Derek, can't you do anything right? Come down from there."

"I'm telling you, Doreen. I can't shift. I'm stuck. Come up and help me."

"Not flaming likely. You're not getting me up no ladders, struggling with a tub of lard thirty foot off the ground."

"Do something, Doreen. I can't hang here all night."

"What exactly do you suggest?"

"Get the fire brigade. They'll know how to release slightly overweight people from window frames."

"This is going to make an excellent first impression on the neighbours, isn't it, sending for the sodding fire brigade."

"Come on, Doreen. Stop messing about. Find a phone and get the brigade out. I'm likely to get exposure stuck like this all night. I can already feel strain on my hernia scar. You know what our family is like for perishing in freak accidents. Hurry."

I was cringing at the prospect of having to trouble one of the neighbours, but I didn't have much option. I could see next door was up. All the lights were on and there was somebody at the window watching it all.

The woman who answered the door seemed a bit startled when she saw me.

"Don't I know you?" she said. "Aren't you Doreen Blenkinsop?"

"Blenkinsop as was," I said. "Potts as is."

I was trying to place her. Her face had a familiar ring to it, but I couldn't quite think who she was. Then it dawned on me. "Beryl Jennings. Form 4C. Mrs Calvert's class — special needs and challenging behaviour. You look different without glasses on."

"It's nearly twenty-five years since I last saw you, Doreen. There's more than a pair of glasses that's different. I've been married four times and had me womb removed in the intervening period."

"Never!" I said. "Boring Beryl Jennings has had four husbands? It doesn't seem credible. We've got some catching up to do."

So I went in and had a cup of coffee with her. What a laugh. She's called Beryl Cathcart now, although she says she's had that many names she'll answer to just about anything these days. It seems that Beryl's first husband died early on — inherited condition apparently — then her second husband ran off with her best friend, and the third had made his fortune in small tools. Unfortunately, Beryl says, small tools were his personal as well as professional speciality, and she couldn't get no satisfaction.

She says: "When I first met him, I used to say: size isn't everything, but when he failed to consume the marriage, I divorced him."

However, what the marriage lacked in orgasms it more than made up for in cash. Her divorce settlement was generous.

"All that money just because your husband had a tiddler!" I said. "I think I've been badly advised somewhere along the line."

Her latest husband is an international business man, big in all departments, including his bank account. "It's the best marriage so far," she says, "because I hardly ever see him. He's always off on business trips abroad. Months at a time he goes for. And that's how I ended up in Evergreen Close. What about you?"

Well, I decided to give her an edited version of the events that had brought us here. I left out the bits that I thought might alarm her, although I could see that she didn't believe a word I was saying. She knows that we can't afford to live here in the manner to which we would like to become accustomed, but she also knows what its like to want to better yourself. After all, when she left school she was wearing these milk bottle bottomed glasses with national health frames. How she ever got one man, let alone four, I'll never know, but get one she did, and he paid for her to have laser treatment on her eyes. Now she wears contacts and looks more like an ordinary person and less like Mrs Magoo.

"We've jumped in a bit at the deep end," I said. "I get worried that I won't fit in around here. What are the other people on the Close like?"

"Be careful, Doreen. There's some terrible snobs. They could make your life a misery if you let them. You can expect a visit from Mrs Henshaw soon. Number eight. She's formed a residents committee which we've all had to join. She'll expect you to become a member. She'll be round with the welcome wagon soon, and she's a cow. She runs the committee like Stalin ran Russia. Everybody's scared stiff of her — and she'll be looking for your weak points, so if you've got any skeletons in your closet, keep them hidden. Otherwise she'll use them against you."

I began to panic. I thought: I'll bet they all watch BBC2 round here. If I want to watch Coronation Street I'll have to do it with the curtains drawn. All the same, it was nice to find a friend living next door.

"Now, what was it you wanted? A cup of sugar?" she said.

I nearly jumped out of the chair. "Oh God, it went clean out of my head. It's my husband. He needs the fire brigade."

"A bit of a hot number is he, Doreen?"

"No, he's a bit of a misery actually. But he's stuck in the upstairs bathroom window at the moment, and I forgot all about it. Have you got a phone I could use?"

I went into the hallway to dial 999, but by the time I got there I could see a bright blue light flashing outside on the Close. I looked through the door. It was a police car.

"Aye, aye," said Beryl. "I see the coppers' narks — otherwise known as the community policing initiative — have been busy. They're on to the police station if you so much as put your rubbish out on the wrong day."

I rushed out to explain what exactly a young girl in a skimpy nightie was doing asleep on the doorstep while a man was stuck in the window upstairs.

"Well, I've seen some things in my time," says the policeman, "but this takes the biscuit."

"Don't be too hard on my Derek," I said, "He's got a mother on the danger list."

By this time Beryl had rung for the fire brigade and the engine came whizzing on to the close, sirens going, lights flashing, men shouting. It were bedlam. The curtains around the Close weren't so much twitching as palpitating. Beryl was standing beside me in her dressing gown when they extricated my Derek from his predicament. She thought it was hilarious.

She laughed that much she had to hold her side. "You want to count yourself lucky that Adolf Henshaw and her husband are away for the weekend or she'd have written your name down in her black book. Mrs Henshaw doesn't hold with hilarity. She probably thinks immoderate laughter brings property prices down."

More curtains twitched, more doors opened. The whole Close was watching us make a spectacle of ourselves, and our Sylvia slept right through it.

* * *

Doreen's Diary 8th February 1996
Our first few days on the Close were taken up with getting things as I wanted them. We moved the furniture from room to room until I'd worn Derek out. I got the curtains up and the beds made. I can't stop going round with the Hoover because I want the house to stay looking sparkling for as long as possible.

As soon as anybody sits down I have to plump the cushions behind them so they don't look untidy and spoil the effect. Derek says I would be happier if I lived here on my own, then other people wouldn't be able to spoil my fantasy. I told him not to be silly, but in reality I agree with him.

The fly in my happiness ointment is Iris. Just as she predicted, they never found nothing wrong with her at the hospital. They tried everything, but they couldn't get to the bottom of it.

Well, we took it in turns to go and visit her. Derek went on Tuesday, Wednesday, Thursday, Friday and Saturday and Sunday and I went during the restricted visiting times on Monday afternoon. She gradually regained conscienceness — well, if that's what you can call it. She was sitting up in bed shouting: "Mother! Mother! There's a fire up the chimney!"

There was this big West Indian cleaning lady, and Iris would shout at her: "Have you seen my mother knocking about, love? Only I'm waiting for her to take me home. Could you see if she's in the lav?"

You could tell the nurses were sick of her. She kept punching them every time they tried to turn her over to avoid bed sores. "Where's me mother gone?" she kept saying to Dr Ahmed. "If that lass keeps messing about with me I'll hit her."

I pestered that doctor from morning till night, just as Iris had recommended in her instruction manual, and eventually he seemed to run out of steam. He started talking about her "having to live with it" — whatever *it* was — and we would have to start thinking in terms of long-term care for her.

Hospital wasn't the right place, he said.

I said to Derek: "We can't have her at home in that state, Derek. How are we going to cope?"

I was all for getting the social services to find her a nursing home — you know, in Bournemouth or somewhere even further away — but Derek insisted that she come and share our dream home with us, even though she's gone ga-ga and is in no fit state to appreciate it.

He's eaten up with guilt. He says it's all his fault that she's turned out like this. Something else for him to maunder on about.

So, they discharged her and we brought her here with all her paraphernalia. Wheelchair, bathing aids, commode, mouth care packs, you name it. At first all she did was sit in her wheelchair watching me. It was like having one of them statues where the eyes follow you wherever you are in the room. You can fair see the hatred oozing out of her. Then all of a sudden she'd shout: "Send for the bobbies! There are bell-ringers in my wardrobe! I'm not safe. Get the police!"

It scared the hell out of me — she'd be that insistent about it I sometimes found myself going upstairs half expecting to find the bloody bell-ringers.

I felt sorry for her in a way, when you think about how lively she used to be, cocking her leg up at the Derby and Joan club sing-song. All the same the physical and mental torture of having a completely dependent person around the house is exhausting.

Anyway, back to her instruction manual — get an assessment from the social services and ask what benefits we are entitled to as regards looking after a semi-cabbage. That was Iris's advice and that's what we did.

Well, the social worker was very helpful but it turns out that the Government have got all these new regulations that if you've got more than so much put by, you aren't entitled to all the benefits that you used to be. I couldn't believe it. Iris must have known, but she let us go ahead under false pretences. They'd taken her bungalow back now that she was living with us and we were stuck with her.

I thought yes, you crafty cow, this was all part of the plan, wasn't it. Get your feet under the table and leave us to pick up the pieces.

Still, we do get some benefits from the social and as Iris can only eat soup, we are left with a small profit at the end of it.

Our Gary is well aware of my aversion to other people's bodily functions and what he calls "fluids", and so he comes over to help me in the evening when we have to bath Iris.

He's got a few tips off his boyfriend, Bill, and I'll give the lad his due, he's buckled down perfectly. All the same, it's a backbreaking business having to look after an invalid, lifting her on to the commode and then into the bath, seeing to her bits and pieces and then lifting her out again. Then she has to be lifted into bed. She's shouting out all the time you're trying to help her, saying the lawn wants mowing and that she's being stalked by a Frenchman.

It makes my flesh crawl having to mess about with her, but our Gary has brought a supply of rubber gloves and distracts me by chattering away so as to stop me heaving.

Our Sylvia has also moved in with us. Her five thousand pounds is helping to keep the fear of mortgage repayments at bay, and she also thinks it entitles her to avoid all contact with her granny. She's a lovely girl, or she is when she wears half-way decent clothes. I said to her the other day, I said: "Should a girl with pretensions to holiness, such as yourself, be wearing your skirts quite so short? And isn't the display of so much cleavage likely to inflame lust in men?"

"Don't be silly, Mam, the body is a temple of the Holy Ghost and should be seen as such. Everybody knows that. It says so in the Bible — Corinthians, chapter 1."

She knows her Bible back to front, so whenever I criticise her she's always ready with a quote. How can you argue if it's in the Bible? She's got the upper hand over me as regards scripture, you see, she's studied it and I haven't.

Despite our set-backs, I still can't believe that we've actually got here. I can't stop having cups of tea in my new kitchen, and sitting there looking at the tiled flooring and masses of cupboards. Derek isn't so pleased, though. He spends most of the day pacing about and looking worried.

Then he goes and drowns his sorrows at the Trades with this cronies. He's even talking about making renewed efforts to find a job, something he'd previously given up all hope of.

He goes to the library to look through the situations vacant column. He doesn't want to do it, but he's scared witless that we won't be able to pay our debts. At the moment, we're OK, but a little bit of extra income wouldn't go amiss.

I encourage him to keep trying, although if he goes to interviews with the same hangdog look that he has when he's here, the only job he's likely to get is as an undertaker's assistant.

He's just going to have to learn to cope.

* * *

Letter from Gary Potts

Dear Terry,

Thanks for the tip about the Housing Advice Centre. After Mr Hindley stepped up his campaign to get us out of the flat we went over there to ask about our rights. They said if he was harassing us, we had grounds for legal proceedings. They said we ought to write to him and tell him that if he didn't give over tormenting us, we'd take him to court.

His response to that was to hold a ceremony of exorcism outside our flat. He brought some of his born-agains from the church and they were chanting outside the door and singing hymns. Mr Hindley said he wanted to cast out the devils.

Apparently he does some kind of healing mission where he exorcises devils from women with gynaecological problems.

We tried to ignore him but the racket was terrible, and they went on for hours. And they came again the following night.

That was it — Bill lost his rag. "Right," he said, going into the kitchen and filling his mouth with mushy peas out of a tin. Then he went out on to the landing.

"Give up your evil practices," says Mr Hindley, crossing himself at the sight of Bill. "We can pray for you. We can counsel you. We can rid you of the demons that put these wicked ideas into your head."

The congregation — about eight of them, mostly old women and wild-eyed youths — looked petrified. Old Hindley had worked them up into such a frenzy they really believed there was a devil living in the flat. So Bill gave them what they had come for and he pretended to do a projectile vomit with the mushy peas and it went all over them. Well, they screamed and fled for their lives — they'd obviously all seen The Exorcist, and thought it was a documentary.

Mr Hindley must have convinced himself that he was dealing with Beelzebub, too, because he was first on the staircase. Unfortunately he tripped and went arse over tit down the stairs, with all the old ladies tripping over him as they followed. It was like a cattle stampede, blind panic and people running in fear for their immortal souls. The bottom of the staircase was a great pile up of flailing arms and legs and screaming women trying to get through the door to escape the supernatural.

Bill laughed his socks off and we thought we'd well and truly got shut of them, but they were back the following night, worked into a right frenzy. They were waving their crucifixes, gibbering in tongues and shouting hallelujah.

Out goes Bill again, this time trying to placate them.

"Look," he says. "I'm sorry about last night. It was a joke."

The congregation gasped and drew back. One of the women threw holy water at him.

"Come forth, demon, and show thyself," Pastor Hindley shouted. "Leave this poor sick child in the name of the Lord."

"Mr Hindley — please! I've got to get up early in the morning to go to work at the hospital."

"The devil is come down to you, having great wrath, because he knoweth he has but a short time!" "Mr Hindley!"

"And the smoke of their torment ascendeth up for ever and ever: and they have no rest day or night, who worship the beast and his image. And we walked through the valley of the shadow of death and we were not afraid!"

Hindley was well away by this time, wailing and moaning, and the congregation were all wailing and moaning with him, like a Tamla Motown backing group.

"If I'm possessed by a spirit, it is the spirit of philanthropy," said Bill. "I'm a nurse. I take care of poorly people. I am not Satan, honestly. You've got the wrong person."

Well, obviously the congregation were not familiar with the demon of philanthropy, so they had to look to the Pastor for guidance.

"You practise abomination! You mis-use your body."

He turned to the assembled. "Don't be misled by the forked tongue of the demon," he said. "Be sober, be vigilant, because your adversary the devil, as a roaring lion, walketh about, seeking whom he may devour."

"You can't win with these people, Bill," I said. "You might as well come in."

"We intend to keep up an all-night vigil," said Hindley. "We shall not quit until the Lord's work is done and the demons fled."

"Well," said Bill, "if I'm going to have a headache, you're going to have one with me."

And with that, he nutted Hindley right between the eyes. It's a technique he perfected in his days as a professional footballer. Well, once again, panic gripped the worshippers and they were off down them stairs like whippets. Hindley had to go to Accident and Emergency to have his broken nose seen to, the police came and arrested Bill and took him to the police station for questioning. He was kept overnight and then released on bail. A few days later we had a letter telling him that he was going to be prosecuted for actual bodily harm. We're hoping that Hindley won't proceed. It could be disastrous for Bill's career.

As for my parents, they seem to have gone a bit round the bend since they won that money. I've tried to talk to Mam, but as you know, she's completely incapable of reason. They've moved into a great big house in Evergreen Close.

God knows how they've managed it, and my mother isn't all that keen to tell me any details. I'm pleased for them that they've got away from the Vaughan Williams Estate, but Christ knows what the crack is with this new house. It's enormous.

You should have been at the house warming party — you'd have liked it. My mother said I was to ask my friends round, so all the usuals turned up.

When Alice, from the Lesbian Joint Shop Stewards Committee, had had five cans of Red Stripe and my mother had put a few glasses of sherry away, they got into one of their surreal conversations. It would have amused you. I can't remember it word for word, but it went something like this: Alice: You ought to learn about lesbian feminism, Doreen. It can liberate you from the tyranny of the patriarchal state. It's a great relief not to have to depend on men.

Mam: You don't have to be a lesbian feminist for that, love. It's the other way round as far as I'm concerned. The only reason I'd be a lesbian is to stop men depending on *me*. Like my Derek.

Alice: I think it's every woman's duty to learn about the achievements of their sisters in arms down the years. For instance, what do you think of Radclyffe Hall?

"I don't know. I've never been there," says Mam, "Is it under the National Trust?"

Alice was fuming. She thought Mam was sending her up, she didn't realise that it was genuine ignorance. "Have you no feminist thoughts in your head, Doreen?" she said, frustrated that she'd met yet another woman who didn't share her outlook on life.

"Well, I could let you have some of my depilatory cream if you wanted to do anything about them facial hairs of yours."

Alice stalked off after that to talk to gran, who is presently in a wheelchair and totally incapable of speech or comprehension. Alice says she gets more sense out of her in that state than she ever did out of Mam.

Gran has had some kind of stroke and is now completely out of it. It's sad really, because I love her very much. You wouldn't recognise her these days.

There's one thing to be said about the new house, though — there's plenty of room. And they haven't got the Duddys living next door.

I'll let you know about the flat situation, and how Bill gets on with his court case. We're hoping that Hindley will back down before it gets that far.

Oh, by the way, talking of religious maniacs, you won't have heard about our Sylvia, will you? She's gone and got herself knocked up by Bernard Unsworth — he calls himself "Guru Unsworth" now, would you believe. He's started his own religion and runs it from that building that used to be the slag reduction plant down near Pitt Street. You can hardly credit what people will fall for, but apparently he's making quite a name for himself in cultish circles. People are coming from all over the world to be part of his "ashram".

I went down there the other day to have a word with him about our Sylvia, see what he intended to do about it. The place is surrounded by barbed wire and security cameras. You can't get anywhere near him. I tried to go in, but I was stopped by this burly chap who said it wasn't possible for me to see "the guru" as he doesn't mix with the unconverted.

However, when I said who I was, Unsworth sent a message out saying that the wrath of Khali was coming the way of all apostates and thieves.

I sent a simple message back to him: You're fucking crackers, Unsworth.

Our Sylvia's better off out of it, but you know what she is for holy, holy, holy. Remember how she used to make us play at being Jesus,

Joseph and Mary when we were kids? She hasn't changed. She's as daft as Unsworth in that respect.

God knows what the sprog is going to be like — it'll probably be knocking on doors selling the Watchtower by the time it's three.

I don't like to keep going on about religion, but we're surrounded by it here — there are more churches, chapels, mosques and temples than there are pubs. It sometimes feels as though we're being taken over by them. You can't go anywhere without one of them stuffing a leaflet in your hand or rattling a collecting tin in your face. It must be something to do with the recession that all these people are turning to the irrational for answers. Be in touch. Best wishes, Gary

* * *

Doreen's Diary 13th February

I can hardly believe what happened today, and I'm not sure whether I'm relieved or outraged. Everybody else had gone out — Derek on a further job search and our Sylvia to some kind of Bible study class — there was just me and Iris in the house. I was reading *Home Beautiful*, when I suddenly got wind of this smell. Oh God, I thought, she's filled her pants again; that's the second time today. And so I got up and hauled her to the downstairs loo again. What a struggle when you're on your own, giving her the fireman's lift and then having to see to her particulars without throwing up. I don't know where it all comes from, given that she subsists entirely on Heinz Tomato Soup and the occasional mug of Complan.

But I managed to clean her up somehow and get her a fresh pair of bloomers on, then back into her chair. I felt as if my back was going to give way by the time I collapsed back on to the settee. If this goes on much longer, I thought, she'll not be the only one in a wheelchair.

No sooner had I got her back on wheels than I saw a car draw up at the bottom of the garden. There was the posh looking woman coming through the gate. From the description — enormous bosom, expensive clothes, hair like wire netting — it could only be one person: Mrs Henshaw.

I rushed upstairs and got the air freshener and was still squirting it when the door bell went. I wheeled Iris into the kitchen double-quick and told her to keep quiet. I had an impression to make.

"Good morning," says Mrs Henshaw when I answered the door. "Mrs Potts isn't it?" She stuck her gloved hand out and I shook it. "I'm Hilary Henshaw."

I'd been waiting for this moment. It was like an audition.

This woman could give me the credibility I needed to fit in. If she took to me I could relax.

"Oh yes. You're the lady from number eight. Mrs Next Door said you might call. Very nice to meet you. Do you want to come in for a cup of tea?"

She gave one of them forced, weedy smiles, the sort that says, this smile places me under no obligation to like you. I thought: watch your step, Doreen, or you could come a cropper here.

She came into the house, through the hall and into the sitting room. Her eyes were darting about like a shoal of little fish, taking it all in. Within two seconds she'd priced everything in view, including my picture of the oriental lady I'd bought all them years back from Boots.

Mrs Henshaw's nostrils curled slightly as though she were sniffing something. She plonked herself on the settee and put her crocodile handbag on the floor.

"You've got the house looking...er...very interesting, Mrs Potts."

"Oh call me Doreen, Hilary," I said. "Now can I get you anything in the way of light refreshment? A cup of tea, perhaps, or would you prefer coffee?"

"Do you have filter?"

"I'm afraid it's Nescafe at the moment. I could do you Gold Blend. The coffee maker was somewhat damaged — broke in fact — in the move. We shall have to obtain another."

"Then I'll pass, if you don't mind. I find the instant coffee to be unacceptable as a substitute for the real thing. Now, I've come to officially welcome you to the Close..."

"Officially, Hilary? Are you an official of some kind, then?"

"In a way, yes. I am President for life of the Resident's Association. We think that by banding together we can help each other keep our environment a pleasant one. We want to ensure that Evergreen Close remains as..." she paused as though searching for the right word, "... as *select* as possible. After all, we all came to live here because the area is quiet, discreet and populated by our kind of people. We've managed to keep it that way so far — we're blissfully free of foreigners and others who tend to affect the quality of life of those with higher ambitions. No dole scroungers, unmarried mothers or sellers of the Big Issue round here you'll be pleased to know. Let's hope that we can keep it that way."

I suddenly had the kind of feeling that Mrs Duddy must have got when she was on the road and always being evicted: we don't want your sort here; we don't care where you go so long as you don't hang about on our doorstep.

"Oh, I do agree", I was saying, with the words almost choking me. "We ourselves have been tormented something cruel in our previous home by the neighbours. Terrible it was. Up at all hours, carrying on like something not right. We had to get away, and this area seemed right peaceful."

"And where was your previous home, Mrs Potts?"

"Er...it was an inner city part of town. You know, at one time it would have been very upmarket, but it's gone down now. We had to abandon our old family home. All kinds of rubbish living round about. We didn't have no alternative but to flit, really."

"I think you'll find that we are blissfully free of those kind of self-inflicted social problems in Evergreen Close. A quieter, more respectable set of neighbours it would be hard to find. Even the local newsagent is northern European, so that says everything. And I'm sure you'll want to be part of the Association. When you come to the monthly meetings you'll be able to meet everyone else."

She got this clipboard out of her bag. "Now if I could just ask for a few particulars."

I could see that she had a long sheet of paper with questions on it. I'd have to think fast with this.

"First of all, who actually lives in the house besides yourself and your husband? I noticed a young lady of working class appearance leaving the premises the other day. I expect she's some kind of cleaning help or au pair, is she?"

"That is actually in fact my daughter, Sylvia. I have spoke to her about her mode of dress, tried to get her to smarten herself up, but she's not like other girls. She is of a spiritual bent and her appearance means little to her. She used to be a nun at one bit, so she had to get out of the habit of looking in mirrors. She's still quite high up in the church."

"Really? I'm surprised I haven't come across her before. I'm prominent in ecclesiastical circles myself. Has she attended our local church?"

"I don't think so, not yet. But I'm sure you'll be seeing more of her now that we've moved in. She can't keep out of religious institutions. Something in her character is drawn to them."

"That's reassuring to hear. So many young people these days neglect their spiritual side and prefer drugs and drink and experimenting with deviant sexual practices. Will we be seeing you and your husband at church, Mrs Potts? You'll find the local vicar a most uplifting individual. He was specially commended by Mrs Thatcher once for his trenchant sermons on self-reliance and charity."

"Oh, I hexpect we shall be attending whenever possible."

I was that desperate not to drop any aitches that I was beginning to put them in where they didn't belong, just to be on the safe side. This woman was making me so nervous I could hardly talk.

"Yes, you should count yourself lucky to have a girl going in the right direction, morally speaking. Most of them — well, it's lamentable. I'm a JP and see it all the time in my court. Anyone else on the premises?"

"Well, there is my mother-in-law. My husband's mother, sort of thing. She is confined to a wheelchair as of at the moment, due to a little-hunderstood brain disease. Tragic. She's gone a bit... you know how they do. Not quite all there any more. I thought it was just her hadvancing years, but apparently she might have got it from heating beef burgers."

"Beef burgers?" Mrs Henshaw's lip curled in distaste.

"Not properly defrosted, you see."

"Oh," she said, "I'm sorry to hear that. But, on the other hand, it is a joy to learn of someone not abandoning their aged parents when the going gets rough. There are too many in our society depending on the welfare state these days. Single mothers and goodness knows what just gobbling up our taxes. What career does your husband pursue?"

I resisted the urge to say invertebrate gambler and said: "Er...actually he's retired now. Made his money in the field of butchery and cooked meats. But he keeps busy with his many 'obbies and that."

"I shall look forward to meeting him, Mrs Potts. He sound fascinating. I'm a great admirer of the self-made man. What type of car does he drive? I always think that says so much about a person. I haven't noticed your vehicle."

"Well, in actual fact we are between cars — on a waiting list actually for something that isn't immediately available. Mad about cars is my husband, it's got to be just right before he'll have it. Fussy old thing. I used to have a bit of a runaround myself for the shopping and so forth, a little thing it was. I had to get shut of that due to parking problems and vandalisation difficulties at our previous address."

"I see," she said stiffly, and wrote something down on her clipboard. "Have you any other children, Mrs Potts, besides your daughter?"

"There's my son, Gary. He lives in his own flat with his...with a friend."

"No need to worry, Mrs Potts. I know all about cohabiting. These young people of today — they all seem to live together before they get married, don't they? I don't generally hold with it, marriage is the proper way to honour one's body and spirit. But one can't swim against the tide for ever. So long as there is the intention to legalise and formalise the relationship, one has to be a little — what shall we say? — patient. At least it's normal, isn't it? Much better for them to live with their girl friends than to get mixed up with all these other things. I had a man in my court last week — caught in a lavatory with another man. You can hardly credit that such things happen, can you? I said to him: you ought to find yourself a good woman and settle down and stop all this unnatural behaviour. I blame it on the television. They normalise such things, don't they? I refuse to watch soap operas, these days. They're obsessed with the unnatural. I think it should all be illegal again, then they'd think twice. Is your son, in fact, engaged or thinking of marriage?"

I was getting nervous and it was beginning to show, but then the door opened and Iris wheeled herself in. Yes, wheeled herself in! "Iris!" I said. "What are you doing? And how are you doing it?"

"This is your mother-in-law, is it?" Mrs Henshaw said.

"Yes, this is her. You'll have to make allowances."

Mrs Henshaw stretched out her hand, but Iris just shouted out at the top of her voice: "Kaka!" Mrs Henshaw bridled: "What did she say?" she asked.

"I'm afraid she gets like this. She's gone childish. Says things that we might later regret. Please don't take no notice. We have to put up with it all day. And disregard any mention of Frenchmen in her bedroom."

"KAKA!" Iris says even louder. "I want to kaka!"

Mrs Henshaw reared up like some kind of giraffe, her face was the picture of distaste and disgust.

"Oh, I'm ever so sorry, Mrs Henshaw, you'll have to excuse her. I think I'm going to have to attend to her personal functions, if you don't mind. She can't do nothing for herself, totally lost the use of her legs, you see. I usually have help to lift her. I don't suppose you could see your way to assisting?" Mrs Henshaw, gathered up her gloves, handbag and clipboard very quickly. "I'll have to leave you to it, Doreen. I have a severe aversion to any kind of illness or physical imperfection. I can't even join the hospital visiting committee — the very idea of being in the company of the indisposed or unhealthy makes me go quite faint. But I think you are a saint, I really do, and I just hope that my children will do the same for me if ever I reach that stage. God forbid. I'll call again some time when you aren't so busy."

She was out of that door and down the path like greased lightning.

"Iris," I said. "How did you manage that? Wheeling yourself about. The doctor said you had total muscle atrophy and were as helpless as a new born."

No response. She was slumped in her chair like a rag doll again, slobbering down the front of her blouse.

"This is the strangest condition I've ever come across," I said. "Dead to the world one minute and wheeling yourself about like a rally driver the next. I can't work it out."

At dinner time I warmed her soup up and started spooning it into her mouth. However much I hate her, and however persistent these thoughts of mercy killing are, I can't help feeling sorry for her. She really used to like her food, did Iris.

Then all of a sudden, as I wiped the spillage off her chin, she mumbled: "I could murder some fish and chips."

I was that taken aback I wasn't sure I'd heard it right. I thought: it's just one of her random remarks.

"Pop down the chip shop, Doreen, and get me a haddock. I'll pay."

"Is that you, Iris? Are you talking normal?" I said, puzzled. "Or are you going to start on about your mother and them Frenchmen again?"

"Listen, Doreen," she said without moving her lips, "go and shut them curtains. There might be a DHSS spy with a video camera out there, trying to catch us out."

I was that shocked, I was what they call immobilised.

"Go on, then!" she said. "I can't sit here eating this muck all day."

I got up like a zombie and drew the curtains across. I was still speechless. Then, like some kind of nightmare, Iris rose up out of the wheelchair and walked across to the sideboard and got herself a glass of sherry. "I think I deserve this, after a performance like that."

"I can't credit it," I said, rubbing my eyes. "You mean to say...are you telling me that there's been nothing wrong with you all this time? It's all been a put-up job?"

"That was the agreement, wasn't it? It had to be convincing."

"You deserve more than a glass of sherry, Iris," I said. "You deserve a chuffing Oscar. Are you telling me all that time you were in the hospital, you were putting it on?"

"Very realistic wasn't it?"

"And all that time we've been lifting you, and humping you in and out of chairs, breaking our backs and wiping your arse, there was nothing wrong with you?"

"If you hadn't believed it, you wouldn't have been able to convince the DHSS. They'd have known you were lying. They're crafty them people from the social security — they have special training in spotting phonies, watching your body language and asking you trick questions. They're human lie detectors some of them. But they haven't reckoned with me. I've been studying the techniques of Indian yogis. They can reduce their bodily functions to the absolute minimum by sheer will power. One of them was buried alive for three weeks and when they dug him up he was still in tip top shape. It's all done with meditation and self-hypnosis."

I was livid. "When I think of the agony we've been through over the past couple of weeks over you! While we were crying us eyes out and thinking you'd gone for good, you were laughing up your sleeve at us. I could kick you up and down stairs and think nothing of it. I could knife you."

"Don't come it, Doreen. You didn't do no crying over me. Only my Derek and our Gary shed any tears. I know who really cares about me."

"You've played me for a right fool, you old cow. Derek will go mad when he finds out."

"He'll go mad with relief. You've no idea what I've been through to get this far. All that poking and prodding at the hospital, all them wires and needles and nurses using sandpaper towelling to give you bed baths. And I did it all for the sake of the family. You'll see — this disability is going to be very lucrative before we've finished."

"What disability?" I says.

She winked and started cocking her leg up like a can can girl.

"As soon as you open them curtains, Doreen, I'll be a limp rag in that wheelchair again. And I won't let up. Them DHSS bastards have got spies everywhere ready to report you. I'll play it for all it's worth. But remember — not a word to anybody about this, not even the family. If they know about it, there's more likelihood that one of them will crack and give the game away. They'll be much more convincing if they're kept in the dark. You can tell them that I've spontaneously regained my senses, that I'm compos mentis again and capable of holding conversations. But you'll have to crack on that I'm still non-ambulant as regards the use of my legs."

She climbed back into her wheelchair. "You've got a gold mine in me, Doreen, you'll see," she said. "Now, go and fetch them fish and chips. If I have to eat any more of that bleeding tomato soup I'll spew me guts up."

My head was spinning, but I went to get my coat. "And another thing," she says: "You want to watch that Henshaw woman. We fought the last war to stop her sort invading the country, and now they're chuffing running it. It's the likes of her that thinks telling tales to the DHSS is a civic duty. I come in here just in time. You were digging a grave for yourself. Answering all them questions. She'll be wanting to see your bank account next and your birth certificate, just in case you aren't the right nationality. Chuffing nazi. You'll get yourself into bother as well with all them lies. You won't recall who you've told what to who. You haven't got the fully trained memory for it like I have. Bleeding magistrates — I can't be doing with 'em."

"No, and that's because you know you're going to end up in front of her one of these days. And don't expect no sympathy from me when you do."

* * *

Doreen's Diary March 10th

I shall have to tell you about the meeting of the Resident's Association. It was held at Mrs Henshaw's place. I went to call for Beryl Cathcart so we could go round there together.

"This'll be your first rally, will it, Doreen?" she said.

"Rally?" I said.

"Nuremberg of that ilk," she said.

I didn't get her meaning, but we strolled over to number eight without much enthusiasm.

"You'll be amazed by your neighbours," she said. "In fact, you'll be that amazed you won't believe them. Just be careful what you say — and how you say it."

The Henshaw house is lovely, in a very posh kind of way. There's nothing vulgar or cheap about it — you know the sort of thing, Laura Ashley curtains and upholstery, beautiful reproduction vases and ornaments and a few antiques here and there. And all spotlessly clean. She has a woman come in every morning to do the housework for her.

I gulped when I heard that. Only a few months since I might have been that woman.

It was that immaculate, I felt guilty just sitting on the sumptuously appointed settee, as though my frock would dirty it. Everything looked as though it had just come out of the box or from under sheeting. Not a speck of muck nowhere.

All the other lady residents was there, about ten of them. Most of them middle-aged to elderly, all looking as though they had money coming out of their ear holes. And hairstyle to prove it. It looked like I was the only one dressed by Primark, and I felt self-conscious about it.

No men, though. Even Mrs Henshaw's husband had gone out for the evening — drinks at the golf club, apparently.

"We'll have to see about getting your husband into the golf club," she says to me. "There's a lot of networking done there. You're nobody if you're not in the golf club. What's your husband's handicap?"

I restrained myself from saying "erectile failure" and said: "I couldn't tell you, Mrs Henshaw, love. I take no interest in sport nor nothing like that."

"Golf is not a sport in the usual sense of the word, Doreen, it is actually a social lubricant. Oh yes, I must get my husband to have a word with yours."

I couldn't help noticing Mrs Henshaw's bosom again. She was trying to hide it under this enormous tent-like dress, but it stuck out like two great guns on a warship. I wondered what kind of rigging she had to keep them standing up like that — surely they weren't naturally so perky. Most women of her age with a bust that big would have found it hanging round their belly button.

"Anyway, I'm glad you decided to come to the meeting," she was saying, noticing that I was staring at her chest.

"Oh, I like to keep abreast of what's going on," I said, but then could have bitten my tongue off.

I sat down next to Beryl before I said anything else that would get me into trouble.

"Thank you ladies," Mrs Henshaw shouts, bringing the meeting to order. "Have we all got refreshments? Help yourself to nibbles, and the coffee pot will be replenished as and when. Now — minutes of the last meeting. Mrs O'Boyle?"

A woman about my age stood up. Her nose was sore, red and scabby as though she'd had a really bad cold and had been wiping her nose with sandpaper instead of soft tissue.

She was sniffing something alarming, and all through her recital of the minutes of the last meeting she kept having to stop to wipe her nose. Mrs Henshaw looked at her with distaste every time the poor woman's hand went up to her nose, and she kept pushing this box of mansize Kleenex in front of her.

Mrs O'Boyle began: "We discussed the erection of a high fence around the front of the Close with electronic gates, as proposed by Mrs Henshaw. It was thought that there might be planning difficulties and I promised to approach the council about it. I'm still awaiting their response."

Sniff.

"Mrs Henshaw drew the attention of the residents to a bye-law which forbids the fouling of the pavement by animal droppings. All those of you who have pets should be aware that if they do their business in The Close it is expected that it will be cleaned up immediately. Mrs Henshaw said that those who failed in their duty would be prosecuted to the full extent of the law — which includes a twenty pound fine."

She stopped to sniff again, but obviously sniffing was no longer sufficient and she reached down to the tissue box. Mrs Henshaw sighed in annoyance while Mrs O'Boyle blew her nose with the sort of noise you get as the bath empties.

"Notices to the effect that salesmen, hawkers or charity beggars..."

Once more she reached for the tissues and blew out another unbelievable amount of snot. Mrs Henshaw was livid by this time.

"Where shall I put the used tissues, Mrs Henshaw?" asked Mrs O'Boyle, waving this great handful of slimy Kleenex around the room.

Mrs Henshaw indicated a waste paper bin.

"You really will have to get something done about your problem, Brigitte," said Mrs Henshaw sharply.

"Well, I have tried to get to the bottom of it. The doctor said..."

"Could you get on with the minutes, please? I have some polenta nibbles in the oven and they won't wait for ever."

"Oh yes...now where was I? Oh yes...notices aimed at discouraging charity beggars were distributed to all residents.

Mrs Henshaw said that she expected to see them up outside every home by the time of this meeting."

She sat down gratefully, smothering her nose once more in tissues.

"Thank you, Brigitte. Now to this month's agenda. First of all, I would like to welcome our new resident, Mrs Doreen Potts, who has recently moved into number eleven. I'm sure many of you will already know her, as I believe there was a bit of a commotion when she moved in."

"Terrible racket..." somebody mumbled.

"Well, we know how traumatic moving house can be, and so we will make allowances. It's just that, as you know, Doreen, the residents are pretty keen about noise pollution.

Most of us have suffered to some degree in the past, and I know that you've been a victim yourself. Consequently, we are determined that Evergreen Close will remain a haven of peace and tranquillity. I'm sure you'll do your best to adhere to our wishes."

I nodded feebly.

"Doreen has shown a good example to all of us by taking into her home a severely disabled relative. Your mother-in-law is, in fact, in a wheelchair, isn't she? I would just like to bring to your attention that any ramps you are thinking of installing outside your front door must be of a temporary nature. You will see in the deeds to your home that you are not permitted to make any alterations to the front of your house that will in any way alter the uniform appearance of the Close. No cement mixers or workmen without permission, Doreen. Thank you."

I was about to say something, but before I got my mouth open, she continued: "Next item on the agenda concerns unsightly activities on the Close. Namely, hanging out laundry."

I felt a shock of horror go through me. Only ten minutes before I'd been pegging out.

"We have tried hard to maintain a picturesque quality to our Close. We feel indeed privileged to inhabit such delightful surroundings. Only the other day I noticed that a heron had alighted by my garden pond. This is a much more suitable bird than the many pigeons which infest the neighbourhood. Please don't encourage them by the leaving out of bread and other inducements. Coming back to the point — residents are requested to consider their neighbours when doing their washing. Please keep it indoors for drying purposes. And from a wildlife perspective, we feel that bird tables are acceptable in the garden, so long as they are discreet and of good quality."

Her bosoms were heaving with self-importance and suddenly I found myself saying: "Tits."

The group took a breath.

"Blue tits, I mean. We've got them in our garden."

Mrs Henshaw was stony-faced. She obviously didn't like being interrupted.

"We now turn to the issue of barbecues. Last summer several residents held barbecues on their outdoor patio seating areas. Now, as I understand it, barbecues are American or Australian in origin. They involve sausages, beef burgers and" — she looked at her papers — "something called 'ribs'. Now, while I accept that eating preferences are a personal thing, the inhaling of smoke is not. Last summer a great deal of smoke was produced from barbecues, and much of it wafted in to my kitchen. I hope that when the weather improves, and the concept of eating al fresco once more becomes popular, residents will bear in mind that some of us do not appreciate our lungs being coated with wood smoke. And that the smell of chargrilled sausages is not to everyone's taste."

The gathered women looked down, suitably chastised.

"Finally, a perusal of the planning applications indicates that a change of usage application has been made to convert the old community centre — the one just outside the Close — into a licensed mini-mart."

There was an excited buzz round the room.

"The name of the applicant," Mrs Henshaw said, "is a Mr Bannerjee." The hub-bub died down. "I believe that it would be in the interests of the Close to oppose this application."

"Why?" I said. "It'd be nice to have a shop on the doorstep, in case you run out of milk. They stay open till all hours these Indians."

It was as though she hadn't heard me. "All those in favour of lodging an objection, please show."

They all put their hands up except me.

"All those against."

She looked me straight in the eyes. I didn't move.

"Record one abstention," she said to Brigitte, who was taking the minutes. "And now, if there is no further business..."

I half put my hand up, but it was too indecisive to register.

"I declare the meeting closed. Now please enjoy the olives and pesto morsels."

And that was an order.

* * *

Letter from Gary Potts
Dear Terry,

Greetings from Rotherham, and just for once I've got a bit of good news. It's about Gran — she's much, much better. It's quite amazing, the doctor is absolutely bewildered by her recovery. She's gradually regaining her senses and is almost back to her old, sharp-witted self. But her legs seem to have gone for good. They think she'll be confined to a wheelchair for the rest of her life, but at least she's mentally agile again.

When she came home from the hospital she was totally gone. I thought: we'll never be treated to that rasping voice again, slagging the world off. You see, my Gran is a hero to me, it's her cynicism that I admire so much. I think I must have inherited some of it from her because whenever I see her in full spate, abusing any representative of authority she can get access to, I feel like cheering and shouting "Go on, Gran, you tell 'em". Everybody else cringes with embarrassment, but I love to see her in action. She tells off the social workers for being tardy; the local councillor gets and ear bashing about the delays in payment of her benefits; the vicar's been sent off with a flea in his ear for even daring to suggest that he say a prayer for her, and she's written a defamatory tract to the Prince of Wales. She's no time for any of them! Mam brought her round to the flat the other day, just for a bit of an outing. A change of scene, sort of thing. I was that glad to see her I had a little cry.

Poor old Mam had to push her all the way over here in the wheelchair — it's almost two miles. She was knackered by the time she got here and fell asleep on the settee.

Bill says: "I'll put my Music of the Whales disc on. It's supposed to be relaxing and reviving. Might make Doreen feel better."

As soon as it started, Gran says: "What the chuffing hell's that racket?" Bill says: "It's the cry of the humpback whale set to synthesiser rhythms."

"It's enough to give you earache," she says.

"It's New Age," I said.

"New Age it might be," she says "but this is Old Age," and wheels herself over to the music centre and takes the disc out. "Where's them Jimmy Somerville tapes you used to have? Let's have them on. They've a bit more tune to them. Not much, but a bit."

That little visit took our mind of the court case for a couple of hours, at least. The date has been set and Hindley is insisting that he is going to see it through. We are going to plead provocation, and our solicitor is thinking about countersuing him for harassment. Bill is worried sick that if it goes against us he'll have a criminal record that will interfere with his career.

Yesterday our Sylvia came round to the flat. Her pregnancy is now beginning to show, and she'll soon have to abandon her tight-fitting skirts and think about maternity frocks. She looks like some old slapper that hangs around the docks in Portsmouth. Talk about "hello sailor" — she'd be lucky to get 50p a time the way she's looking these days.

And yet she keeps going on about how inspired she is by her religion. I said to her: "Why don't you have a word with Hindley for us — remind him about the virtue of Christian forgiveness?"

But she says that he is being led astray by forces beyond his control.

"That's not real religion that he is preaching Gary", she says, "it's the mock variety. Hindley is praying to false gods. Mark my words, one day the truth will be revealed. Somebody's got the answer, but he isn't born yet."

"I assume you are referring to the forthcoming Unsworth sprog?"

"Whatever you might think of Guru Unsworth, he deserves respect for his spirituality. He's gifted in that department. Stands to reason that his child will be as well."

"Bernard is gifted in a number of departments as I remember. I used to take showers with him at school after football. Yes, he's definitely gifted. But then, you'd know all about that."

"That's the limit of your interest, isn't it? You can't see the size of his spirituality, only his genitals."

"Seems to me that you've not been completely indifferent to them, if I might say so."

While I made tea she sat with Bill on the settee. She was snuggling up to him and invading his space like crazy. He was hutching up, but she followed him and was nearly on top of him by the time I brought the beans on toast through.

"It's tragic that a lovely-looking lad like you should be a homosexual," she says to Bill. "All that gorgeous hair and them blue eyes. And the muscles. What a waste. Have you ever tried it with a woman?"

"What?" he said, not believing her cheek.

"Well, have you?"

"Yes, I've tried it with a woman. Not that it's any of your business," he said impatiently.

"If you must know," I said "Bill was married at one bit."

"Never! When was this?"

"I don't want to talk about it," says Bill. "It was a mistake."

Our Sylvia seemed fascinated by this piece of news.

"Go on, Bill. Tell me. What was her name?"

"It's all in the past. It's forgotten about."

He was annoyed with me for giving her this titbit and took his dinner into the bedroom, closing the door after him.

"Well, would you credit it!" says Sylvia. "He's not really gay after all."

"Of course he's gay. I should know."

"Yes, but there's different kinds of gay aren't there? There's genetic gay — like you, and there's men who take it up because they've had bad experiences with women. Like Bill. He's too masculine to be a real gay. He's shown he's capable of fancying women. And he's played football for Rotherham United."

"Do you ever talk anything but crap, Sylvia?" I said. "You don't know anything about it."

"Oh, don't I? I know what I know — and I know that Bill isn't the same as you. You can see it in his face. You can feel it about him. He has that masculine aura. The kind that you haven't got."

"Sylvia, listen to me carefully. Bill is fully homosexual. He is not bisexual. He is not heterosexual. He is gay. Him and me make love, just about every day. Sometimes three or four times at weekends. I am not a woman."

"No, not as such. But you're not really a man either, are you? I mean, look who cooked the tea. It wasn't him, was it? What I'm getting at is, yes, you are a man in the sense that you have the equipment on your body, but your mind isn't made the same way as other men. I know about these things. I've studied it closely."

"The fact that you've probably had more prick than a junkie's forearm does not make you an expert on alternative sexualities."

"As much as you'd like to be, you aren't a woman. You haven't got that sixth sense that women have. I think Bill could be rescued."

"Rescued from what?"

"This life you've got. I mean, where's it going? No kiddies, no family, no normality. Choose what you say, you can't give him what a woman could give him."

"Sylvia," I said patiently. "If you are setting yourself up as a representative of normality, I think I'll stick with what I've got, thank you. And I wouldn't keep raising the topic with Bill. He's very touchy about people putting gayness down. He doesn't like it."

"That's because he's oversensitive. Defensive. He's trying to justify the decision he's made, but that wall of denial can be broken down."

"Oh get off back to Guru fucking Unsworth. You deserve each other."

She patted her stomach. "I've got as much of Guru Unsworth as I want here. What I'm carrying will make Guru Unsworth's efforts at evangelism look like chicken feed. The only thing this child lacks is a father figure that can support him until the day comes when his destiny is delivered to him."

"OK, that's enough. Can you pop off home now before I lose my temper?"

She smiled pityingly at me. I think she really believes all this claptrap she keeps spouting. But she put her coat on and, as she left, she made the sign of the cross and said she hoped that God would deliver us. She'd shut the door before I had time to throw my shoe at her.

It left me in a foul temper, and Bill was equally unhappy. We hardly spoke the rest of the evening.

Anyway, the following weekend something else happened that has worried me. I went to the local betting shop to put the traditional pound each way on the Grand National for Gran, and there was Dad. He was that engrossed in watching the betting show, he didn't see me come in. Just as one race was ending he screwed his ticket up and threw it on the floor, then stormed out of the shop without even noticing I was there.

Nellie Maddox, the woman behind the counter shook her head.

"You want to keep an eye on your Dad, Gary," she said.

"How do you mean, Nellie?"

"Well, I'm not at liberty to say. Confidentiality between a bookmaker and his client is as sacred as that between a priest and confessor. But take note that I said so."

I was puzzled, but I went over to where he'd chucked his ticket on the floor and picked it up. It was for a £250 bet on the 2.30 at Cartmel. It hadn't won.

I thought: he's trying to repeat his success, obviously without succeeding. I wondered how many other bets of this size there had been, and how many there could be before disaster struck.

I'm going to have a word with him to see what's going on, and I'll let you know the outcome.

Your worried friend, Gary

* * *

Doreen's Diary 4th April 1996

I was woken up last night — well, early this morning actually — by the sound of the phone ringing. Now, I don't know about you, but whenever the phone rings in the middle of the night it puts the wind up me good and proper. It can only be bad news or a wrong number. I jumped out of bed and went downstairs to answer.

"Can I help you?" I said, expecting it to be the hospital or the police.

"Sylvia?" this man's voice said.

"No," I said. "Sylvia's in bed. Where the hell do you expect her to be at three a.m. in the morning? Who's calling, anyway?" "It's anonymous," the voice said.

"Are you anything to do with Bernard Unsworth?" I said.

"I told you, it's anonymous and private. Could you get your Sylvia to the phone, please, Mrs Potts."

I went up to our Sylvia's room and woke her up.

"There's an anonymous phone call for you from Bernard Unsworth," I said.

She sat bolt upright with her eyes wide open.

"How does he know I'm here?"

"Shall I tell him to eff off?"

"No, I'll speak to him."

She jumped out of bed and went downstairs. I stood on the stairwell, listening.

"I know it's you, Guru, and I know what you're ringing up for. You can't scare me," she was saying.

I took a few steps down the stairs so I could hear better.

"No. That money belongs to me. I shall soon have a child to support, and although it's a privilege to be carrying such a unique infant, we'll still have to eat. So no, I won't be handing it back just so you can buy another daft car. Besides, most if it's spent now."

I went down a couple more steps.

"Don't you threaten me...I don't care what you say...No. I've told you. I'm not coming back and neither is the money and neither is the baby."

I charged down the stairs and grabbed the phone out of her hand.

"Who is this?" I demanded. "Is it Bernard Unsworth?" Nobody answered, but I could hear heavy breathing.

"Listen, Unsworth, I'd know your breathing anywhere. Don't get no ideas about our Sylvia coming back to that brothello you're running down there. You've caused her enough problems, getting her up the duff. I could knock your block off for the trouble you've caused this family. But you'll get your just desserts my lad, I'll see to that."

Whoever it was at the other end rang off.

"What was all that about? Is it about that money you pinched off them?" I said to our Sylvia.

"They want it back. I don't know how they've tracked me down, but they've got my number now."

"Did he threaten you?"

"Only with the vengeance of Khali."

"Who the bloody hell's Khali when he's at home?"

"I've told you once, it's a she — the goddess of vengeance and destruction."

"Well, I'm Doreen, goddess of smacks in the mouth, and if that Unsworth comes anywhere near you or that babby you're carrying, I'll cripple him."

She looked that worried I put my arm round her shoulder.

"Get off back to bed, love. You don't want to go upsetting yourself or you'll affect the kiddy — they're sensitive to that sort of thing. We've got enough with one face-ache in the family, namely your Dad."

She went off to her room, and I went round checking the locks on the doors.

* * *

Doreen's Diary 7th April 1996

I don't know what Derek's up to, but he never seems to be in the house these days. He goes off straight after breakfast and I don't see him again till well after tea time. He cracks on he's looking for work, but I can't imagine where he can be looking all day every day, there aren't that many firms left to turn him down.

Iris was equally puzzled. "Do you think he's got himself another woman?" she asked. "Only they sometimes do when they're depressed."

I said: "I think there's about as much likelihood of Derek committing adultery as there is of Mrs Henshaw doing the hokey-cokey."

Still, it keeps him out of the house, and there's less likelihood he'll come across Mrs Henshaw and start answering her questions in a way that contradicts what I've said to her.

The DHSS benefits relating to Iris's incarceration in a wheelchair are now on stream, so that's relieved the financial pressure a bit. Our Sylvia continues to contribute from her own dwindling nest egg, but that's not going to last for ever. She's also looking into the benefits she can get when she's a single mother. It all adds up.

Yesterday our Sylvia got a letter which upset her. It had been sent anonymously although the handwriting was unmistakable. It had Unsworth written all over it.

It consisted of a picture of this Indian god with six arms.

"Khali is coming," our Sylvia wailed.

"Good," I said. "I could do with somebody to help me with the housework. Somebody with six arms would be just the ticket."

She wasn't amused and ran upstairs to her room.

She's looking quite the little expectant mother now, and she's bought herself a range of lovely maternity dresses from Marks and Spencers. The problem is that she's taken them all up, well above the knee, which gives her the look of a boiled egg perched on two matchsticks. She thinks it's sexy, though.

All the same, she's not a happy girl.

And our Gary's no better. What with this court case coming up, Bill's getting right bolshy. I think their relationship is under something of a strain. I try to help, but it isn't appreciated. I said to Bill the other day, I said: "I don't know what you're worried about. I mean, what's the worst that can happen to you?"

"I could get sent to prison, that's what could happen," he snapped.

"That's nothing these days. They've got colour televisions and table tennis in there."

He just sniffed and went into the bedroom.

He wants to be grateful he's got our Gary to support him through the crisis. He can be a rock can our Gary.

He's as loyal as a labrador, that lad.

* * *

Letter from Gary Potts
Dear Terry,

I don't want to burden you with my problems, but I've got to talk to someone; my whole life is disintegrating in front of me. Not only have we got the court case next week, I've been told by the union that my job is under threat.

You know that I work at the cleansing department.

It's my job to co-ordinate the dustbin men on their rounds. Well, the council are selling the whole department off to a private firm, and we've all got to apply for our own jobs again under this new regime. The problem is, this private firm is cutting down on the administration. Some of us in the office are going to be made compulsorily redundant. So that's yet another sword of Damocles hanging over us.

I must say, I haven't made things any better by what I did last Friday. Bill was working nights so I decided to go out with Darryl. That was mistake number one. We went to that new gay club they've opened just outside town. Well, the upshot was I dropped a couple of tabs of E and then brought somebody home for the night. It didn't mean anything, I just wanted to cheer myself up, and there's nothing quite like a big dick for putting the smile back on your face, is there? Kevin he was called. Nice lad. I couldn't resist it.

Well, we were just about to have another go when Bill came home unexpectedly and caught us. The flat reeked of poppers and it was all a bit embarrassing because this Kevin had me over the back of the settee in a somewhat acrobatic position. As you can imagine, it hasn't helped the situation.

Bill's gone into a crisis of confidence and hardly talks to me; he's maundering over the Hindley business and, well, it's all getting a bit much.

Wish us luck for next week — that's if we're still together.

best wishes, Gary

* * *

Letter from Gary Potts

Dear Terry,

I hope you don't mind me sharing it with you, but I think I've just had the worst week of my life.

Bill was found guilty and fined £500 and made to pay £1,500 compensation to Hindley. The judge took into account his previous good character and the fact that there had been an element of provocation, but all the same, it's cleaned him out. All his savings gone in one swipe. And he's been sent for by the personnel officer at work. He hopes it's just going to be a telling off and a warning.

He'd been ever so quiet over the last few days. Introspective. Worried. Then one day he came home from work and said: "I've made arrangements to move into the nurse's accommodation at the hospital."

"But why?" I said. "You've always said you'd never live there — nobody on the premises after eleven, people making noise all night. You said you'd rather live in a cardboard box."

"We're going to have to move out of here eventually, anyway. Hindley won't rest till he's moved us on."

"But we can find somewhere else together. Not all landlords are nutcases."

He looked at me. "I don't think I want to."

"It's what I did the other week, isn't it? I've said I'm sorry — it was something I'm not proud of. It won't happen again. I'm ashamed."

"That hurt, yes, but that's not all of it. I've been beginning to wonder about where our relationship is going for a while now. I don't think I want to live with you any more."

I fell on to the settee, stunned. "Well, thanks for letting me down gently," I said.

"I'll be moving out tomorrow if that's OK."

"What? This is all a bit sudden, isn't it? You know I can't afford to live here on my own. You're going to leave me right in the shitter."

"I'm sorry."

"Look, Bill," I said. "I know all this has hit you for six and I don't blame you for being angry and depressed. Give yourself a bit of time. We can work on our problems together, perhaps with one of those counsellors down at the complementary living centre. Don't pack it in at the first sign of a hiccup. Will you try?"

He looked at me with a little tear in his eye and said, with a crack in his voice: "I'll go and put my things into boxes. I'll be gone by the time you get back from work tomorrow. You can keep the CD player."

Well, true to his word, he was gone when I got home, having removed all signs of his presence from the flat. It didn't matter really, as this was my final return from work, too. There was a letter on my desk at the office this morning regretting that the firm no longer had need of my services and could I be off the premises by lunch time. Statutory redundancy money enclosed — £125 — many thanks and cheerio.

The upshot of it is that I've moved back in with my parents, into their new house at Evergreen Close. Mam thinks it's wonderful that we're all back together under one roof.

She's living in a fantasy world, but I go along with her. Talk about being forcibly returned to childhood — there's my old Dandy and Beano annuals on the bedside table and she's put a Star Wars duvet cover on the bed. Every time I go out of the door she shouts: "Don't forget your curb drill." She'll be insisting I sleep with a night light next.

I'm in a reasonably large single room, but the house seems really crowded with our Sylvia taking up the space of two and Gran going about in her wheelchair. It's difficult to adjust to living in this kind of large communal household again.

Although there are three lavatories, they still seem to be occupied all the time. Women are always on the lavatory, every five minutes.

I pay what I can out of my dole money, but that's not exactly a king's ransom. God, I miss Bill. It seems so strange sleeping on my own again and waking up every morning with nobody beside me. Our Sylvia has been gloating a bit, saying I told you it wouldn't last and all that. If she wasn't pregnant I'd beat her up.

She was writing her stories the other night. She's always been a great one for writing stories, has our Sylvia. She gets these exercise books and fills them up with the most stupid tales you've ever heard. She was sitting at the table, scrawling in this spidery handwriting. I looked over her shoulder. She was writing about St Bernadette, because her and me Gran had been watching that film with Jennifer Jones on the telly this afternoon, the one where this really camp Virgin Mary hovers over the rubbish dump and Vincent Price gets throat cancer because he thinks it's all a con job.

"I could do that," she was writing. "I could be a saint, just like Bernadette, and have everybody thinking I was lovely and kind and holy. If only the Virgin Mary would appear to me everything would be all right. That would be one up on Guru Unsworth."

I said: "There's about as much chance of you seeing the Virgin Mary as there is of me fancying Sharon Stone."

She slammed the book shut. "Bog off, reading my private thoughts. It's nowt to do with you." She threw a cup at me but it missed.

Talk about a return to infancy — I can't stand it.

It just goes to show that however carefully you plan things, they can go wrong so quickly. I'm depressed, Mam's depressed, Sylvia's depressed, Dad's suicidal. There's only Gran who seems to be keeping her chin up, and she's got least to be happy about.

Any suggestions you might have about improving our lot would be greatly appreciated. (I'm attending a group therapy session at the Whole Earth Alternative Living Centre, but I might pack it up. The facilitator is crackers.)

Your desperate friend,

Gary

* * *

Doreen's Diary 14th April 1996

Beryl Cathcart came round this morning for a cup of coffee.

She looked at Iris, slumped in her wheelchair and then looked at me pityingly. "Tragic," she said, "I don't know how you cope."

If only she'd been there ten minutes previous she'd have seen Iris on her hands and knees, scrubbing the kitchen floor. Now the old twister was back in her wheelchair, putting on the act. I felt terrible. I really like Beryl, and the thought of Iris laughing at her behind that pretend-dementia got my goat.

"I'll just put her away while we talk," I said, and shoved Iris out of the room and shut the door.

"Will she be all right in the kitchen on her own?" Beryl said.

"Forget her," I said. "She's forgotten us."

Beryl said: "You know, Doreen, Mrs Henshaw is expecting you to host one of the coffee mornings she arranges for members of the Resident's Association."

"Here? I couldn't, Beryl. I can't host social functions, I've no experience at it."

"She'll mither you till you do it. It's nothing, Doreen, really. Just make a few cakes, brew some coffee and leave them to it. No need to make a fuss."

"Yes, but, they'll expect me to sparkle. You can't be a hostess without sparkling."

"Oh, I don't know. Most of them seem to manage it."

"I suppose I'll have it to do, although I don't like the idea."

Beryl put her cup down and bit her lip. "Look, Doreen, I don't want to worry you, but I think it's only fair to warn you."

"Warn me?"

"They're speculating. The neighbours. They're wondering who you really are. None of them believe your story, you know."

I gave a shudder. "What's not to believe? We've done nothing wrong."

"That's not the point. It's not a matter of right or wrong it's a matter of whether they take to you or not. For instance, your Sylvia. It's becoming increasingly unbelievable that she's not pregnant."

"How did you know she's pregnant? She hasn't told you, has she? She's under instructions to keep her trap shut."

"No, she didn't tell me. She didn't have to. When I asked how far gone she was she gave me some cock and bull story about having an eating disorder that causes her abdomen to swell up like a balloon. I ask you! It's risible."

"I told her to say that."

"Well, it's pathetic. That voluminous maternity wear tells the whole story. People know she's not married. And then there's your Derek. Only ever seen after dark. People want to know where he is and what he's doing. You'll never get on the dinner party circuit unless you make yourselves a bit more transparent."

"I've been avoiding it, trying to keep a bit of distance from them. I know the more the neighbours see of us, the less they'll like us. I'm in a bit of a cleft stick really."

"Doreen. I think you know that I'm a bit of an outsider here, too..."

"Not as much as us."

"No, but I don't fit in. I'm not sure I want to fit in. There are some nasty people living in this Close, small-minded, insular. You've seen them in action."

"But I want to be like that. Respectable."

"You'll have to forgive me for being brutally honest, love, but I think you've blown your chances of respectability as far as this lot are concerned. They're just waiting for you to trip yourself up."

"I know that, Beryl. That's why I'm trying not to get involved in social events. I suppose I'm just putting off the hateful day."

"Can I ask you something, Doreen? Why did you move in here? Wouldn't you have been happier somewhere more..."

"Working class?"

"Well, for want of a better description. Somewhere more homely and relaxed?"

"I wanted us to better ourselves. I still do. I think we can if we're given a chance."

"There are no learning curves permitted here, Doreen. You're either one of these people or you're not. And I've a feeling you're not. And you know what, I like you better for it."

* * *

Doreen's Diary 20th April 1996

Well, I did it. I offered to host a coffee morning and Mrs Henshaw was as pleased as punch.

"We shall so look forward to seeing you on your own ground, Doreen. It'll make the house feel much more part of the community if we've all been there. Oh, one thing, as regards your mother-in-law. Will she be on the premises during the festivities? Or will you be able to get her out for the day? Don't get me wrong — I'd love her to be there, but I feel she'd have little to offer the occasion, and as I've explained, I cannot tolerate the company of the seriously disordered for very long without becoming quite ill myself. Silly I know, but there we are."

"Don't worry, Mrs Henshaw. I'll slip her two or three Valiums and put her to bed. She'll be no trouble."

"Excellent. Well, I shall look forward to sharing patisserie with you."

Well, they turned up at half past ten this morning, like a gaggle of geese. Iris was safely tucked up, our Sylvia was off the premises (further religious studies, there can't be much more for her to learn) and Derek was off doing whatever it is he does. Our Gary had helped me bake a few buns — I was going to make a crack about fairy cakes being his speciality, but he's not in the mood and would probably have took it the wrong way. Then he went off down the Labour Exchange to sign on.

Brigitte O'Boyle was there, sniffing like a bloodhound and blowing her nose every five minutes. Listening to it makes you feel a bit sick after a bit. Mrs Henshaw whispered to me: "It's all psychosomatic, you know. Hysterical in origin. Before she started with this she had agoraphobia. I think she could get it under control if she pulled herself together. I sometimes feel like shaking her."

I smiled as I thought: Yes, and there are one or two who wouldn't mind shaking you — by the throat.

85

Mrs Henshaw sat on the high-backed chair like Queen Victoria. I handed her a cup of coffee, but she pulled a face after the first sip and put it on my occasional table in a way that said everything.

"I'm actually very much a tea person, myself," I said. "Never really mastered coffee. It's difficult to know how it should taste if you never drink it. I'll have another crack at it."

I went in the kitchen and started struggling with this coffee percolator I'd bought. Beryl Cathcart followed me in.

"Is it all right?" I said to her.

"So far so good," she said. "Here let me make the coffee. You go back and make sure they're not going through your bank book."

Mrs Henshaw was clinking the side of her cup with her spoon. "May I have your attention ladies," she was saying. "I'd just like to say a few words."

Mrs Henshaw loved holding court.

Silence descended on the room (all except for Brigitte O'Boyle who kept up the barrage of sniffing throughout).

"I'd just like to say that it is so pleasant to see you all here today, our first visit to Mrs Potts's delightful home. I'm sure we'd all like to welcome her in the traditional Evergreen Close manner."

They all reached into their bags and brought out little gifts, wrapped up lovely in silver paper with ribbons and that.

"These," says Mrs Henshaw, "are tokens of our welcome. May we all enjoy many happy years together as neighbours."

They all handed me their presents, and I unwrapped them one by one. There was a vase, an imitation Capodimonte figure, a coffee cup and saucer with a lovely design on it and a box of top quality Belgian chocolates. I was that touched I started to fill up.

"This is ever so kind of you," I said. "I'm right chuffed with it."

They all laughed.

Mrs Henshaw gave a little clap of her hands. "Right chuffed! This is the kind of picturesque speech we all love. I could listen to you talking all day, Doreen — it's so refreshing to hear working class accents from people other than servants. We mustn't forget that Doreen comes from a mining background. I believe your father was a pit worker wasn't he Doreen?"

"Oh yes, worked down the mines all his life."

"Salt of the earth, miners," Mrs Henshaw said. "Or at least they were in D.H. Lawrence's time, when they knew their place in the scheme of things. Then they became rather too left-wing for their own good, and now look what's happened. Still, they've no-one to blame but themselves."

"Our family's got coal in the blood," I said proudly. "My husband's father was a miner, an' all."

"Well, as long as the coal is in the blood and not in the fireplace, that's fine. We became a smokeless zone some years ago, so it would be quite illegal to carry on your family traditions here," said Mrs Henshaw, with a hacksaw smile.

She turned back to the group. "But, you know, our origins are not the most important thing about us, are they — however lowly they may be. It's our destination in life that counts. What we've made of ourselves. I take my hat off to you, Doreen, in your determination to better yourself and improve life for your family. Despite your many disadvantages. It takes enormous strength and determination to pull yourself up by the bootstraps as you have; to have made your fortune in butchery and cooked meats is nothing to be ashamed of. If I had champagne, I'd toast you."

I wasn't sure whether to thank her or chuck the pot of coffee over her steel helmet of a hairstyle. Instead of calling her a patronising cow I found myself saying: "Thank you Mrs Henshaw. How nice of you to say so."

"You know," she said, "Doreen is an example to us all of true family values. She has a successful husband, a daughter, a son who has recently moved in and, to cap it all, she has extended her family to include her mother-in-law, presently disabled and little more than a turnip..."

"I think you mean a cabbage," whispered Brigitte O'Boyle.

"Well, certainly not completely in command of her faculties. Doreen is an example to us all of raising a family that feels good enough about itself to stay together. So many families these days are estranged and this is the source of many of our social ills. In my court room I see many examples of the fallen — many could have been saved if only their family life had been more wholesome. Crime, vandalism, single parenthood, deviant sex, drug-taking, divorce, alcoholism, unrestrained gambling — I see them all.

And the thing they all have in common is a damaged family."

There was a general murmur of agreement from the assembled Henshaw fan club. Gloria Longbottom from number two tried to start a round of applause, but Mrs Henshaw stopped her with a raised hand, and continued: "Look, I know that life is complicated and difficult these days. We all have our problems, but we have to keep faith with ourselves and particularly with our families. The family is the bed-rock of civilisation. Divorce is the enemy of the family."

From the kitchen I heard Beryl start having a coughing do.

We was all sitting there, chit-chatting when I heard the front door go. It was our Sylvia back earlier than she said.

She came into the room — stomach first.

"Oh sorry," she said. "I didn't realise you were having a party, Mam. I'll go upstairs out of the way."

"Sylvia, isn't it?" Mrs Henshaw called out.

Our Sylvia turned back. "Yes, that's me."

"Pop upstairs, love," I said. "Do your exercises for that disorder you've got that causes your stomach to bloat. The doctor will go mad if he finds out you've not been doing as you're told."

"Oh, I'm sure she could join us for just a few minutes," Mrs Henshaw said, realising that at last she had me in a corner as regards our Sylvia. "Come and sit with me, my dear."

Our Sylvia looked at me, and I tried to signal to her with my eyes to get out before Mrs Henshaw prised the truth from her, but she didn't realise what I was trying to say and she sat next to Mrs Henshaw on the settee.

"Now, then, dear, this condition you have. It's quite extraordinary. Have you seen a specialist about it?"

"Oh yes," I interrupted. "She's had the best advice money could buy. Haven't you, Sylvia, love?" "Er...yes," says our Sylvia.

"And what is the condition called?" says Henshaw.

Our Sylvia was struggling. She looked at me, but I couldn't help her.

"Isn't it Westheimer's Syndrome?" says Beryl Cathcart from the kitchen door.

"Oh that's it. Westheimer's Syndrome. Thanks for remembering that Beryl. I've no memory for these medical names," I says.

"Westheimer's Syndrome," says Mrs Henshaw, writing it down in her little black book. "I'll look that up in my medical reference when I get home. And," she says, returning the spotlight to our Sylvia, who now looked like a frightened rabbit cornered by a fox. "Are you engaged or seeing a young man at present, my dear?"

"No, actually, I'm..."

"She's been engaged in the past, haven't you, love? Er...but he was tragically killed. Terrible it was. She was devastated."

There was a silence as they waited for me to supply further particulars.

"Shocking wasn't it, Sylvia?" I said.

"What?" she says.

"When he was killed."

"Who?"

"Your fiancé."

"Oh, er...yes."

"What exactly happened my dear?" says Mrs Henshaw with this mock kind of sympathy. Her eyes narrowing as she saw us floundering.

"Was it a street crime, Mam?"

"No, love," I said, giving a weak laugh, "What on earth are you thinking about? It was a motorway pile-up. On the M1. Street crime! I don't know where she gets her ideas from. Oh yes, it tipped her over the edge for a bit. She was even thinking of going into a convent."

"So, no intention of getting married?"

"Not at the moment, no. Have I Mam?" says our Sylvia.

"She's still in a state of grief. She couldn't even consider moving on yet."

Mrs Henshaw appeared to be satisfied with that, and we all started to relax. But that was just a ploy. As soon as we'd let our corsets out, so to speak, she pounced. "Is the ante-natal clinic still up at Dobney Hill?" she says to our Sylvia, ever so casual.

Before I could intervene, our Sylvia blurts out: "Yes, I go on Tuesdays and Fridays."

Mrs Henshaw was triumphant, but before she could revel in her victory, the front door went again.

It was our Gary. He called through as he took his coat off: "It's only me, Mam. I've been to see a solicitor about suing the council for unfair dismissal on the grounds of my homosexuality."

Everybody gasped. It was like a wind running through the room.

"That's my son, Gary," I apologised. "Always having his little jokes. He'll say anything, however disgusting, to get a laugh. He's as normal as the day is long."

He walked into the room, wearing a T-shirt saying "Nobody knows I'm gay" in large pink letters.

Then there was complete silence. It went on for what seemed like minutes, with everybody waiting for me to say something. I couldn't think of anything. Then Mrs Henshaw dropped her pencil, and broke the spell.

"I thought so," Mrs Henshaw said. "Well, Mrs Potts. I'm afraid we have to be going now. Don't we ladies?" Her voice was as cold as ice.

They all started gathering up their bits and preparing to leave.

"Oh, don't go yet," I said. "You've only just got here. I haven't properly thanked you for your presents."

Mrs Henshaw swept past me and knocked my imitation Capodimonte figurine over as she went out. The little shepherdess's head broke off as it hit the floor.

The rest of them left without a word. All except for Beryl.

I sat there surrounded by the wrapping paper, unable to speak.

Beryl shook her head. "Well, at least you don't have to keep up the pretence any more, Doreen. The cat is well and truly out of the bag now."

"I'm sorry, Mam," says our Sylvia.

"I didn't realise there was anybody else in the house," says our Gary.

"Oh, don't worry, love. We're all out of the cupboard now. Who needs that old cow anyway? She can take a running jump — and take her snotty crew with her. We can live without her and the likes of her."

"Not in Evergreen Close you can't," says Beryl. "You'd better start putting the barricades up, Doreen, because those on the wrong side of Hilary Henshaw have got themselves a formidable enemy."

"Don't let her frighten you, Beryl. She can't do nothing. It's not illegal to have an illegitimate bastard child these days. And there's nothing to stop you being a pervert, neither. We pay our way. She can stick her Residents Committee up her arse."

Our Sylvia laughed, but I know that big words are easy to say. It's different when you've got to face the enemy.

* * *

Doreen's Diary 21st April 1996

I wasn't happy. Every time I went out I was cut dead by one or other of the neighbours. When I saw Mrs Henshaw getting into her car one morning I went out specially and tried to strike up a conversation. It was as though I didn't exist; she looked straight through me.

Right, I thought, if that's the way you want it, so be it.

And I went in and did three full loads of washing and hung it out in the garden — lines full of it flapping in the breeze.

Then I went and put the rubbish bags out by the gate, three days before it was due to be collected.

Then I said to Derek: "We're having a barbecue for our tea tonight. Go and get it lit."

"I can't light no barbecues, Doreen. I don't know how to do it. Besides, we can't be eating out in this weather, it's too parky."

"Well go and burn some rubbish in the garden. Some old tires or something. I want that Henshaw bag well and truly upset."

"You'll only make it worse by tormenting her," says Iris.

"Shut up you," I said. "When I need your advice, I'll ask for it."

I was that mad I could have gone over there and chucked a brick through the Henshaw's window. But I restrained myself.

Then the afternoon post came, and that took my mind off revenge good and proper.

There was a bank statement. I nearly dropped through the floor when I saw it. In the red by £1,692. 47. I said to Derek: "It must be a mistake. We can't be overdrawn, we had a little nest egg in that account."

"I'll be off then," Derek said, going for his coat.

"Did you hear what I just said, Derek? We're in debt to the bank. All the money's gone."

"Mustn't be late for the library opening. Time is of the essence when you're job seeking." he said.

I grabbed his arm. "Just a minute, you. What's going off here?"

"I'm sure you'll be able to sort it out, Doreen. Give them a ring. Talk it over."

"I'm not giving nobody no ring till you've told me what's to do. I want to be armed with all the facts before I go charging in there."

Derek looked shame-faced, as well he might.

"Have you drawn this money out?" I said.

He shuffled and looked down at his shoes. A family trait.

"Have you?"

"Derek — answer her!" Iris commanded from her wheelchair.

His face crumpled up and he started sobbing. "I only did it for the best. I thought I could do it again."

I looked at Iris. She looked at me.

"Do what again?" Then it dawned on me. "Oh, my Jesus, the bookies!" I said. "You've spent it at the bookies."

"You soft sod," Iris shouted. "Haven't you learned by now that only fools chase their winnings? His dad were just the same."

He slumped down on to the floor and wept like a baby.

"Oh my God," I said, as the full horror of what he'd done dawned on me. "We've got the mortgage payment due this week as well. What are we going to do?" Derek sobbed even more loudly.

"Stop that snivelling, Derek, it's getting right on my chest," says Iris.

"I'm sorry, Mam," he cried. "I'll make it up to you."

"Oh get out of my sight," she said. "Doreen, lock him in his room. He'll have to be kept away from that betting shop or we'll end up with a debt the size of Soviet Russia. Now let me have some space, I don't want disturbing for a couple of hours. I've got some conniving to do."

* * *

Doreen's Diary 23rd April 1996

We have to face the facts. We are stony broke and haven't got a penny to our name. Worse than that, we're in thousands of pounds of debt. No jobs, no prospect of any jobs — our sole and only income comes from the Government. And half of that we're getting under false pretences. So I called a conference for all members of the family today. We all sat round the kitchen table for a barnstorming session.

"Come on," I said, "let's have a few ideas about how we are going to get ourselves out of this mess."

"We can't," said Derek. "We're trapped. I said this would happen. I said events would overtake us."

I looked at him severely. "Events haven't overtaken us, Derek. You have brought events about with your gambling mania. It didn't just happen accidentally."

"What about selling up and going back to the Vaughan Williams?" our Gary suggested.

"No," I said firmly. "Going back isn't the way forward. I'd rather chuck meself under a bus than go back to that hellhole."

"Besides," says Iris, "there wouldn't be room for all of us there. I'd have to go into an old folks concentration camp again."

"I'm all for that," I said.

"I don't know why we're even bothering to talk about it," chips in Derek in his doom-laden voice. "There's nothing to be done. It's hopeless."

"I'll pray for us," says our Sylvia. "I'll pray harder than I've ever prayed before. I could pray to St Jude, patron of lost causes. After all, I'm a Catholic now and Father Donaldson says God hears the prayers of all good Catholics."

"A Catholic?" I said. "Since when have you been a Catholic? You were christened in the Church of England like all the rest of us."

"I've been taking lessons in it for several weeks now, down at Father Donaldson's place. He's coached me personally. I was converted at a moving service last week."

"A moving service?" I said. "Why didn't you tell us about it?"

"Because you'd have tried to stop me."

"You're bloody right about that," Iris says. "We've never had a Catholic in our family. I'm shocked. The Pope's a bastard, everybody knows that."

Our Sylvia crossed herself. "May God forgive you for saying such a thing. And anyway, I thought you didn't like religion? You're always going on about how stupid it is, why should it bother you what denomination I subscribe to?"

"Just because I don't believe any of it doesn't mean I can't despise some more than others."

"Don't get excited about it, Gran," says our Gary, "She'll be a Buddhist this time next week."

"Look — what about the emergency?" I said. "Where are we going to get the money to pay the mortgage? Let's have a tot up. How much has everybody got?"

Our Sylvia had two hundred quid left from her Unsworth dowry.

"Where's it all gone?" I said.

"I've had to live. And besides Father Donaldson wanted a donation to the Lourdes fund. He's getting a bus up to take the disabled to the shrine. I could put your name down for it, Gran, if you like."

"No thanks," she says. "I don't want no favours from the Romans. And I don't want to go to France neither. Another set of dirty buggers."

"What about you, Iris. How much can you put in the kitty?"

"I've got seventy pounds in the Post Office and a marquisette necklace from my grandmother. That should be worth something."

"Gary?"

"Seventy five pounds in Premium Bonds. Eighty pounds in the building society and that's it, really."

"And your dad and me have got a debt of £1,962. 47 with the bank and another one of many tens of thousands with the building society. And rising. The social security benefits we're getting between us are hardly enough to feed us and keep the electricity and gas on. What the hell are we going to do?"

I dismissed Iris's suggestion of an "accidental" barbecue catastrophe and ensuing insurance claim. "No," I said. "I'm not having my dream turned to ashes literally as well as metaphysically. I like this house. I want to stay here, and I'm going to stay here. Look, if we put all our money together, we'll be able to see to this month's mortgage payment.

That'll give us thirty days to come up with a more permanent solution. Get your thinking caps on, the lot of you. And start looking for jobs."

* * *

Doreen's Diary 15th May 1996

The Close has come into bloom. All the trees are laden down with blossom and the sun has started shining a bit. I really think winter's finally over. But our troubles are only just beginning. Nobody in the house has managed to find a job.

Our Sylvia is coming near to her time, and the next mortgage payment is approaching. Beryl Cathcart thinks Mrs Henshaw might be planning something to make life even more unpleasant for us. She's pouring through the bye-laws apparently, looking for a loophole to lever us out with.

I try to pretend that everything's hunky dory, but being sent to Coventry by your neighbours is not a pleasant experience. The weather might have improved but there's still a cold wind blowing in Evergreen Close.

All except for good old Beryl next door and, strangely enough, Brigitte O'Boyle at number 14. She had to wait until Mrs Henshaw had gone out to one of her court duties this morning before she slipped across the road and knocked on the door.

"Mrs Potts," she says, "I want to tell you how sorry I am that people are being so nasty to you." She looked uncomfortable and kept glancing over her shoulder to see if anyone was observing her at the door. I couldn't help noticing that there was this little candle of snot hanging off the end of her nose. It was still running like a river.

"Come in, love," I said. "I'll make us a cup of tea. If that isn't considered as consorting with the enemy."

"I think it's awful what Mrs Henshaw is doing, setting everybody against you like that. She can be right vindictive can Hilary. I sometimes think she enjoys being horrible to people."

"Well she certainly got a buzz out of showing us up," I said.

"I'm just glad that they've done away with the death penalty," says Brigitte, "or she'd be dishing it out to people who eat at McDonald's and shop at Kwik Save." There was a pause then she said: "I hate her!"

She put her hand over her mouth as though she'd shocked herself by saying it. "I didn't mean that, Mrs Potts. I don't know what made me say it. I don't hate her. I'm a good Catholic and I'm not allowed to hate people, except abortionists and condom manufacturers. I'll have to go to confession."

"Don't you worry about that, Brigitte, love, people will understand. I think even the Holy Father might have trouble keeping his hands off Hilary Henshaw's throat if ever he had the misfortune to meet her."

Just then our Sylvia comes in. She looks radiant in her present state. Carries herself beautiful considering her size.

"Hello, lovey," Brigitte says. "How are you?"

"I'm fine, thank you. I'll be glad when it's all over, though."

"She's a lovely girl," says Mrs O'Boyle. "Never misses mass do you, lovey?"

"Oh, do you go to the same church as her, then?" I says.

"Oh yes, under the guidance of saintly Father Donaldson. Lovely man. Very understanding. He's as pleased as punch that your Sylvia never even considered the unspeakable option when she discovered that she was pregnant. As you know, it's not really a choice at all for a serious Catholic."

By now her nose was running like a torrent. I didn't have any tissues, so I got her a toilet roll. Ten minutes later she'd nearly used it all up.

"I'll see you on Sunday, then," our Sylvia says. "I'm just going to put the rubbish out."

"Well you take care, and don't do no heavy lifting," I said.

"She's a smasher that girl of yours. It's her that made me feel so guilty about what Mrs Henshaw is doing to you." She sniffed deeply. "I'm sorry about the state of my sinuses. I've tried everything to stop them. I seem to spend my whole life apologising to people. I know it's revolting."

I could see she was distressed.

"I had a row with my husband this morning," she said. "I was making his breakfast when the snot dripped into the frying pan. He just blew up. You see, he's had to live with it as long as I have. He's been very supportive, but there's only so much a person can take, and I think he's reaching the end of his rope with me."

"You can't help it, love," I put an arm round her. That just made her even more emotional. "It's not your fault that your nose is a revolting spectacle. It shouldn't be held against you. It's a disability in a way, isn't it?"

"Do you know, Doreen," she said, "that's the first sympathetic word anybody has ever said to me over my condition. Most of the time they're tutting or pulling disgusted faces. Nobody knows how I suffer."

"Here, have a cup of tea, Brigitte, love. Replenish your fluids."

Well, we were having a grand old chat, and it was cheering me up no end, when all of a sudden our Sylvia lets out this almighty scream in the yard.

"Oh my God!" I said, jumping up. "Her waters must have broke."

I rushed out to the dustbin hole where she was filling a black plastic bag with rubbish. Our Sylvia was on her knees, hands together in front of her, staring into space.

"What's happened?" I said. "Have you seen a rat? Are you going into labour?"

Mrs O'Boyle was standing behind me, sniffing like a warthog. It must get worse when she's frightened.

"She's here! I can see her!" our Sylvia says.

"Who?" I says, looking round.

"She's speaking to me."

"Who is?" I couldn't see nobody. "If you're on drugs, Sylvia Potts, I'll have your guts for garters. Have you no more sense than taking drugs when you're pregnant?"

"It's not drugs, Mam, it's real. It's Our Lady."

Mrs O'Boyle took in a sharp intake of breath. "Jesus, Mary and Joseph and all the saints," she says, crossing herself like mad.

"Our Lady," I said. "It can't be. Not here."

"She's having a vision, Doreen. It's wonderful. I've longed for something like this to happen to me all my life. Look at the expression on her face. She's in ecstasy." Mrs O'Boyle was nearly in tears.

I have to say, I've never seen our Sylvia look quite so lovely. Her skin was shining and she had this like contented smile.

"Yes, Madam," our Sylvia was saying to this invisible vision. "I will, Madam."

I looked round, but I still couldn't see nothing.

Mrs O'Boyle whispers to our Sylvia: "Is she as beautiful as everyone says? What's she saying?"

"I will tell them, Madam," our Sylvia says, quite oblivious. "I'll make sure they understand."

Mrs O'Boyle knelt down besides our Sylvia and put her hands together as well. I didn't know what to do, after all, I'm a Protestant so I wasn't entitled to kneel down — Our Lady is actually Their Lady as far as my beliefs is concerned.

Our Sylvia then closed her eyes, like she was in a trance.

She still had this smile on her face. "Hail Mary, full of Grace," Mrs O'Boyle was chanting over and over again.

After a few minutes, our Sylvia opened her eyes. Brigitte O'Boyle was on to her straight away. "What did you see, Sylvia. Was it Her?"

"Oh yes. Yes!" says our Sylvia. "It was Her. Holy Mary, mother of God — and she showed herself to me."

"What was she like?" Brigitte said. "Was she gorgeous? Did she say anything?"

"She said I was to tell the world that she has a message. She is going to return with a special message."

Mrs O'Boyle was crossing herself like something demented. "Praise be. Praise be." she kept saying. "I'm going to tell Father Donaldson."

She jumped up like an Olympic athlete, but then suddenly stopped. It was a though she'd been instantly frozen. Her hand went up to her nose.

It was dry.

She blew down it. Still nothing.

"It can't be!" she said. "It can't be! But it is. It's gone! I'm cured. It's a miracle!"

She rushed over to our Sylvia and embraced her and then kissed her on the cheek. "Oh my dear Lord — it's a miracle. A genuine fifteen carat gold miracle."

She did a little dance, then stopped to check her nose again. Still nothing.

"You don't know what this means to me, Sylvia. You've saved my life."

"Not me," says our Sylvia. "Her."

She glanced up into the sky.

I glanced up with her, only to notice that Iris was at the bedroom window watching the whole proceedings.

Mrs O'Boyle thanked our Sylvia again and then set off running. Last I saw of her she was racing out of the Close towards St Agnes's. I turned back to our Sylvia.

"I don't know how you think them up," I said. "What's it going to be next? UFOs from outer space?"

* * *

Doreen's Diary 16th May 1996

"You know what this is all about, don't you?" Iris says to me.

"She's been watching that film, The Song of Bernadette on the telly. I saw it with her the other Friday afternoon on Channel Four. A lot of old cock it was, but she was taking it all in. I could see it on her face, identifying with this young lass in France. She wants a good hiding. She's transparent, and not only that, you can see straight through her."

"You weren't there when it happened, Iris. There was *something* going on."

"Yes, and I'll tell you what it was. A bloody daft girl trying to draw attention to herself. She's always been the same. Do you remember when she used to come home from school covered in scratches and crack on she'd been attacked by a hedgehog on Bradwell Street? You used to smack her legs in them days and tell her not to be such a little liar. This is exactly the same thing. Don't give it credence — she'll soon forget her bleeding vision when she realises that we're not falling for it."

"Brigitte O'Boyle was convinced, anyroad. She's as pleased as punch that her nose has stopped running. She says it's the first time she's been free of excess mucous for over five years."

"She's as soft as a brush, an'all. A snotty nose is nothing, everybody has them from time to time. That's what hankies were invented for."

The door bell went. It was Brigitte O'Boyle.

"Speak of the devil," Iris says as Brigitte joins us in the kitchen-stroke-breakfast room.

Brigitte's face was a picture of happiness. Now that she's stopped having to wipe her nose all the time it has returned to its normal colour, all that soreness and redness has gone.

"I wanted to come round and thank your Sylvia again," she says.

"She's in bed at the moment with her back. You know how it aches when you're carrying a lump like that around twenty-four hours a day."

"Haven't you thanked her enough?" says Iris impatiently from her wheelchair. "It's starting to turn her head. I think it'd be better if you'd let the matter drop. We don't want to be encouraging these attention-seeking devices of hers."

"There's nothing wrong in what happened in your back yard yesterday, Iris. It was something wonderful. And I feel privileged indeed to have been present."

"Well, I'm sure I don't know what to think about it," I said.

"I'm telling you, Doreen," Iris says, "if that girl isn't curbed she'll get herself into trouble. Tell this woman to stop egging her on."

"I understand your worries, Iris," Brigitte cooed. "It must be disturbing to find that your own grand daughter had been chosen in this way."

"The only thing she's been chosen for is inconvenient motherhood," Iris said nastily. "Now, leave it. Don't go filling her head up with this Holy Mary tripe."

"You're only a minor player in this, Iris, so I'll not take offence," Brigitte said. "Your harsh words can't diminish the revelation that's been made in this house. Now, I said I'd come to thank the girl, and so I have. But I want to do it in a practical way. I want to show my gratitude by giving her this."

She reached into her handbag and handed me an envelope.

"It's a cheque, Doreen. I want Sylvia to have it to help with the baby."

"She couldn't possibly..." I started to say, but Iris had it out of my hand before I could give it back.

"Let our Sylvia decide what she will and won't accept in the way of gifts. It's rude to throw generosity back at people. You should know that."

"It's a small price to pay for the relief your daughter has given me, Doreen, and the happiness that she can bring to the world. She is a conduit through which Our Lady is going to speak. You can't imagine what it means to those of us who have devoted our lives to the Virgin."

"Well, that's so kind of you, Brigitte, I don't know what to say."

"Just rejoice that you have such a special child. You are the mother of the Little Mother."

"Well, yes, I suppose I am," I said, blushing.

"And now I've got to be getting along. I've a meeting of the Mother's Union at eleven. I can't wait to tell them the news — I'm donating my hundreds of handkerchiefs to their next jumble sale. All hygienically laundered, of course. Oh, and by the way, don't be surprised if you get a visit from Father Donaldson later. I had to tell him what happened. He above all had to know."

I was in a state of bewilderment as I showed her to the door.

When I got back to the kitchen, Iris had opened the envelope.

"Here, what're you doing?" I said, "That's our Sylvia's letter."

"Two hundred and fifty quid," Iris says, her eyes shining. "Look at that."

I took the cheque from her. "Isn't that nice of her."

"Nice!" says Iris, "Nice! Don't you realise the implications of this cheque, Doreen?" She wheeled herself into the lounge with one of those concentrated looks on her face. The sort that indicates that she's scheming again.

* * *

Letter from Gary Potts

Dear Terry,

Just to bring you up to date with all the latest. Living at home is proving to be something of a downer. I've been reduced to being a ten-year old again with Mam insisting on cooking me the kind of meals that I thought I'd finally left behind — all based on meat.

Our Sylvia is really getting on my nerves. I do nothing but argue with her. Then Gran's wheelchair seems to be everywhere in the house. She hasn't really mastered it yet and I'm constantly colliding with it. As much as I love Gran, she can be very demanding. And my parents are at their wits' end with money worries.

I'm desperately looking for a job so that I can get out before I go mental. I've got a couple of interviews coming up, so keep your fingers crossed.

As you suggested, I've been trying to contact Bill at the hospital, but he's avoiding me. I ring up his ward and they always say that he's not available. They never used to say that when we were together. And he never returns the calls. The other day I decided to go round to the nurses' home to try and see him face to face.

There was no answer when I knocked on the door of his room and I was about to go home when the chap in the next room along stuck his head out. It was Harold Thirkettle — a fellow nurse — middle-aged, rotund sort of chap. I've seen him around on the scene, so I knew I'd be able to talk to him.

"Have you seen Bill?" I asked.

"He's doing a double shift today. Trying to get some money together apparently. Working all the hours God sends."

"Is he OK? In general I mean?" "He seems to be. I have a drink and chat with him sometimes — he's doing all right."

"Only, I haven't seen him for a while." I tried to sound casual as I said: "Is he seeing anyone at the moment, do you know?" "I don't think that's any of my business," he said, meaning it was none of *my* business. "But as it happens, yes, he does have someone visiting him here. During the day mostly. I don't know if there's anything in it, though."

"Any idea who it is?"

"Listen, Gary, I don't ask. It really is none of my concern who he sees. All he's told me is that he's finished with you and is trying to make the best of it. Let's just say it's not somebody I'd choose to have a date with myself. But then, I'm not into rough trade. You'll have to get him to fill in the details."

"Does he ever mention me?"

"He was a bit down in the dumps at first, what with the court case and then having to move into this place. But he seems to be getting over it."

"This other chap — do you think it's serious?"

"You'd better talk to him yourself, old son. I'm not getting involved in this one. I've got problems of my own at the moment, with my piles. Emotional entanglements only set them throbbing."

So, Terry, it looks as though he's found somebody else.

Didn't take long, did it? I'm shattered, because I was living in hopes that when I got a job we'd be able to get together again.

Now I can't eat or sleep for thinking about him and wondering what's going to happen. I'm trying to hold it all together, but if you can offer any words of comfort, please do.

Your friend, Gary

* * *

Doreen's Diary, 22nd May 1996

When I heard that Father Donaldson was coming round to visit our Sylvia, I couldn't give over tidying up. Iris said if I didn't stop I was in danger of hoovering the pile off the carpet. He arrived about eleven o'clock.

"You go into the kitchen while me and our Sylvia talk to him," I said to Iris.

"Not chuffing likely," she said, putting the brakes on her wheelchair. "I want to know what's going off. We're going to have to play this canny. I don't trust you, you're too naive."

So Father Donaldson comes in. Our Sylvia was sitting there in her most loveliest maternity smock with this beautiful smile (Iris called it an 'idiot grin', but I took no notice).

The Father was a youngish man, no more than forty I should think, hair thinning a bit but with very handsome features. Lovely Irish blue eyes. I got him settled and fetched a pot of tea in.

"Now Sylvia," he says, taking our Sylvia's hand, "this is quite a story you're telling."

"If by a story you mean it's made up, then it's not a story," our Sylvia says, without letting the smile waver.

"Well, why don't you tell me exactly what it was that happened."

"She had a vision," says Iris.

"So I gather," says the priest. "But a lot of people claim that. Visions mean different things to different people. Sometimes it's their imagination playing tricks."

"Are you calling her a liar?" says Iris. "Because I won't have it. She's not that kind of child. She's always been honest."

"I don't doubt it. I just want to get to the truth. Now, I know that you've got Sylvia's best interests at heart, Mrs Potts Senior, but I would very much like to hear this from the girl's own lips."

I gave Iris a push in the shoulder to shut her up. "I apologise for my mother-in-law, Father. I told her that she was superfluous to requirements as regards this conversation, but she would insist on staying. I'll just put her away."

I got up to shove Iris into the kitchen out of the road, but she locked the brakes. "Touch this vehicle and I'll chop your arms off," she said.

"Well, if you're staying in the room, shut it. The Holy Father wants to have a word with our Sylvia. Now be quiet," I said. "I'm terribly sorry Father. She'll not interfere any further."

"Now Sylvia," he said. "Let's start at the beginning."

Our Sylvia looked out ahead of her, and the smile continued unabated. It was as though she was reliving the whole thing again, and it was giving her the greatest of pleasure.

She said: "I was putting the rubbish out, when all of a sudden, I became aware of this blinding light. When I looked round, I saw it was coming from over the dustbin hole. At first I was dazzled, but as my eyes got used to the glare, I saw a lovely lady stepping out of the light. Her face shone with beauty and kindness and she smiled. She was dressed in robes of red and green..."

"Red and green?" said the priest.

"She means blue and white," Iris said. "She's colour blind, you see."

"Sssh," the priest said to Iris, and then returned to Sylvia.

"And what did this lady say to you, Sylvia?"

"She said welcome to my embrace, little mother. Yes, that's what she said, welcome to my embrace."

"And what did you take that to mean, my dear?" Our Sylvia just smiled and looked as though she were hypnotised.

Iris was impatient: "It's obvious, isn't it? She was welcoming her to the Catholic church."

Father Donaldson ignored her: "Did the lady say anything else?"

He was talking to our Sylvia like a doctor talks to you when he's trying to get embarrassing particulars from you, all sympathy and reassurance.

"She said: 'I am the light and the way, follow me. Tell the world, little mother, that I bring tidings. This is your destiny. Alert the world to my message and I will return.'"

The priest was transfixed. "And then what happened?" he whispered.

"She reached out and pointed at me, and smiled again. She was lovely, and there was a kind of warmth coming out of the light."

"Anything else?" "No, she walked back into the light and it started to fade. And then it was gone. But I was filled up with the warmth. It was going all through me as though I'd got a hot water bottle on my tummy."

"Is that all?" Our Sylvia said nothing, she just looked as though she were very happy with her memory of the event.

"Well," I chipped in, "there was Mrs O'Boyle. You heard what happened to her?"

"It's a mystery, to be sure," said Father Donaldson. "I've been trying to intercede on behalf of Brigitte O'Boyle for many months

103

now. I've offered up numerous prayers asking for help for the poor woman."

"Well, there's your answer," says Iris, triumphant.

The priest shook his head and looked puzzled. "I'm sure I don't know what to make of it."

"You're not the only one," I said. "I mean, why would Your Lady choose our Sylvia to make her appearance to? She's just an ordinary pregnant unmarried mother-to-be. Nothing special. What I can't understand is why, after she's only been a Catholic ten minutes, the Holy Mother should favour her with a visit? And why over the dustbin hole?"

"There are precedents for this."

"Yes," said Iris, "she once appeared over the council tip in Lourdes, didn't she? And then there was that place in Yugoslavia. She certainly helped the people there, didn't she? I believe it's bombed to buggery now."

"It really isn't our business to question these things," said Father Donaldson. "They are mysteries beyond human understanding. Although it's true that most visions of the Virgin have been granted to young innocent girls."

Iris had a bit of a gagging do at the mention of innocence in connection with our Sylvia, but I let it pass.

"What is your opinion, Mrs Potts? Do you believe?"

"Well, of course I believe," I said. "I go to church every Christmas regular as clockwork. And sometimes at Easter as well. But it isn't *your* church, Father — no disrespect intended. I go to the Church of England."

"Whether you're a Catholic or a Protestant seems insignificant at times like this, Doreen," he said.

Iris mumbled: "Try telling that to the IRA,"

The priest chose to ignore her.

"I said we don't generally hold with the Marian cult in this family," says Iris, "My old dad wouldn't have had you in the house. But given that this has happened in our own back yard, we haven't got no option but to modify our dogmas."

"It certainly is fascinating. I may have to take it further, if that's all right with you, Mrs Potts. There are higher levels in the church much more qualified to deal with such things than I am."

"Whatever you think is best, Father Donaldson. What do you think, Sylvia?"

Our Sylvia put her hands together and said: "I'm only interested in Her. I'm just living for the day she comes back."

"I'm sure you are, my dear," says the priest gazing in awe. "But I want you to be absolutely certain about all this. I don't want to set wheels in motion unnecessarily."

"There he goes again," says Iris, "blackguarding her honesty. He doesn't know her like we do, does he Doreen? That girl couldn't tell a lie to save her life."

The priest nodded, put his hat on, and with a look of contented bewilderment, left the house.

"I'm going to my room to meditate," says Sylvia, still smiling.

"If you're having us on, madam, I'll throttle you," I said to her.

She drifted up the stairs like a sleep-walker.

I poured me and Iris another cup of tea.

"What do you think's going on, Iris?" I said.

"She's a lying little cow, that's what I think. She's revelling in all this. What with folk giving her money and priests coming to see her as though she were something special — it's like having all her birthdays come at once."

"But you just said to the priest..."

"I know what I said to that barmy article — he *wants* to believe it. It's *got* to be true, or otherwise he's been wasting his time all these years, hasn't he? Besides, if he can prove that there's been a one hundred per cent, kosher miracle in his parish, it'll do his career no harm at all, will it? You notice he couldn't wait to rush off and make an appointment with his boss."

"Well, if she is lying, how do you explain Brigitte O'Boyle's hooter? She's been everywhere with it."

"Another hysterical tart."

"But why were you cracking on to the priest that you believed our Sylvia? I can't make you out."

"Because, Doreen, my dear, this could be the answer to our problems."

"I don't get you."

"There are hundreds like Brigitte O'Boyle out there, just dying to be miraculously cured. Give it a few days to get round on the grape vine and see what happens."

"Don't be silly, Iris. We're not exploiting our Sylvia like that. Whether or not she's telling the truth, *she* believes it and we have to respect that."

"Respect it my arse. Them with too much respect get trodden into the ground. No, Doreen, scepticism is the way forward, that's the only healthy option. Faith only leads to you being subjugated by tyrants. So keep your guard up when you're moving among the faithful, they'll have you caught up in their delusions before you know what's happening. And then you're ripe for exploitation."

"It's all beyond me. This kind of talk just gets me confused."

"Of course it does, and that's only the beginning. Confusion is going to be the making of us, Doreen. Now listen. I've been thinking. We're only going to get one shot at this, and I want to make sure we get maximum returns. I'm going to prepare a battle plan and I want the whole family round that table at six o'clock for an emergency meeting. And nobody is excused."

"What are you conjuring up now? It doesn't sound legal — or nice."

"Do you want to stop in this house or not, Doreen? Because a lifeline has just been chucked to you."

Doubts were swirling about in my head but I thought: humour her, Doreen. Perhaps it's not going to be as bad as it sounds.

"Go on then," I said. "Six o'clock. We'll be there."

And so it was. At six o'clock sharp, we'd finished our teas and Iris got us all round the table. She was full of herself and had a sheaf of papers spread out in front of her.

"Now, we're having this meeting because something important has happened," she said. "Something that could affect us all. If we act in a united fashion, we might find it very much to our advantage." Having got everyone's attention and interest, she continued: "Now, as you know, as of yesterday our Sylvia has been possessed by the holy spirit..."

Our Gary blew a right loud raspberry.

"Yes, she has, and the Catholic Church is, at this very moment, being alerted to the fact that there has been a possible visitation from the Virgin Mary at this address. A miracle has already happened, in that a woman has been cured of a snotty nose by our Sylvia."

"Stop this!" says Derek, trying to be masterful. "I'm not having it. I can see where it's leading. We're all going to end up in purgatory as well as Parkhurst. I want you to pack these lies in, Sylvia. I'm your father, and I'm ordering you to stop having truck with the supernatural. If you don't, I shall be forced to do something."

"Sit down, Derek, and listen to what your mother's saying," I said.

He sat back in his chair and put his head in his hands.

"Now." Iris was relishing it. "We've got to ensure that we all tell the same tale. We've all got to be convincing about our sincerity, whatever our private thoughts might be."

"I don't have to pretend," says our Sylvia quietly. "I *am* sincere. I know it's true."

"Whatever you say, love," says Iris, indulging her.

"There's liable to be media interest in what's happened now that word's got out. We have to put up a united front to the papers and television. We've to make sure they see it from our point of view."

"That's manipulation," says our Gary. "Aren't there enough lies in the papers without us feeding them more? If anybody asks me my opinion, I shall tell them straight out. It's fake news, a lot of bollocks."

"God forgive you," whispered our Sylvia.

"Bollocks, crap, shite and bilge," says our Gary.

"Stop that language in my kitchen," I said.

Just then, the phone rings.

"If it's that Unsworth again, don't worry Sylvia. I've got a referee's whistle. If he starts that breathing again I'll give him a blast with it."

"Hello, is that Mrs Potts?" says this man's voice down the phone.

"Yes."

"Could I speak to Sylvia, please?" "Who is this ringing up?" I asked. "Only, depending on who it is, she might be indisposed."

"It's the Rotherham Advertiser here. Could I have a quick word, do you think?"

"What is it in regards to?"

"It's about the miracle."

"The miracle? How do you know about that?"

"We journalists have our sources, Mrs Potts."

"Well, I'm not sure. I'll have to have a word with her about it. Give me your number and we'll call you back."

So he did. I went back into the kitchen.

"Don't tell me," says Iris. "The paper."

"How did you know?"

"It's as inevitable as night following day."

"But how did they find out?" says Derek.

We all looked at Iris. She shuffled in her seat and said: "They'd have got to know about it eventually anyroad. These things get round. I just saved them the trouble of having to track us down."

"What have we to do?" I said.

"Tell them to go away," says Derek. "We're inviting trouble, Doreen. We'll be the laughing stock of the town if this gets in the paper. I'll never be able to show my face at the Trades Club again."

"What do you think, Gary?" I said.

"I don't want anything to do with it, mother. For once, I think me Dad's right. Once it gets in the paper anything could happen."

"Exactly," says Iris.

"What about you Sylvia?" I said. "You're the one who's going to have to answer all the questions and have your photo took."

She looked up at me. "Have me photo took? Yes, get in the papers. Have everybody taking notice of me."

"Exactly what she wanted," says Iris.

"No!" says our Sylvia. "Not for myself. For Her! She said I had to alert the world to her message. I never thought about it, but of course we couldn't alert the world without the help of the mass media. Stands to reason. Tell the reporter I'll speak to him, mother. Tell him to come round immediately and bring his photographer with him."

"Hang on, Doreen, you'll do no such thing," says Iris.

"Ring him up and tell him that you've got no comment. Tell him that there is no story and that any rumours he might have heard of Vatican involvement are exaggerated. Tell him to leave you alone and then slam the phone down."

"But I thought you *wanted* it in the paper?"

"So, I do. But we want it on the front page, not inside. If the reporter has to come round here rooting for the story it'll seem much more important to him. If we hand it to him on a plate he'll be suspicious. Don't court the media, let them dig for it. Then he'll think he's got a scoop. That's why I've started with the Advertiser. That'll set the ball rolling."

"Eeh, Iris," I said. "I hope you know what you're doing. Because I don't."

"Anyway," she said, "the main thing is to stick together. And if you aren't with us, Gary, don't be against us. This is a matter of survival for some of us. If you don't want to be involved, make yourself scarce."

She gathered up her papers and wheeled herself into the lounge. Our Gary followed.

Derek was sitting there biting his lip, brooding.

As I got up, he grabbed my arm.

"Doreen," he said. "There's still time to stop this."

He was that serious it made the hair on the back of my neck prickle.

"Are you listening to me, Doreen? There's still time."

He had desperation written all over this face.

"I know you're worried, love. I am, too," I said. "But I think you're wrong. Wheels are in motion. There's no stopping it now."

As I said it, little sort of electric shock type of sensation passed through my stomach and into my back.

I couldn't work out whether it was fear or excitement.

* * *

Article from Rotherham Advertiser

"Exclusive! BACKYARD MIRACLE: 'Little Mother' stays quiet — Catholic church denies inquiry into unexplained 'healing'.

A pregnant Cankersley girl has caused a storm in the Catholic church by claiming to have had a vision of the Virgin Mary.

The vision was accompanied by the apparent miraculous healing of a woman who says that the medical authorities had given up hope of curing her chronic sinus condition.

At the centre of these sensational events is Sylvia Potts, a twenty-four year old local woman who has only recently converted to Catholicism. Ms Potts lives with her parents in Evergreen Close, where the supposed miracle occurred. It is understood that the Vatican has ordered a high-level investigation.

Ms Potts refused to speak to The Advertiser, but another witness to the events — neighbour Mrs Brigitte O'Boyle, 57 — told us: 'I was just paying a neighbourly call on Sylvia's mother, when the girl cried out in the back yard. We rushed out to see what had happened and found her on her hands and knees, talking to the Holy Mother.'

Mrs O'Boyle has suffered for many years from a medical condition which she says had 'made her life a misery'.

Doctors have been unable to help, but she now claims that after stumbling on the encounter between Ms Potts and the Virgin her symptoms have completely disappeared.

'I have no doubt at all that I was cured by being in the presence of Our Lady,' said Mrs O'Boyle. 'I'm absolutely convinced that there is something amazing and wonderful happening here, and I'm thrilled to bits to be part of it all.'

She said that the Virgin had referred to the girl as 'Little Mother' and had inferred that she would reappear with a 'message for the world'.

109

Father Liam Donaldson, 43, the local Catholic priest who recently converted Ms Potts to his faith, refused to confirm that the matter was being investigated by the authorities within his Church.

'I have visited the Potts family and spoken to them about their claims, but beyond that I don't want to comment,' said Father Donaldson.

A spokesman for the Catholic church in London claimed that they had heard nothing about the case.

* * *

Doreen's Diary 24th May 1996
I was cleaning the windows this morning, about eight-ish, when this woman comes walking up the garden path.

"Can I help you, love?" I says, expecting her to be selling something.

"Do you know where I can find Sylvia Potts?" this woman says.

"Depends who you are. Are you from the catalogue company? Or the DHSS?"

"Oh no, nothing like that. Just a private individual."

"Well in that case, she lives here. She's still in bed at the moment. Can I help you?"

"I wonder if she'd see me. Only it's personal."

I climbed down from my step-ladder. "What is it? Are you a friend of hers?"

"No, it's in regard to this..." she pulls a copy of The Advertiser from under her arm and shows me the front page.

"Oh, my God," I said, reading it as fast as I could. There was full details as provided by Brigitte O'Boyle.

"Only, it's about an internal lady's problem I've got. I wonder whether she could intervene on my behalf with her friend the Blessed Mary."

"Oh, no, I don't think so, love. No. I'm sorry. She'll not be able to do that. I mean, after all, she's only met her once, they're not exactly on intimate terms."

"If I could just have a word with her...?"

"No," I says and gathers my chammy and bucket together. "You'll have to seek assistance elsewhere, love. Our Sylvia can't do nothing to help."

"Please, Mrs Potts. I'm desperate."

"Go home, love. Go on. Don't believe everything you read in the paper."

She looked crestfallen as she walked back out of the gate.

I ran in the house and shut the door and locked it.

"Iris!" I shouted. "Where are you?" She was in the kitchen having some All-Bran.

"We're all over The Advertiser," I said. "There's a woman at the gate wants her insides sorting out."

"Excellent," Iris says, doing her best with the All-Bran despite having loose-fitting dentures.

"I hope this isn't going to get out of hand," I said.

"Of course it is. That's the whole point."

Then the phone started ringing. It was a man wanting to know when the next sighting was going to be because he was considering bringing his eighty-nine year old father over with a view to having his cataracts removed by holy intervention.

He said it would be quicker than waiting on the hospital lists.

I put the receiver down on him. He rang back. I rang off. He rang back. I left the phone off the hook.

"That's the way to do it, Doreen," says Iris. "Let them get desperate. They'll soon be hysterical. That's when the money will start rolling in."

"Oh no," I said. "There are limits. I'm not making money from the weak and suffering, nor the halt and the lame neither. I draw the line at that."

"We won't have to. It's the papers and the television that are going to provide the money. As for the halt and the lame — well, you never know what might happen. They always say that if they *believe* they're feeling better, they will do. Faith healers have been working on that principle for years."

"It's wicked making money from sick people."

"Go and tell that to the authorities in Lourdes," she snapped. "I'm not going to take a penny from anybody who's poorly, Doreen, and neither are you. If it makes the afflicted feel good to believe that our Sylvia has been chosen, then who are we to tell them different? Maybe she has been."

"Yesterday you were saying she was a little liar and wanted her face slapping. Now you're saying it might be true."

"I've had time to ponder on it. I've become an agnostic now."

"What's that? It's some kind of Greek religion isn't it?"

"No. Agnostic means you don't know. Haven't made your mind up. You're willing to be convinced. Now then, keep our Sylvia out of sight for the day, don't answer the phone, don't answer the door and let them stew for a bit. Brigitte O'Boyle is doing a grand PR job for us out there."

Memo from Philip Bolam, journalist, to Mark Howard, editor of The Daily Chronicle, London

Dear Mark, I've just picked up this story from one of the wire services about a "miracle" in Yorkshire. All the usual bollocks. I know you aren't too keen on religious stories, but I've heard that *The Sun* are going to go big on this and I thought it might be fun to let them build the story up for a day or two and then shoot it down. I'll raise it at our planning meeting tomorrow morning.

Phil

* * *

Doreen's Diary 25th May 1996

I'm glad I took Iris's advice and laid in plenty of grub because it's turning into a bit of a siege. We can't get out of the house for sightseers and reporters.

After the story had been in The Advertiser things went a bit barmy. The "pilgrims" as Iris calls them, started arriving one by one. All sort of folk we had knocking on the door. In the end I had to shift them off the garden and make them stand on the pavement outside the gate. I put a notice up saying: "Private property. No trespassing beyond this point. No miracles today."

That didn't stop the reporters, though. By half past two they were knocking at the back door, at the front door, tapping on the windows, pushing notes through the letterbox and ringing up every couple of minutes.

"They're monstering us," says Iris. "That's a good sign. Every time they ring up, tell them you have no comment and put the phone down."

I was following her instructions to the letter. Mainly because I had no idea what else to do.

Our Sylvia stayed in her room most of the time. I told her to draw the curtains and try to take no notice. I don't want her to get over-excited what with the baby being so near. Derek also stayed in bed, but that's because he's in the grip of one of his clinical depressions and is

112

unable to motivate himself as regards getting up. I've only seen him like this a couple of times before — once when his penis was mocked by lads in the changing rooms and then when we had our first house repossessed. He's good for nothing when he's this low down.

He becomes unable to function, really. If it carries on, we'll have to have the doctor out to him.

There's now quite a crowd of people in the Close, all standing there looking at the house as though they expect something to happen. Needless to say, Mrs Henshaw was horrified, and sent for the police. But they were unable to influence the mob who just came back five minutes after they'd been moved on.

"What next?" I said to Iris, as I looked out of the window at the milling throng. "Where do we go from here?"

"Shut all the curtains," she said. "They'll have them long lens cameras trained on every window, trying to catch us out. The best thing is to keep them waiting. We'll put another titbit out tomorrow."

* * *

Article from front page of The Daily Chronicle, London 26th May
"Little Mother 'Miracle House' Under Siege
Extraordinary scenes of religious hysteria were seen today on a quiet Yorkshire housing estate **writes Philip Bolam**.

Crowds have gathered in Evergreen Close, Cankersley in the hope that The Virgin Mary will appear once more to a pregnant young girl.

"Sylvia Potts, the unmarried 24-year-old at the centre of the controversy, remained silent yesterday as hundreds of believers and curiosity-seekers gathered outside her home to find out what was going on.

One of those who was waiting patiently in the Close was Mrs Hilda Berkshore, 69, a grandmother of seven, who had travelled from Bridlington to catch a glimpse of the so-called 'friend of the Virgin'.

Mrs Berkshore said: 'I've always wanted a religious experience and this is a wonderful opportunity to have one. I believe in this girl, I really do.'

Mrs Brigitte O'Boyle, the woman supposedly cured of a sinus disease, was yesterday enthusiastically handing out cups of tea to those who had travelled to Evergreen Close in the hope of witnessing something extraordinary. 'I'm thrilled to bits that the word is spreading. If Sylvia could intercede with Virgin on my behalf there is no reason why she shouldn't be able to do it for others. I'm walking on air because I never in a thousand years thought I was going to be free of my condition. I prayed for a miracle, and I got one.'

* * *

Message from Philip Bolam, journalist, in Sheffield, to Mark Howard, editor of The Daily Chronicle in London
I expect you've seen pictures of the madness up here on the television. The crowds are getting bigger by the minute and people are actually camping out on the bit of spare land outside the Close. All the local hotels are full. The police say they can't clear the place because of the emotional state people are in — they're afraid of the consequences of trying to shift all the grannies that have arrived. There'd be a riot if the police got heavy-handed.

This story is taking on a life of its own, even though there's absolutely no word from the Potts family themselves.

I haven't been able to get them to talk, even though I shoved an offer of five grand through the door. I believe The Mirror is offering double that. Can you let me know what I can spend? The Sun is determined to be first with an interview with the 'Little Mother'. Either the Potts's are playing it very craftily or they're genuinely innocent. Haven't decided which yet — mainly because I haven't seen any of them.

However, I have got a lead on some background information on Sylvia Potts which will take a few days to unearth. Sounds like it might be interesting though. I'll keep you in touch.

Phil.

* * *

Doreen's Diary 27th May
It's utter madness. I've had to get Beryl Cathcart to bring some groceries in for me. She says that the press are pestering her from morning till night for information about our Sylvia.

They want to know what she's like — what's her history? Is she genuine? Who's the father of her child? I said, "What have you told them?" She said, "Nowt."

She's a good friend, and I think she's enjoying all this palaver, although she's getting fed up of people wanting to use her lav. Some of them aren't that particular.

She says Mrs Henshaw has been on to solicitors and barristers and her MP to try and get it all stopped. Apparently she's hopping up and down with fury that 'her' precious chuffing Close has been invaded by this lot, chucking litter all over and playing wirelesses at full pelt.

I said: "It'll all have been worth it if only for the satisfaction of seeing her nose put out."

Our Gary has absented himself from the house in disgust.

He's gone to stay with his hairdresser friend Darryl.

I said to Iris, I said: "How are we going to cope with this? I've never seen nothing like it. And just when we need him most, Derek gets melancholia. He's put himself out with a couple of Iris's sleeping tablets."

"Typical of him, that is," I said. "Absenting himself to unconsciousness just when he's needed."

Also today we had a visit from another priest. Came in what he called "mufti" which apparently means disguised as a normal person. Apparently he was doing a bit of a reccy for the Vatican. Very cautious they are, have to be absolutely certain that everything is hunky dory before they're seen to be involved.

It was then that Iris went a bit off her head with him. She was that abusive I was cringing with embarrassment.

"I don't care who you are," she said to him, "we don't need no endorsement from Pope John Paul nor George or Ringo neither, thank you very much."

She wouldn't let him see our Sylvia and she said some really nasty things about Catholic priests spending more time in frocks than a drag queen. This man was horrified and left in high dudgeon.

I said to Iris: "I don't understand you, I thought you wanted this miracle to be confirmed as genuine by the Vatican."

"We don't need the Vicar of Rome for our purposes," she said.

"But you needn't have been so nasty to him."

"Getting the top side of people in authority is something I've always enjoyed, Doreen — you know that. Putting the high and mighty in their place has always been a hobby of mine. And just at the moment we've got the power to do it in a big way."

"Well, if you ask me you're cutting your face off to spite your nose."

"We'll see about that. I've got the whip in my hand for what will probably be the last time in my life, Doreen, and I'm bloody well going to crack it. So the so-called top nobs had better watch their arses."

"Well you've gone and shot yourself in the foot with that whip, because you've made a powerful enemy in the Catholic church. You'll be internally damned."

"I'm already internally damned. Why do you think I'm eating All-Bran morning, noon and night? Listen, when that priest's picture appears in the papers tomorrow — and it will, because I made sure the press knew who he was before he even got here — the speculation will be rife. I can see it now: 'Vatican sends emissary to confirm Evergreen Miracles.' That's all we need. Rumour and speculation will do the rest."

At that moment Derek came down the stairs. He looked terrible — unshaved, hair all over the place, big bags under his eyes.

"Hello, love," I said. "It's nice to see you up and about. Your mother's just been abusing a priest."

He groaned loudly, turned round and went back up the stairs.

"Let him be, Doreen, he's useless when he's like this," says Iris. "The two of us will have to manage single-handed, that's all. Now then, I think it's time for our Sylvia to show herself to the multitude. Just make an appearance at the window and wave a bit. Are you up to it, pet?"

"Of course I am," says our Sylvia, her eyes gleaming at all these stories about her on the front pages of the papers.

They'd got this picture of her that was took a couple of years back by a pal of hers at Blackpool. Horrible it was. She looked like a right slut, drinking a can of lager, slouched on this moth-eaten settee with her knickers showing.

"I hate this picture," she said. "Kathy Hales took it when we stayed at that scruffy boarding house. I wonder how much the papers paid her for that."

"Never mind," Iris says. "We'll change your image in an instant. Dress up in your nicest maternity smock and be moderate with your make-up. We'll change you from a slag to a saint quick enough. But don't say anything. Don't utter a word. The spell will be broken if they hear you talking like a tripe hound."

Our Sylvia went up to her bedroom to prepare herself, "What's going to happen now?" I said.

"It's anybody's guess, Doreen," Iris said, "But let's enjoy it. Now then, wheel me to the front door and open it. I want to have a word

116

with them reporters. And when I give the word, tell our Sylvia to draw the curtains upstairs and stand at the window and wave. But tell her to keep her gob shut. Under no circumstances is she to say anything."

I did as she told me. As soon as the front door opened, the shouting started again.

"Where's the Little Mother? We want Sylvia!" Iris raised her hand to silence them and, as word passed to the back of the crowd that something was happening, the hubbub died down.

"Ladies and gentlemen," says Iris in this really loud voice that carried across the Close. "I am Sylvia's grandma, and I am speaking for the family. Please understand that my grand daughter is very near full term in her pregnancy and we don't want to upset her. She is spending most of her time in prayer, waiting for the moment when she might again be chosen to receive words from above. However, she understands your feelings and is happy that you have come here today. She is going to come to the window upstairs so that you can see her."

At the signal I shouted upstairs to our Sylvia. As soon as she drew back the bedroom curtains there was a great cheer, and some people fell on to their knees and started praying.

Our Sylvia was waving and smiling as though she were born to it. She had this right pious look on her face, like you see in these holy paintings. All she was short of was a halo.

After a couple of minutes the crowd started to go silent and people just gazed up at her. It was a bit weird to look out of the front door and see these hundreds of pairs of eyes all staring in awe at my daughter. Even the reporters and photographers had stopped their shouting and clicking and were just looking at her.

"There's something strange going on," I whispered to Iris as I saw the effect our Sylvia was having on this crowd.

"It's called mass hysteria," Iris whispered back without moving her lips.

Then our Sylvia moved away from the window and went to the toilet. The tension in the crowd relaxed and they began to talk quietly among themselves.

"Ladies and gentlemen of the media," Iris called from her chair to these reporters and photographers who were all lined up outside the gate. "We will be holding a press conference at six pm. Please be cognisant of my grand daughter's condition and let's not have no shoving and pushing. Conduct yourselves with restraint please."

Then she shut the door.

"What are you going to say to them?" I said.

"Only what I want them to know," says Iris.

* * *

Memo from Philip Bolam, to Mark Howard, editor of Daily Chronicle, London

As you've probably seen from the report I've filed, the Potts family held a press conference this afternoon. They had little choice really because the house was just about totally surrounded, and there was no way out for them. They had to say something or the press would have stormed the front room. They don't seem to have any professional advisers, so I didn't know what to expect from the briefing. The girl's father was conspicuous by his absence — ill in bed, apparently, no miracles for him — and the spokesperson was the grandmother, a game old bird in a wheelchair. Sylvia just sat there with this beatific smile on her face. She's a real mystery. There's no doubt that she did something to that crowd this morning, it was bizarre. She's heavily pregnant, looks as though the kid will drop any second.

What the old lady said didn't amount to much. They don't seem to be all that interested in the money they're being offered — a hundred grand by The Sunday World News — so I can't make out what's going on. I collared a priest that was coming out of the house this morning. He would only speak off the record, but he said he thought it was the genuine article. He seems totally convinced by the whole shebang.

After that Vatican chappy visited yesterday it looks as though the Church is really taking it seriously.

However, I've been doing a bit of digging and it turns out "the Little Mother" is not as saintly as she's cracked up to be.

There are convictions for soliciting, shoplifting and one for possession of a Class A drug. She's also been involved with another religious cult, "The End-Time Charismatics", who have their headquarters in Rotherham, just down the road from here. She's a bit of a religious nut from all accounts and the Catholics are only the latest in a long line of her victims.

It seems the family is deep in debt, all of them out of work, living beyond their means. Benefit swindlers *par excellence* I don't doubt. The brother is a notorious poofter, the father a depressive, the mother three sheets to the wind and the grandmother has a mind like a calculator. I don't think this information would make much difference to the gathered faithful. As things stand, they won't hear a word said against Sylvia Potts. I was talking to one of the nuns that have arrived here and she said it didn't matter that they were poor and in debt — Jesus had never had money, and his parents couldn't afford a room on the night he was born, so poverty was no bar to holiness. And whatever dirt I told her about Sylvia, this old nun could turn it round to sound like a virtue. A prostitute? So was Mary Magdalene, says the wimple-wearer. A thief? Jesus forgave thieves — it says so in the Bible. A fornicator? Ditto. You can't win. There's nothing that they can't turn to their advantage if it suits them.

The way things are going, this story still has some mileage in it. I think we should let it play for a while before we shop the lying little cow. I'll try and find something absolutely rock solid that will bring her down.

None of the other press lads up here seem to be on to her yet, or if they are, they aren't saying anything. The hysteria is growing and there's an incredible amount of interest. There are TV crews here from from Tokyo, Canada, Brazil as well as European stations and CNN. They're beaming it out all over the place. The Little Mother is an international celebrity.

All she's got to do now is conjure up the Virgin Mary again — a small thing to ask.

Let me know what you think.

Phil.

* * *

Letter from Gary Potts

Dear Terry,

I expect you've seen and read about what's happening at our place. There's been nothing like it since the loaves and fishes.

I didn't want to be involved – you know what I think about religion — so I went to stay with Darryl at his flat. He's over the moon about it all — he knows a celebrity at last. He must be pretty desperate if he thinks my family are celebrities.

Mind you, they are certainly having their five minutes of fame in a big way. But you know what these newspapers are — they'll drop the story as soon as something more interesting comes along. All it will take is a train crash or another MP being outed and the Potts's will be history.

I've tried phoning them, but the line is engaged all the time, so I decided to go home and give them a bit of moral support yesterday, but when I arrived I could hardly get through the crowds. The media has whipped up a right frenzy.

It was like a fairground on the piece of waste land outside the Close, with tents and ice cream vans and hot dog sellers. I'm not joking, there were literally thousands of people there, and in the Close as well. Old ladies most of them, sitting in deck chairs having tea out of thermos flasks and comparing rosaries. And nuns! I didn't know there were so many, like black beetles scuttling all over the place.

All the usual religious leeches are there preying on them, handing out leaflets, selling luminous plastic statues of the Madonna and holding candlelit services. Hindley was at the forefront, of course, trying to recruit for his Baptist barmpots, talking about evil spirits and the need for women to be exorcised.

I was that sickened by it that I decided to abandon my visit and go back to Darryl's, but as I turned to go, who should I spot but Bernard Unsworth — incognito, this time, no saffron robes, and wearing a bobble hat to hide that shaven head of his. He had two of his heavies with him, but I decided to tackle him anyway.

"Hey up Unsworth," I said.

As soon as he heard his name he recoiled instinctively behind one of his minders. When he saw who it was, he stepped back to face me.

"So, a member of the holy family," he sneers.

"What are you doing here? Looking for more idiots to do your dirty work for you?"

"Just checking out the competition. After all, I am in the business myself. I taught your Sylvia everything she knows. Besides, if there's anything truly significant going on here I, above all, should be part of it."

"You snivelling ratbag," I said. "It's you above all who deserves a good hiding. What about our Sylvia and that babby she's carrying? Anything to do with you, is it?"

"I make no secret of being the father of the said infant. I've told Sylvia that she has no right to keep it to herself. I shall want more than intermittent access when it is born."

"What's that, some kind of threat?"

"We are all interconnected. When the child enters this world, we will be re-united to form the ultimate family in Jesus, Shiva, Buddha, Mohammed and Bernard. The world will be one, and we will be there to make sure that war and pestilence are no more."

"And I expect you might get a few more cars out of the deal as well? I've a feeling the world is going to find it a pretty expensive business being saved by Guru Unsworth and his favoured family."

"You're a pitiful specimen Gary, but you can be saved. Meanwhile, you'd better shut it, or you might find that you'll not be around for the joyful day."

I looked at the dim-witted blokes he had with him. Dimwitted but beefy. Slow but with big fists. I decided the best course of action was to leave it alone.

"Looks like you were a good teacher, Unsworth. Our Sylvia has got this religious con-trick down to a fine art. I think you might find that she's got her own ideas now, and won't be all that bothered about being re-united with you. She's bigger with her followers than you'll ever be with yours."

"The child will return, whether its mother does or not. Mark my words, and relay them to your sister."

"Piss off," I said and walked away. I made sure I went back to Darryl's through well-lit streets, though, checking all the time that I wasn't being followed. Unsworth has a crazy look in his eyes. Scary.

I'm glad I'm out of it all. I just wish I had Bill here with me to hold my hand. I feel quite frightened about what's going to happen to Mam and Dad and our Sylvia — they're so vulnerable stuck in the middle of all that lot. Although they get on my nerves, I still love them. I wish this would all go away.

No doubt by the time you receive this letter something else will have happened. But I can assure you that it makes me feel better to get it out of my system by writing it down.

Hope all is well with you,

Your pal, Gary.

* * *

Doreen's Diary 29th May
I was getting sick with worry. I said to Iris: "What is the point of all this? Why are we doing it? I thought it was supposed to help us out with our debts? You keep turning down all that money the papers are offering us."

"Timing is everything, Doreen and I think the time is just about right for the next phase. Get our Sylvia down here for a pow-wow."

The three of us sat round the table with our tea. (Derek had to have his taken upstairs on a tray. He won't even have the lights on in his bedroom. He's turned into a hermit.) "Sylvia, love, have you had any word yet about when you next might be in touch with you-know-who?"

"Not really," our Sylvia said.

"Only all these people outside are waiting for a sign. The trouble is, they won't wait for ever. It's a bit parky at night, and just waiting about is starting to wear them down. Similar with the media. They're unlikely to keep all these resources focused on us much longer. Interest will start to wane if there isn't some movement. Do you think you could chivvy her along."

"You can't go giving orders to the heavenly throng, Gran. Demanding that they come and satisfy the whims of the curious."

"I realise that, love, but given you're on such good terms with her and, after all, she has promised to return..."

Our Sylvia looked thoughtful.

"And as I've said," says Iris, "your moment will pass very soon. If she wants to get her message over, she ought to take advantage of the fact that the world is watching. The world has a very short attention span in my experience."

"Do you think four o'clock this afternoon would be too late?"

"No, that sounds champion. Now listen, what I want you to do is rendezvous with the Virgin in the same place as before. Get her to give you this here message she's going on about and then we can relay it to the awaiting world media. I'll invite a select few to be present — the American networks, the BBC and perhaps *The Sun*. Depending on what they offer for the privilege."

"I'll go to my room and pray," says our Sylvia.

"That's right, love," I said. "And take your Dad the *Sporting Life* as you're going up. It's the only paper that hasn't got you on the front page."

Off she went.

"Now," says Iris. "Have you got that letter they sent you from the hospital about my illness?" I went to the drawer and rifled through the papers till I found what she wanted. It was a letter from the specialist who'd dealt with her, saying that her condition was a mystery but didn't seem life-threatening. He said that she appeared to have complete muscle atrophy of the legs and would probably never walk again. They had no idea why. They said she'd have to go back every so often for physiotherapy and would be provided with a wheelchair and other requisites.

I have to say, she's played the part very well. Only at the dead of night, when everybody's in bed and all the curtains are drawn, does she get out of that wheelchair. Then she gets her exercise: pops up and down stairs a few times, does an aerobics-for-the-elderly routine and then returns to her supposedly crippled state. I'm the only one who's seen it happening. I'll give her full marks for will power, because I couldn't bring myself to be voluntarily out of commission on a long-term basis — not for any amount of money.

"What do you want this letter for?" I said.

"Just keep it handy."

* * *

Article from The Daily Chronicle
"LITTLE MOTHER PULLS IT OFF AGAIN Millions saw TV pictures of events unfolding in Evergreen Close last night. Was it a miracle or, as some say, a rather pathetic hoax? The nation is split on the truth or otherwise of Sylvia Potts's story.
Here our religious affairs correspondent Gilbert Bagnall gives a personal account of what he saw and felt yesterday afternoon in Yorkshire.

The long-awaited re-appearance of the Virgin Mary, in what has been dubbed 'Miracle Close' in Yorkshire, came yesterday amid scenes of unparalleled religious fervour. The young girl at the centre of the controversial claims, Sylvia Potts, 24, suddenly announced to the waiting media that a voice had informed her that the Virgin Mary would appear to her again that day.

"Selected members of the press and television crews were invited into the modest back yard to see Ms Potts — heavily pregnant and unmarried — fall to her knees and gaze towards a cupboard used to store rubbish. I was one of those chosen to witness the event.

As the time approached, the rumours of the imminent appearance of the Virgin spread rapidly among the crowd, and there was a huge display of spiritual passion. Some people fell to the ground in hysteria, some prayed silently on their knees. Others simply clung to each other in smiling anticipation of some great revelation.

A small group sang hymns and held hands while another group spoke in tongues. Three people had to be taken to the St John's ambulance tent for first aid.

As one who has, in the past, heard of numerous 'visitations', I was, of course, sceptical about the story.

Having said that, I could not help but be affected by the apparent sincerity of the young woman as she appeared to listen intently to a voice only she could hear. It may have been my imagination, influenced by the powerful sense of faith surrounding the event, but I saw what appeared to be a strange luminescence shining from the girl's face. Divine light said the believers, over-exposed film said the doubters.

Around her were gathered her mother, Mrs Doreen Potts, and her grandmother, Iris, who was confined to a wheelchair.

I use the past tense because as Sylvia appeared to come out of a trance-like state, her grandmother groaned loudly and her legs became rigid, rising up in front of her. These strange scenes were recorded for the world by TV cameras, although what the TV audience could not have felt was the almost unbearable tension in the air.

After a moment, Iris Potts's legs relaxed again and she placed her feet on the ground. Then, with a look of complete terror on her face, she lifted herself from the wheelchair and stood unsteadily before it.

'No, no, it can't be!' she said. 'It's not possible.' And with that she staggered across the yard and into the house screaming. Her fear seemed genuine and it was distressing to behold.

All the same, the media crews were utterly unconvinced at first, some of them actually laughing out loud at the unlikeliness of the new 'miracle'. But as Sylvia rose from her knees, their mocking laughter subsided. With an authority which I have never seen before from someone of her age, she silenced this gang of hard-bitten, cynical journalists without saying a word. That really *was* a miracle.

After a moment, a woman from the BBC said: 'Did you see the Virgin?'

'Yes, I saw her,' said Sylvia quietly.

The journalists were anxious to know what the Holy Mother's long-awaited 'message to the world' might be, but Ms Potts was saying nothing. Enigmatically she walked back into the house, accompanied by her stunned-looking mother, whose mouth was hanging open. The door closed behind them.

Whatever we are to make of this latest turn of events, there can be no doubting that something remarkable is happening in Evergreen

Close. Whether it is a true supernatural manifestation or an elaborate confidence trick, 'Little Mother's' miracles are holding the world spell-bound and are providing a focus for deeply felt religious needs.

To the devout and the sceptical alike, there is an anticipation that is palpable. Some say that crowd hysteria is the cause of this phenomenon, but having been there and seen it for myself — and more importantly *felt* it — I'm not so sure.

Whatever the explanation for the 'miracles' and 'visitations' in Evergreen Close, I am more convinced than ever that there is a spiritual momentum gathering around this modest Northern girl and her family. A momentum that strikes fear and envy into the heart of the established churches.

The 'little mother' is providing a focus for long-suppressed religious feelings in this country. Not for many decades has religion been discussed and debated in so many pubs, offices and factories. Evangelists who have been trying for years to convince the population that they need God in their lives are admitting that Sylvia Potts seems to be succeeding where they have failed.

For the first time in an age, God is in the air.

* * *

Story from The Daily Chronicle, 28th May
"Doctor confirms that 'miracle woman' was disabled.

"Mr Andrew Ahmed, 39, the surgeon who treated Mrs Iris Potts — the woman supposedly miraculously cured by her grand daughter, the 'Little Mother' of Evergreen Close — has confirmed that his patient was totally incapacitated by her illness **writes Phil Bolam**. Dr Ahmed, who works at St Gilpin's Infirmary in Rotherham said today: 'Mrs Potts appeared to have some kind of muscle atrophy which made it impossible for her to walk, or even stand. The last time I saw her, she was totally unable to support herself.'

"Asked if he believed that Mrs Potts could have been miraculously cured, Dr Ahmed said: 'I work with facts not superstition. I do my job to the best of my ability, but we doctors are human and we don't have all the answers. Having admitted that, who can say what is possible when the supernatural is at work.'

Iris Potts later issued a statement saying that she didn't believe that what had happened was in any way connected with the alleged 'visitation' from the Virgin Mary.

'My own feeling is that it was some kind of spontaneous remission brought on by the excitement. I don't want anyone to get their hopes up on the strength of my experience.'

Others harbour no such doubts, and hundreds of sick and disabled people are arriving at Evergreen Close in the hope that they will be chosen next.

"In the meantime, Sylvia Potts is saying nothing about the latest message from the Virgin Mary. Her mother says that she has written it down and placed it in an envelope to be revealed at the 'appropriate moment'."

* * *

Message from Phil Bolam in Yorkshire to Mark Howard, editor Daily Chronicle, London

I know I'm as guilty as anyone for keeping this story on the boil, but seeing the parade of crippled and disabled people gathering here, I'm feeling a bit sick. Despite my efforts — and your money — it seems that The Sunday World News have got the rights to interview Sylvia. Apparently she's going to reveal the 'message' from on high to them. They're going to go big with it over the next three Sundays, TV advertising, the lot. They've been negotiating with that old granny who says her cure wasn't miraculous. Very clever.

I'll do my best to stop these shenanigans. If I can get something before Friday, we might be able to scupper the World News's story before they get the chance to run it.

Phil

* * *

Doreen's Diary, 30th May

Another exciting day. Iris certainly knows how to make things happen.

To start with there was the offer of money from the Sunday paper: £210,000. I had to rub my eyes when I saw it.

All we had to do was talk to a reporter for a couple of hours, have our pictures took and let them have exclusive rights to the Blessed Virgin's message. I would have preferred it to have been another paper, mind. The Sunday World News is a bit on the disgusting side — full of nude women and stories about film stars and politicians having sex with each other and whatnot. Last week it was pictures of the royal family behaving filthy beside a swimming pool. Next week it looks like it's going to be us getting the treatment, although hopefully with our clothes on.

It makes you sick the way these papers invade folk's privacy, I mean who wants to know the intimate details of people's bedroom activities? The Government ought to put a stop to their snooping and make them leave people alone.

Showing people up like that — goodness knows what their mothers must think when they see it.

Our Gary always says: "Why do you buy it if that's the way you feel?" He's got a point but, well, Derek follows their racing tips and I like the scratchcard Bingo, so I never get round to cancelling it, somehow. But that doesn't mean I don't think it's absolutely sickening, and if it weren't delivered every week, I wouldn't have it in the house.

Anyway, after we'd agreed terms with them, they told us we weren't to speak to anyone else or let on what was in the envelope containing 'the message'. Not much chance of that — our Sylvia insists she's not revealing it until the appropriate moment. We've no more idea what it says than anybody else.

I think the people outside are getting a bit impatient. The crowds are beginning to disperse a bit now. The cold snap is driving all these old biddies away. A couple have ended up in the hospital with hypodermia and exposure. They were saying in the paper this morning that there's a feeling among the faithful that we've kept the miracles a bit too much in the family.

Anyhow, the reporter arrived from The Sunday World News. Tiggy Fenwick-Hudson she was called. Beautiful camel-hair coat, expensive ear rings, talked down her nose.

Iris said she was a Hooray Henrietta, whatever that means.

Tiggy brought this film team with her to record our Sylvia doing a TV advertisement for the paper.

"Super to meet you, Mrs Potts," said Tiggy, shaking my hand. "And what a fab house. Now, time's short and the deadline's looming, so let's get down to business, yah?"

"Yes, let's," Iris chips in. "Where's the money?"

Tiggy turns to Iris and looks at her, as though she'd just crawled out of the drain.

"And you are?" she says, as though Iris had no right to be in the house.

Well, any kind of hoity-toityness directed at Iris is like a red rag to a bull. "I am the grandmother of the little mother as it happens, and as such I don't appreciate being patronised. So get that superior look off your face, lady. I don't care how important you think you are. It cuts no ice with me that you come from London."

"I came here to do business with Mrs Potts," says Tiggy. "Not to suffer abuse from some ghastly old hag."

"*I'm* Mrs Potts," says Iris severely. "Mrs Potts Senior. I am conducting this negotiation. And you want to watch your lip, Miss Fenwick-Goball, before you get it fattened."

"Is this true, Doreen? Do I have to speak to this...this creature?" Tiggy says to me. I nods. "Well then, let's start again. I'd better know your name."

"If there's money involved, my name's Iris. If not, it's Mrs Potts."

"Very well, Iris. Could we see Sylvia, please, and have a little word?"

"Sylvia will make herself available when the business end of this transaction is complete," Iris says.

"We really need to be sure that we'll get our money's worth," said Tiggy. "My editor doesn't part with that sort of cash easily."

"I am well aware of that," says Iris, "which is why I want to see the colour of it before you get anything out of us."

Tiggy turns to me. "Doreen — perhaps *you* could get Sylvia to come downstairs to see us?"

"Please refer all enquiries as regards this matter to my mother-in-law," I said. "She's the head of the family."

Head of the family! It nearly choked me to say it, but Iris is much better at standing her ground than I am. If it were left to me I'd give them my full life story free of charge and chuck in a meat and potato pie as well if they asked nicely.

"Well, then?" says Iris, hard-faced as anything. "Where is it?"

Tiggy went into her handbag and pulled out the cheque.

£200,000.

Iris looked at it with disgust and then handed it back. "The agreed amount was £210,000."

"I don't think so," says Tiggy. "I think you must have misheard."

"My hearing's perfect, thank you, and if that's the way you're going to carry on we'll call this meeting to a close right now. This interview is at an end. The deal's off. Good morning."

Iris stood up. "Doreen — see if you can contact that chap from the Sunday Globe and Echo" she said.

"You can't do this, Iris. We've arranged a TV tie-in for Saturday evening. We've booked peak time slots," says Tiggy. "We're linking our scratch card game to your grand daughter's story. Scratch off three Holy Mothers and you win a car. It's all set up. We had an agreement."

"And you've gone back on it. Now get the £210,000. And you can forget about the cheque, I want cash and I want it transferring directly into our No 2 account today. Electronically. I know it can be done, I've looked into it."

"This is out of my hands. I'll have to call the editor."

"Well," said Iris, fully aware that she had this clever-dick of a girl dancing to her tune. "Go on then, get on with it instead of standing there like a spare part. Here's the details of our bank account. The branch have been alerted and are awaiting your newspaper's call. The phone's over there."

Tiggy looked miffed but went to make the call.

"And don't forget there's a money box at the side of it when you've finished. Calls to London aren't cheap."

"You're being a bit hard on her, aren't you, Iris?" I whispered.

"Just saying her name makes me want to throw up. Anybody calling themselves Tiggy Fenwick-Hudson deserves shooting. She's no better than the rest of her kind, Doreen, riding round on horses and hitting the servants. They hold us in the deepest contempt. We're just money-making fodder as far as they're concerned. And they'd diddle us out of that cash without a second thought. Oh no, I wouldn't trust her with a tuppence ha'penny stamp. Now, get the kettle on. These film people will want a cup of tea."

Tiggy comes back. "The editor has reluctantly agreed your terms, Iris, but only under protest. We don't usually operate in this way. We're making an exception."

"I should think you bloody well are. This is the story of the century is this. It's not every day you get an exclusive from heaven above, is it? There are journalists from every corner of the globe queuing up out there. Now then, sit here and have a cup of tea. I'll give it an hour and then I'll call the bank for the emergency clearance. Then we can begin."

Iris has missed her vocation. By rights she should have been in high finance instead of in the boot and shoe factory where she spent most of her working life.

As we waited, she gave Tiggy what she called 'the background' on our Sylvia. I was mesmerised by the flights of Iris's imagination. She told of what she said was our Sylvia's early childhood, how she'd been a gentle child who kept to herself and how she'd always been spiritually gifted.

"She was strangely drawn to churches and chapels, even as a youngster," Iris was musing. "In fact one time when she were no more than five, she went to Sunday school and within minutes she was taking over the class because she knew her Bible better than what the teacher did. Do you remember that, Doreen?"

"Oh yes, I'd forgotten about that."

In truth, our Sylvia was playing doctors and nurses at seven, menstruating at ten, smoking at twelve, caught in possession at fourteen and in the juvenile offenders unit the year after that. She's calmed down a lot since then, though.

But Tiggy was writing down Iris's load of cock in shorthand and kept checking that her tape recorder was running.

It took two hours and three phone calls before Iris was satisfied that the money was safely in the bank, and only then did she call up the stairs to summon our Sylvia for her big moment.

She come down very slowly, clutching a Bible in front of her. She looked radiant. I could see Tiggy, who was as hard as nails under that posh exterior, begin to soften up as soon as our Sylvia came into the room.

"Sylvia, how sensational to meet you," she says. "Are you ready for the cameras, sweetie?"

Our Sylvia sat at the table and waited without saying a word. The film team got the camera set up and arranged their lights, then Tiggy held up this piece of cardboard with the words that our Sylvia had to say written on it. An idiot board they call it. Most appropriate.

"Now when the cameras roll, I want you to give it a bit of oomph. You know, really make the room light up. Give us that divine expression of yours — the one that stops the traffic and makes everyone gasp."

Our Sylvia faced the camera and intoned: "I'm the girl who the Virgin Mary called the Little Mother. You can read my story exclusively this week in The Sunday World News. I'll be revealing the message which the Holy Virgin wanted me to pass on to the world. You'll know the truth behind the miracles in Evergreen Close that have gripped the world. Don't miss my own story in my own words — this week only in The Sunday World News."

Tiggy looked slightly put out. "Sylvia, sweetie, do you think you could do it again, only this time with a little bit of feeling? You don't sound very...well, enthusiastic. In fact you sound as though you're under the influence of Horlicks."

Our Sylvia shrugged her shoulders, said she had a belly ache, and did it again. It sounded exactly the same, just like a robot, no expression on her face. Tiggy realised she wasn't going to get her hopping up and down and shouting, so she just nodded at the film crew and they started to pack their gear up. "They'll jolly it up with a few of those manic graphics," she was saying to them.

After they'd gone, Tiggy put another tape in her recorder and started a new notebook. The photographer was snapping our Sylvia from all angles.

"Now Sylvia, I have to ask you: why do you think you were chosen in this way. What makes you special? Any thoughts?" Tiggy said.

"Who knows? Our Lady seems to have took a fancy to me, that's all."

"When did you first realise that something out of the ordinary was happening?"

"It was one day some weeks back when I had this urge to turn Catholic. As soon as the conversion was finished, I realised that it was for a special purpose."

She winced as though she had a pain. "It must have been them sausages we had for breakfast," she said to me.

"Are you saying that the Virgin Mary is specifically a Catholic? Not just a general Christian? Would she, for instance, appear to a non-Catholic?"

"I wouldn't be so bold as to say nothing regarding her personal allegiances. She can speak for herself," our Sylvia says.

"Can you tell me what she looked like? I'm sure our readers would be fascinated."

"She was adorable in every way. Lovely skin, gorgeous figure, nice smile. She's looked after her teeth. She hadn't plucked her eyebrows, though, they were a bit thick. She was wearing like these flowing robes and a pair of bedroom slippers. Very much like her pictures and statues. Such a nice lady. Kindly. Warm. She was surrounded by a strange light."

"How did she sound? What was her voice like? Did she speak in English?"

"She spoke soft, in a whisper. I had to strain a bit to hear what she was saying."

"And what *was* she saying, Sylvia?" Tiggy was entranced by this time.

"She gave me a message. She said I was to tell it to the world. I've written it down so's I don't forget it. It's here, in this envelope."

131

She opened her Bible and there inside was this brown envelope with the words "Our Ladies Message" scrawled in our Sylvia's terrible handwriting.

I could see Tiggy was having to restrain herself from snatching it there and then. I was dying to know what was in it myself. And I'm sure Iris was curious, too.

"You know that we've got an exclusive contract to reproduce the message, Sylvia? You *are* going to hand it over, aren't you?"

"At the right moment."

Tiggy looked worriedly at Iris.

Iris reassured her: "She'll give it to you before you go."

"And these supposed miracles, Sylvia," Tiggy continued. "What about them?"

Our Sylvia turned and narrowed her eyes. "*Supposed*? What do you mean. *supposed*?"

"I mean," says Tiggy, "did she say anything about them, or were they something that happened separately? Were they in fact miracles at all?"

"I shan't dignify that with an answer," our Sylvia said.

"The money was paid on the assumption that you'd answer all questions," said Tiggy. "Now, did the Virgin authorise those miracles?"

"Yes, of course she did. It wasn't just a coincidence."

"They weren't very impressive miracles were they?" Tiggy said. "Hardly on a par with raising the dead or walking on water. What I don't understand is why, if she has such powers, the Virgin Mary doesn't just cure everyone in sight. Why some and not others?"

"That's a question that will have to be referred to someone more au fait with theological matters," says Iris.

"Now, Sylvia. Will the Virgin come to you again, do you think? Or is her mission complete?"

"There was intimations that she would return," Sylvia says. "She said she wanted to know how I got on with my baby. And she has more to say to the world."

The interview went on and on. Tiggy wanted to know what colour the Madonna's eyes were. Had she said anything about her relatives? Was she going to favour anybody else with a miracle? After four hours I made us all a sandwich. Tiggy wanted to go on a bit longer, but our Sylvia was getting tired. I could see it in her face.

"I've got this pain, Mam," she said to me. "In me back."

She flinched. "Now it's in me front." She took a sharp breath and I got all tensed up.

"I think it's happening, Mam. It's just like how they described it at the ante-natal."

"Take deep breaths," says Iris. "Are you having contractions?"

"Ooooh, mam, it doesn't half hurt," our Sylvia says. She's never been a great one for pain and suffering, especially when it's her having the pain and doing the suffering.

"You'd best get the ambulance," Iris says, so I runs to the phone.

"This is marvellous," Tiggy was saying, clapping her hands. "The baby could be here in time for our deadline. That would be icing on the cake. If she could have the baby in the ambulance it would be so dramatic — the back of a taxi would be even better."

"There'll be an extra charge for exclusive rights to pictures of baby," says Iris, quick as a flash.

"Fuck off, Iris," said Tiggy. "You're not getting another lousy penny, and I'm having the baby pics."

Our Sylvia was doubled up with contractions. It was coming ever so fast, faster than I've ever seen it before.

"Get the envelope," the photographer says, and Tiggy snatches it up before anybody could do anything about it.

"We've paid for this," she says.

"Aren't you going to let us see what's in it?" Iris says.

"Buy a copy of the paper on Sunday, you wicked old vulture," says Tiggy. She could let rip, now, you see — nothing to lose.

Well, what happened after that is all a bit of a blur. The ambulance came, and they took our Sylvia out, screaming on a stretcher. The people who were still hanging around the Close cheered as they realised that she was in labour. They were shouting things like: "Good luck, Little Mother. Can you do anything about my migraines?" I went with her to the hospital, together with Tiggy and the photographer who had by that time got through hundreds of flashes. Iris stayed at home to try and wake Derek up and tell him what was happening.

There was no doubt about it, we were only just in time.

Her waters had broke before we got the hospital and Tiggy nearly got her wish to have it delivered in the back of the ambulance. We just made it into the casualty theatre.

There was a lot of shouting and screaming, accompanied by effing and blinding, on the part of our Sylvia. As the baby started to pop out, Tiggy puked and then fainted, but I saw it all. Talk about an express delivery! The upshot is that I am now the grandmother of a bouncing girl, seven pounds two ounces, everything perfect.

Our Sylvia's immediate reaction was to say she would name the child Mary, but I said that might be construed as blasphemious by some people, so she changed her mind to Charmaine Bernadette Potts. The whole birth had been photographed from beginning to end, and as soon as the photographer lad had the final picture of the baby in her mother's arms, he went off to deliver his work to the paper.

When she'd recovered, and sponged the sick off her coat, Tiggy pronounced herself satisfied with the day's events and went off back to London to file her story. God knows what she's going to write, but at least our money troubles are over.

I sat with our Sylvia for a bit, while she came round. The hospital had had to put her in a private room — she couldn't go in the general ward now that they'd announced on the telly that she had delivered. The other patients would never stop tormenting her for instant cures.

About seven-ish who should come waltzing in to her room but our Gary's Bill, who had been on duty in men's surgical.

"It's all round the hospital that you've been brought in, so I came straight down to see you as soon as my shift was over."

He sat on the bed beside our Sylvia and they suddenly fell into this passionate embrace. He swept her up in his arms and kissed her on the lips. She clung on to him like something out of a Bette Davis film.

I pulled them apart.

"What's going off here?" I demanded "I know you're a friend of the family, Bill, but a peck on the cheek would suffice."

"You don't understand, Mam," says our Sylvia. "We're in love. I've been seeing Bill for some time now. We've formed a bond. We're going to get married."

"What are you talking about? This is our Gary's Bill," I said. "He's a homosexual gay person. They don't get married. Not in the same way that real people do."

"He's changed sides, haven't you Bill? He's moved on from being gay."

"Don't talk so silly, our Sylvia. A leopard never learns new tricks. It'll all end in disaster, I saw a programme about it on BBC2 the other day — women who marry gay men. They was all as miserable as sin."

"I'm sorry if this has come as a shock, Mrs Potts," says Bill. "I'd intended to say something to you before this, but I never got round to it."

"I dare say you didn't," I said, up in arms. "Now let me get this right. You've chucked our Gary and took up with his sister?"

"I need to fulfil my biological imperative," says Bill. "I need children."

"I've never liked you, Bill, if I'm honest," I said. "Just when I thought we'd got you out of our lives, you now come telling me that you're going to be a legally binding member of the family."

"I know it's hard to take in. But you'll get used to it, and I promise that I'll take care of Sylvia and the baby."

"I seem to remember you making a similar pledge about our Gary not so long back. Does he know what's going on?"

"Not yet..."

"Oh, you've 'not quite got round' to telling him, either, then? What a bastard *you've* turned out to be. And as for you, Sylvia — going behind your own brother's back and pinching his boyfriend! I'll tell you this, milady, if I wasn't so over the moon about that babby I'd bat you into the middle of next week."

I gathered my belongings and after kissing little Charmaine Bernadette, stormed out.

I expect it'll be up to me to break the news to our Gary.

Poor little bugger. Nothing seems to go right for that lad.

* * *

Letter from Gary Potts

Dear Terry,

They say that truth is stranger than fiction. Well, you're never going to believe what's happened. Bill — the man I've spent so many sleepless nights worrying about — has only gone and shacked up with our Sylvia! Yes, it's true. I've been well and truly shitbagged.

Have a glass of brandy before you read any further.

Well, she's done it this time — the gloves are coming off.

The chuffing so-called Little Mother is nothing but a lying, cheating pig! And as for Bill! He's the biggest son of a bitch of all time.

When Mam told me about them, I thought she was joking.

And then it occurred to me — Mam doesn't know *how* to joke. The more I thought about it, the more it all began to fall into place.

I expect you've read all about our Sylvia dropping the kid.

Ugly little bastard. Wizened up prune of a thing. Don't believe anything you might read in the papers on Sunday. It really does,

135

literally, look like a monkey — complete with vile red bottom and too much hair.

But can you believe what the two-timing, lying turds have been doing behind my back? I haven't slept at all for the last two nights. And Darryl is getting sick to death of me moping around his flat having crises. When I go knocking on his bedroom door at three o'clock in the morning he always provides a shoulder to cry on, never complains, but I can see it's getting him down. It's only a matter of time before he asks me to move on. Which means I'll have to move back to Evergreen Close and the pandemonium there. And be inside the same house as those two liars.

Apparently The Sunday World News — the filthiest rag in the world — has paid a fortune for the story, but I can't help thinking that the family are riding a tiger there. Those kinds of paper aren't noted for their compassion, are they? I sincerely hope that Mam and Dad don't come a cropper dealing with that lot.

It makes me sick all the fuss that our Sylvia has generated, all the people she's taking for a ride, all the fucking lies she's telling. And as for Bill! They fucking well deserve each other, the gobshites.

The worst thing about it is that I've lost him to a woman. I think you'll understand what I'm saying. I've always maintained that straight men are sub-human and ought to be kept in cages, and now I discover I devoted four years of my life sleeping with the enemy! All those nights of passion we had and he didn't mean a single one of them! In all that time there's never been so much as an inkling that he was straight or even bisexual. He hasn't even had the decency to ring and tell me what's happened, he left my mother to do his dirty work.

I'm so pissed off I could cry. In fact, I am crying. I'll sign off for now or this letter will be just a shapeless lump of papier mache by the time it reaches you.

Your despondent chum, Gary

* * *

Headline from Sunday World News
World Exclusive: Little Mother Delivers the Goods World News reporter delivers miracle girl's baby in ambulance.
"Inside today – the truth about the Evergreen Miracles. And exclusive revelation of the long-awaited Message from the Madonna. What does

it mean for you? Our astrologer Mystic Morgana gives an individual interpretation for each star sign.

"Read the true story of Sylvia Potts in her own words.
Only in the *Sunday World News*!"

* * *

Letter from Gary Potts

Dear Terry,

I hope you don't mind me writing to you again so soon, but I've just got back from the paper shop after buying The Sunday World News. Did you see it? "Little Mother Delivers the Goods" — what a pile of shite! And where did they got all that about our Sylvia? You know what a slag she's been, but to read that lot you'd think she was Snow White. The bleeding lies! I can't bear it. And did you see the so-called message from the Queen of Heaven? "As the rivers flow, so you will flow to me. I open my arms and they will embrace you." What the chuffing hell is that supposed to mean? In one way it's very clever — vague enough not to cause any ructions and portentous-sounding enough to give the holy brigade something to "interpret" and fight over for the next five hundred years. As far as I'm concerned, it's the same as all the other so-called sacred texts — meaningless bollocks.

You've got to give it to our Sylvia, though, she's crafty.

Anyway, it looks like Armageddon might be approaching Evergreen Close. Darryl came home from the pub at dinner time and said a reporter from The Daily Chronicle had been going round asking if anybody knew where I was. Apparently they're doing a story about our Sylvia (aren't they all?) and they're gathering 'background'. And we all know what that means.

Darryl told this chap that he didn't know where I was, and that, anyway, he was sure I wouldn't want to speak to him.

Then this reporter started asking Darryl what he knew about the family. Did he know anything about our Sylvia's convictions? Did he know anything about the family's finances? Darryl said he didn't. The chap flashed a great wad of money at Darryl if he could come up with any information.

The landlord of the pub thought Darryl was a rentboy plying his trade and kicked him out. Darryl is dead chuffed to have been mistaken for a prostitute, and he's going to dye is hair blonde and start working out.

Anyway, it looks like The Daily Chronicle might be digging the dirt. This reporter gave Darryl one of his cards and said that if he saw me, he should tell me that it would be worth my while to contact him.

I'm seriously thinking of doing it. Let's see Bill and our Sylvia squirm when I tell the papers the true story of their nasty little lives! I'll keep in touch, Gary Potts

* * *

Message from Phil Bolam to Editor, Daily Chronicle
Hope you'll bear with me for a couple more days, I think I'm getting there. I've got some excellent shit on the lousy "Little Mother" and her equally iffy family. What toe-rags! And after reading the snow job they did on her in the Sunday World Screws, I'm really looking forward to kicking that stinking little phoney Sylvia off her pedestal. Get the demolition crew ready, you're about to see a plaster saint smashed to smithereens. And as for the rest of the family — the country is going to be traumatised when they find out the truth about the swindling, scrounging, worthless Potts crew.

The mother is three hail Marys short of a novena and the old granny thinks she can "manipulate the media" — how many have thought that before now and lived to tell the tale? The brother Gary is a raving nancy — or 'gay activist' as he likes to call himself. Poofter Potts would be a good handle when we get round to him. The father's a psycho, spent time in a madhouse for "depression". An embarrassment of riches, really.

Phil.

* * *

Doreen's Diary, 31st May 1996
Everybody's thrilled to bits about the way The Sunday World News wrote that story about our Sylvia. They made her out to be a right lovely girl. It was that convincing I almost believed it myself.

I said to Iris: "Well, we've all got things in our pasts that we'd rather forget. Our Sylvia's entitled to a fresh start. This could be the making of her."

Iris just sniffed.

You've got to give our Sylvia her due, she takes a lovely photo if you get her on her good side. And then there were the pictures of little

Charmaine Bernadette, newly-emerged from the womb. She's an angel, that child. Absolutely beautiful with ever such a lot of hair. I think she must have nappy rash, though, because her little bottom looked a bit inflamed.

Bill dotes on her. He's cooing over her at every opportunity, although I don't encourage him coming to the house. I dread him and our Gary meeting up one day. Not that we've seen much of our Gary since all this started — he doesn't approve, even though it has solved our financial problems, with knobs on.

Iris is pleased with the success of what she calls her "master plan", and now thinks that we can forget everything and get back to normal. I don't think it's going to be as easy as that — she's uncorked a Pandora's box of tricks that she can't put back in the bottle.

Since that torrential rain started the crowds have gone.

Mrs Henshaw has persuaded the police to remove the remaining stragglers. Every so often somebody new arrives from abroad and they'll come to knock on the door. Iris just tells them that no further communications from above are expected and why don't they go and find something better to do with their time. They look downcast.

Every post brings thousands of letters. The spare room is crammed with them. There isn't time to open them all, let alone write back. Iris says there's likely to be money in some of them, so we're not to chuck them away, as suggested by Derek.

He emerges from time to time from his hibernation, but he's still in the throes of misery and despair. He seems to have lost his reason for living since we banned him from the bookies. And he says he can't ever face his cronies at the Trades and Labour Club again after what's happened. He has cups of tea and the occasional pikelet, but most of the time he just sits in the living room staring into space. Iris hasn't got time for him when he's brooding. She never went to see him when he spent them three days in St Joseph's that time. Self-indulgence, she said it was. She's never really understood his depressive nature. She just whacks him on the back of the head as she walks past and says "Don't be so bloody mardy, Derek. I know you're my only child, but you're a grandfather now. You should be handing out cigars instead of moping about. Pull yourself together, lad."

And then there's the babby. I can't stop looking at her.

Every time she gurgles or smiles or cries I get all excited and have to do a bit of washing or hoovering to calm myself down. Even shitty nappies have me clapping my hands, and I never thought I'd say that again. It's lovely to have the smell of a new-born around the house.

139

Our Sylvia really is living up to her title of "Little Mother". She's took to motherhood like a duck takes to a drake. She won't let nobody do nothing for the baby, she insists on doing it all herself. I'm dying to get my hands on that little Charmaine Bernadette, but Sylvia will only let me have hold of her for five minutes when we're sitting watching the telly of an evening.

But then, our Sylvia has become a bit of a prisoner. She knows she can't go out very easily, what with her being so well known now, on the box and in the papers all the time.

She found out what fame means when she popped out for twenty Rothman's yesterday and ended up getting manhandled at the newsagents. People were pestering her to cure their ingrown toenails and whatnot.

Iris is turning down all further offers of interviews. They wanted our Sylvia to go on breakfast telly, but Iris said no.

"We'll pay you well," they said. But Iris put the phone down on them. She says the more of our Sylvia that people see, the less they'll like. It's best to keep the mystique intact. "Look what happened to the royal family," she says. "The instant they opened their gobs they lost all credibility. They should have stuck to smiling and waving and then folk wouldn't be up in arms about how much they spend on shoes."

She's hoping it will all be a seven day wonder that will be forgotten in a fortnight.

* * *

Letter from Gary Potts
Dear Terry,

I've turned into a bitter old queen. I'm traumatised by what our Sylvia and Bill have done to me. Darryl says I should just give it time and I'll get over it, but it's getting worse rather than better.

I've spent night after night lying awake, plotting dreadful vengeance on them. I dream about running them down with the car or stabbing them as they sleep or, best of all, strangling them with my bare hands. Have you ever experienced jealousy like that? It's horrible, isn't it? I had to do something, it was driving me mad, so I decided to see that journalist chap I told you about, Phil Bolam. Quite nice looking and a great bod. He's only small but correct in every detail.

Anyway, he took me for a drink after I'd said I was interested in talking to him.

He was all smoothy, but I could tell straight off that he wasn't a friend of the family, let alone a friend of Dorothy.

Judging by what he told me, he's been working overtime on his research. He's probably been handing out bribes like confetti, although a lot of our Sylvia's friends (like our Sylvia herself) can be bought for a small handling charge.

He knew all about our Sylvia's past. He had her complete criminal record, her history of religious mania, testimony from her slaggy mates — he'd even unearthed some nudey photos she'd posed for when she was eighteen. Not a pretty sight.

When I told him that there was no love lost between me and her he became even more interested. "Anything you want to tell me?" he said.

"I could tell you plenty," I said.

He started mentioning money, but I told him I wasn't talking to him for profit.

He said he was glad I was talking freely because "volunteered information was usually of greater reliability than that which had to be purchased". And so he got the real low-down on her childhood, which is quite different to that dross they printed in the Sunday paper. I don't think he could believe his luck.

"This is all fascinating, Gary, but I'm going to need some kind of evidence. How am I going to prove that your sister has been lying, and that all this Virgin Mary nonsense has been invented to make money?" he said.

"There's a book," I said. "An exercise book where she wrote down what she was going to do. It was after she saw that Song of Bernadette film, that's where she got the idea. If you could get your hands on that book, you'd see she was planning it all from the start. It's all in her own handwriting."

"Could you get it for me?"

"No. I'm not going back there while she's in the house. You'll have to get it yourself."

"How? That old grandma of yours guards the place like a rottweiler. She'll not let any journalists near."

"That's not my problem. I'll give you a plan of the house, showing where our Sylvia's room is. She usually keeps her exercise books in the bottom of her wardrobe. If you can get into the house, you might be able to get your hands on the incriminating one."

"How do you suggest I do that?"

"Pretend you're the gas man or something. Tell them you're from the council and have to inspect all the bedrooms. I don't know. It's up to you."

"This is going to be difficult. I'm not happy about breaking the law."

"I didn't think people in your game worried about minor matters like that," I said. "Look, I've got a spare front door key. If you make a donation to Gay Switchboard — say, £2,000 — I'll let you have it."

He didn't like that idea. His paper spends so much time slagging gays off — or "poofters" as they call us — that the idea of giving money to a gay organisation nearly choked him. But he agreed and I took the cheque made out to Switchboard from him.

I knew that what I was suggesting was strictly illegal, and he probably wouldn't do it. But at least I've done something to get back at the bitch who stole my boyfriend. Hey, that'd make a good song title, wouldn't it? The Bitch Who Stole My Boyfriend.

I just hope that it won't hurt anybody else in the family.

Except that traitor Bill. I wouldn't mind hurting him.

Hope you don't think I've done the wrong thing. I know you don't like the tabloid papers, but sometimes you've got to play them at their own game. I'm sorry about Mam and the others, but they've already got their money safe and sound.

We'll see what happens now.

best wishes Gary

* * *

Doreen's Diary 3rd June 1996

It's almost midnight and I'm still up and about. My hours have become really weird since all this happened. I can't get to sleep so I stay up till all hours, then when I do eventually go to bed I need sleeping pills to get me off. Then I'm out till the middle of the next day. Nobody else seems to be having problems, they're all sleeping like logs. It's quite nice, actually, hearing them all at peace. I went upstairs a few minutes ago and stood on the landing listening. If I stand by the doors I can hear our Sylvia's gentle breathing coming from one room, and Derek's snoring coming from another, and Iris's wheezing in the next. It reassures me to know that they're all present and correct and at home.

Anyroad, here I am, sitting in the kitchen, writing in my faithful diary, which has been such a comfort to me throughout all this. Despite

142

the house being full, I've been feeling a bit lonely and isolated. I'm helpless in the face of it all, what with Iris getting us deeper and deeper into the mire.

She's definitely turned into a manglermaniac, lashing out at all and sundry and thinking she can get away with it. She's under the impression that she's incapable of error. It's frightening to see.

Derek has sunk into profound melancholy — so much so that I'm getting worried about him. Our Sylvia is obsessed with the baby to the exclusion of all others, and our Gary has fled the nest. The only drop of comfort I have is my darling little Charmaine Bernadette. I love every inch of her from her frizzy little head to her perfect tiny little toes. I could eat her on a sandwich, she's that lovely.

For the first time in ages there was no mention of us in the papers today. Iris says she hopes that we're yesterday's news now and that things will start to cool down. I'm not so sure.

There's been a chap hanging about all day, from The Daily Chronicle. He was very persistent. Kept knocking on the door and asking if he could just come in and use the lavatory. Iris told him to have a pee in the grate, he wasn't coming into the house, she said, as we had nothing further to say. Then he came back a bit later and said he'd pay us £500 if we'd let him take a photograph of our Sylvia's bedroom. That's all, just the bedroom. He said his editor was on his back to get something — anything — and if he didn't, he'd get the sack.

He was almost begging.

I said to Iris: "Poor bugger. It's no fun being out of work these days. What harm could it do? It's not as if he wants an interview. A picture of the bedroom's nowt is it? I've tidied it up and hoovered today so nobody could accuse us of not being spotless. And it'd be another five hundred quid in the coffers. Remember, Iris, a bird in the hand."

She thought for a minute, then said: "All right, come in. But don't try anything. Just one photograph of the bedroom, and that's your lot."

He came in, all smiles and thankyous.

"Where's the money?" says Iris, hard faced as hell.

He gets a cheque book out.

"Cash only," she says He goes back into his pocket and pulls out this great roll of notes. He counts out five hundred quid, just like that. They've got money to chuck away have these papers.

"Come with me," says Iris. "And remember, one false move and you're out."

She led him upstairs, and I followed. She opened the bedroom door.

143

"Go on, take your picture and then hop it."

He looked in the room. "Would you mind if I used the toilet?" he said.

Iris bridled. "What are you on with?"

"I've got prostate trouble. I can't hold my water."

"Tie a knot in it. Now take the picture and fling your hook. You've got two minutes and no lav."

He went into the room. "Where's the wardrobe?" he said.

"What difference does that make?" Iris asked.

"Well, it's a pretty strange bedroom with no wardrobe."

"We've shifted it out on to the landing, actually," I said.

"To make room for the baby's crib."

He quickly took his pictures and then came back on to the landing. He looked at the wardrobe standing up against the wall. Iris was suspicious.

"What is it with you and this wardrobe?" she demanded.

"Oh nothing. I was just wondering what wood it was — it's very attractive. I wouldn't mind one of those myself."

"It's a chip board do-it-yourself job from MI5," I said.

"Can I have a look inside?" he asked.

"Give us that camera," says Iris suddenly and grabs it off him, opening up the back. "There's no chuffing film in it. What the hell are you on with?"

"No film? How stupid of me. I'll load up now."

"Right," says Iris, "That's it. Go on. Out."

She hustled him back down the stairs. He protested, but before he could do anything about it, she'd got him out through the front door and shut it on him. He lifted the flap of the letter box. "Give me that money back."

Iris shoved the notes out into his face and they fell all over the front doorstep. As he grabbed for them before they blew away, she shouted out to him: "And don't come back." She turned to me: "Don't let him in again, Doreen. No matter what tale he comes up with. He's up to summat that's not to our advantage."

He was round by the window by this time, glaring in. He was staring at us with this really hateful expression on his face. I shut the curtains on him.

So that was today's events. What time is it now? One fifteen a.m. I'll have one more cup of tea and then I'll go to bed and try and get some sleep.

I'm sure I've just heard something while I was making the tea. It sounded like somebody opening a window upstairs.

And then I thought I heard the front door opening. My hair's standing on end. It's probably nothing, it's just that my nerves are in shreds and I'm imagining all sorts. All the same, I'm carrying the carving knife with me everywhere I go — just in case.

There it goes again! There's definitely something going on up there. I can hear men's voices on the landing. Oh God, the babby...

* * *

Doreen's Diary 4th June 1996

If I can keep my hands still long enough to write this I will put down the events of last the 24 hours as best I can. I think it is as well to get it down on paper while it's still fresh in my memory, just in case it ever comes to the stage where I need to give an account to the...authorities. It's been a nightmare of horror from beginning to end.

Oh God, how did we get into this mess? Now somebody's dead! Anyhow, I was sitting here writing my diary last night when I heard men's voices on the landing upstairs. I picked up the carving knife, which I always keep by me since we became celebrated throughout the land, and I went to have a look what was happening.

I crept up the stairs, but when I got to the landing I just saw someone climbing out through the window. It was dark, and I could only see his silhouette, but there was definitely someone hopping it. I shouts: "Hey up, what do you think you're doing?" When he heard me he panicked and launched himself off the window sill.

My heart was going like a foundry hammer, but I was relieved that he was going rather than coming. But then, as I made my way to the window to see what direction he was going in, I tripped over something on the landing. I went head over heels and almost fell on the knife. Then Iris comes out of her room.

"What's going off?" she whispers.

"We've had a burglar, Iris," I says, in a quiet voice so as not to wake our Sylvia or the babby. I didn't want them to get frightened.

"What's that on the floor?" she says, and puts the landing light on.

Well, I nearly fell backwards down the stairs. This man was laying there motionless in a big pool of blood. And I was standing there with this carving knife in my hand.

"What have you done, Doreen?" Iris says.

145

I realised what it must have looked like. "It wasn't me," I said. "He was already here when I arrived."

"Was he attacking you? Is that why you knifed him?" She came out and felt for a pulse in his neck, like they do on the telly.

"He's as chuffing well dead as a dodo," she said. "You'll have to claim self-defence at your trial."

"No, you've got it wrong. There was somebody else here.

I heard them arguing. I saw somebody climbing out of the window. I never did nothing. I fell over him."

"I never heard no arguing, Doreen, and as you know, I'm always on full alert."

"Get an ambulance!" I said.

"He's beyond ambulances."

"Well, ring the police, then."

"Just a minute, Doreen. Here you are with a dead body on your landing, great holes in his chest, blood everywhere and you with a carving knife in your hand. And then you tell some cock and bull story about one burglar murdering another in the house. It doesn't make sense. The police will make mince meat of you."

I was that shocked I let go of the knife and it fell into the pool of blood.

"I didn't do anything. I'm innocent."

"Yes, about as innocent as I am of obtaining money under false pretences from the papers. And our Sylvia of misleading the world's established religions."

"But we can't just pretend it hasn't happened. Get the police in. They'll have to sort it out. There'll be fingerprints, evidence."

"Evidence. What, you mean like the carving knife with your finger prints all over it and now with his blood on the blade?" "Yes, but they'd sort it out. I'm going to ring them."

She grabbed my arm. "Wait on a minute, Doreen. Just think this through."

"I've done nothing, Iris. I'm innocent of all charges. When I've told the police what happened they'll sort it out."

"Like they sorted out the Cleckheaton Seven you mean?"

"Yes, but that was a freak miscarriage of justice. The police made mistakes."

"Exactly — that's what I'm saying, Doreen. If they don't believe you — and why should they because I don't — they'll construct a case against you. You'll be had up for murder."

"No. No. I'm having the bobbies in."

"You'll end up in prison for the rest of your life. Just like the Guildford Four did until they were released."

"We can't just pretend it hasn't happened. There's a body on the landing. There'll be folk looking for him — his mother, his wife. They're bound to catch up with us in the end."

She was looking at his face. "It's that reporter isn't it? Him that wanted to take the picture."

I forced myself to look. It was.

"What's he doing in the house, anyway?" I said.

"He's after something. He's one of them investigating journalists trying to find evidence against us — that's why he's here. Searching. Prying."

"There's nothing for him to find. We've done nowt to be incriminated about."

"You have now, Doreen. You've stabbed him to death."

"I haven't, Iris! Will you be told. There was somebody else in the house. A third party."

"Aye, well, if you say so. But if you get the police in you'll regret it. You'll be persecuted to hell. Put under lights and grilled. Made to confess through being deprived of food and water. There'll be a nice one and a nasty one."

"No. They're not like that round here."

"Aren't they? You'll see. Remember, Cleckheaton's only just down the road."

"Well what do you suggest?" I said. "Burying him in the cellar?"

"We can't do that. As you say, they're bound to come looking for him. We'll have to dump the body somewhere."

"Dump it?"

"Under a hedge. On a golf course. Somewhere like that.

You read about it in the paper. A man was walking his dog when he stumbled on the body."

"We can't go dumping bodies. How would we get it out of the house without being seen to start with? The only person entitled to carry dead bodies round the streets is an undertaker. The whole idea's ridiculous. I don't know why I'm even hesitating. I'm calling the bobbies. I'll have to take my chances."

She held my arm in a painful grip. "Think, Doreen, think. It's not only you what's going to end up in the clink. We'll all be going with you. Do you think the police are going to stop at just investigating this crime? They'll start looking into everything else that's been going on, then the lot of us will be for it. Do you want to see our Sylvia separated

147

from little Charmaine Bernadette? Do you want to be put away so you'll never see her again until she's old enough to be wearing make-up and hanging around the bus station? Imagine what she'd think with three generations of her family in jail on charges ranging from murder one to grand larceny. She'd be scarred for life. She'd end up a juvenile delinquent taking drugs and leading a sordid life of petty crime. Just like her mother."

I started to cry. "I used to have a clear-cut sense of right and wrong. I was all right with my morals until I got involved in all this religious business. Now I don't know what the hell to do. I just don't."

"Shush, Doreen. You'll wake the whole house up. Think what effect this would have on the kiddies if they stumbled on this scene."

"Tell me what to do, Iris. Advise me. I'm that confused."

"First of all, help me get this body down the stairs."

"I couldn't, Iris. I just couldn't. He's still warm."

"Look, he's on this rug. We could wrap him up in it and then you wouldn't have to touch him."

First she went down to the kitchen and got a couple of pairs of Marigold gloves for us to put on. Then she started wrapping the bloody rug round the body. I could feel the sick rising in my throat when it started squelching.

After she'd completely enclosed him, she signalled me to pick up the other end of the parcel. Fortunately he wasn't a big man, and so getting him down the stairs wasn't too difficult. Most of the blood came with the rug. When we got to the bottom of the stairs, I said: "Now what?"

"Get the babby's pram."

I looked at her gone out.

"Go on, Doreen. Get it."

I went into the hall and brought in Charmaine Bernadette's pram. I'd bought it at the Oxfam shop some weeks earlier.

Nice quality. Gorgeous colour. Aquamarine with gold highlights. And given the size of it (I think it was originally intended for twins) a bargain at £22. 50.

"Now help me get him into it."

I was beyond reasoning with her by now and I just hauled my end of the body into the pram. I had to look away while she arranged his legs underneath him so that he'd fit in. She used to lay out her deceased neighbours when they died at one bit, so she knows how to do it. As she was pushing the arms into place she suddenly said: "Look what

148

he's got in his hand. It's one of our spare keys. Where did he get that from?"

The arm was hanging over the side of the pram, like something out of a horror film. She could see it was making me feel woozy, so she shoved it back in and put the layette over him and the rain hood up.

"Right, we're taking the baby for a walk," she said.

"But Iris, it's two-thirty a.m. in the morning. You can't take babies for walks in their pram at this time of night. People will be suspicious. They'll report us to the police and that will be that."

"Well, have you got any other suggestions?" I hadn't, so I opened the door, had a look round the Close, which, for the first time in days, was deserted.

Iris manoeuvred the pram out through the front door and on to the garden path. "We'll go over to that bit of spare land and tip him out there."

"There'll be evidence, Iris. Forensic evidence. They look through microscopes and brush talcum powder all over everything. They'll have us under arrest in no time."

"We'll fetch the rug back with us and burn it, then nobody will be able to connect it with the house. You can give the landing and the stairs a good fettling tomorrow morning. Remove all traces."

We pushed the pram into the Close and started towards the entrance. But before we got there, a car drew in. It was Mrs Henshaw's Rover.

"Quick," says Iris through the corner of her mouth. "Get them gloves off and put them in the pram, under the cover."

The car pulled up beside us and Mrs Henshaw got out.

"So, at last, I can pin you down. The famous and elusive Mrs Potts," she said. She was dressed in a long evening gown, obviously returning from one of her functions.

"What's been going on here has been disgraceful Mrs Potts, and I want you to know that I've been doing everything in my power to have it stopped. I've spent a small fortune in legal fees. I am furious with you. I sincerely hope that all this nonsense has now come to an end."

"Oh, I hope so, an'all, Mrs Henshaw. But as I'm sure you realise, it was completely out of our control," I managed to say.

"I don't think so, Doreen. And I'm disappointed in you for exploiting these events in the way that you have. You've brought notoriety to our beloved Close. And what on earth do you think you're doing with that baby at this hour?"

"She was crying," I said, "So we thought we'd take her for a walk."

"It's terrible," said Iris "but she is one of the most famous babies in the country at the moment, and it's difficult to get her any fresh air during the day. She's tormented terrible by the general public, you see. They all want to see her."

"So you see," I said. "The middle of the night is the only time we can let her see daylight, so to speak."

"It's quite extraordinary," said Mrs Henshaw. "But, like everyone else, I've heard a lot about her. As you say, she's very famous. May I see her?" She peered into the pram, but it was too dark for her to get a good view. Iris had covered the body well with the baby's pink layette.

"Oh, I'd rather you didn't disturb her," I said, pushing myself between Mrs Henshaw and the pram. "We've had hell on trying to get her to sleep."

"Anyway, Mrs Potts, while I have your attention, I want you to know that I am not leaving it there. I intend to do everything in my power to get you out of the Close and back where you came from. What's happened here over the past few weeks has been a nightmare. The other neighbours are agreed. You and your dreadful family will have to go. And I shan't rest until you do."

In normal circumstances Mrs Henshaw would have been courting disaster talking to me and Iris like that — she might well been next for a ride in the pram herself! But under the circumstances, we decided that discretion was the better part of value.

"Well, we're very sorry for any inconvenience caused," says Iris. "We'll do our best to ensure that everything is back to normal as soon as possible. We really will."

"I'm pleased to hear that. Your usual response is belligerence, Mrs Potts, and it makes it very difficult to negotiate with you. Now that we have broken the ice, perhaps we can talk about a mutually satisfactory conclusion to all this. Perhaps the other residents could arrange some kind of financial incentive in order for you to move on."

"I'm sure that would be possible," I said.

What I really wanted to say was: shove off, you interfering old witch, before I screw your neck round, but instead I said: "We'll talk about it."

"When?"

"Tomorrow."

"Why not now?" she said. "I'll walk along with you. It's a pleasant evening and I'm sure we could come to some preliminary agreement."

"Oh no. You go along, Mrs Henshaw," Iris was saying. "It'll be much better if we can talk about it in a civilised manner during the hours of daylight. I always think that decisions taken at three o'clock in the morning are generally regretted later. Perhaps we could have a chinwag over a cup of filter coffee."

"You mean, you really are prepared to seriously consider moving? Genuinely?"

"Oh, we'll consider anything for a quiet life," I said, forcing a smile and trying to push the pram past her.

She started walking beside us as we made our way out of the Close.

"What I thought might be possible," she said, "was if all the neighbours contributed a reasonable amount — and they will — we could perhaps pay your legal expenses and your removal fees when you've chosen somewhere else to live."

"Whatever you say, Mrs Henshaw," I said, quickening my pace. We were out of the Close by this time and walking along the pavement. Mrs Henshaw was full of it now, smiling from ear to ear. This was her dream come true — getting shut of us.

"Anyway, Mrs Henshaw," says Iris, trying to engage her in conversation in a stationary position, while I pushed the pram on. "I'm sure everything will work out to your satisfaction. Now you go along home and have a good night's sleep. I'm sure you've found it just as difficult as we have recently."

"I have to say," Mrs Henshaw said. "This has taken a load of my mind. I think I probably will sleep tonight for the first time in weeks."

I turned round to see what was happening, but as I did so, my attention slipped and the wheels on the left side of the pram went over the edge of the pavement. The whole thing started to tip over. I struggled to keep it upright, but the weight inside was pulling it hard. It was balanced at a precarious angle. Any moment now, it would topple and the dead reporter would be rolling in the gutter — best place for him, according to Iris.

When they saw what was happening, Iris and Mrs Henshaw come running to help. They got the pram upright again and gave it a lift back on to the pavement. My head was spinning and I thought I was going to faint.

"Goodness me, what a weight," Mrs Henshaw said. "It must be a very big baby. Either that or it's something else. You aren't transporting coal are you? I've heard about people from mining backgrounds such as yourselves storing their coal in the bath and carrying it from place to place in prams."

She gave out a little, tinkling laugh.

My breathing was out of control and I was seeing stars.

Iris elbowed me aside and took over the pram.

It was just in time because I couldn't stand it a moment longer and my legs gave way. I had the sensation of falling, but I didn't feel the pain when my chin hit the pavement.

"Oh my goodness, Mrs Potts!" Mrs Henshaw said, and hauled me back to my feet. "Are you all right, dear?"

I couldn't get myself together enough to speak, but Iris was saying something about the strain of the last few weeks overtaking me.

"We'd better get you home, Doreen," Mrs Henshaw was saying, and was dragging me back towards the house. Iris was obliged to follow, furiously pushing the pram.

When we were back at number eleven, Mrs Henshaw supported me until Iris had opened the door. Then she took me into the living room and dropped me on the settee. Iris was struggling to get the pram back indoors, but couldn't get it over the doorstep.

"I'll help," said Mrs Henshaw, and she pulled while Iris pushed and eventually the pram, with its gruesome cargo, was back in the hall.

"I'll make Doreen some tea," said Mrs Henshaw, and went into the kitchen.

Iris rushed over to where I was sitting and started smacking my face to revive me. She was doing it a bit overenthusiastically I thought, and in the end I had to grab her wrist in order to restrain her.

"Shape yourself, Doreen," she was whispering. "Don't peg out at the crucial moment."

Mrs Henshaw came back into the room. "Don't you worry, Doreen. I've got the kettle on and a nice hot, sweet cup of tea will be just the thing to get you back on your feet."

"Well, that's very kind of you, Mrs Henshaw," says Iris. "Very neighbourly. But I'll look after her now, thank you. You pop off back home."

"I wouldn't dream of it. I'll sit for a while and make sure Doreen is all right. What about the baby? I'll take her back to her cradle."

She was up on her feet and walking over to the pram.

Iris was up after her like a shot. "No, honestly, we'll make sure she's OK. She doesn't take to strangers. Your bust might give her a start, you know, the size of it."

Iris was standing in front of the pram like a guard dog so that Mrs Henshaw couldn't get to it.

"Well, I think it's terrible, leaving a child of that age in a pram. It can't be comfortable."

I was beginning to steady myself, but then our Sylvia comes walking down the stairs in her dressing gown, carrying little Charmaine Bernadette.

"What's all the commotion?" she said. "You've woke the baby up with all this racket."

Mrs Henshaw turned round and looked at our Sylvia. Then she turned back and looked at the pram.

"If the baby's with her mother — whose baby is in the pram?"

"Actually," says Iris. "You were right the first time. It's coal. We were just shifting a bit of coal. It's in our blood."

"You know very well this is a smokeless zone, Mrs Potts," says Mrs Henshaw. "It really isn't good enough."

"That's it, you see, Mrs Henshaw, we was going to dump it. Now that we've got the oil-fired central heating we thought we might as well get shut of it once and for all."

"I hope you weren't thinking of tipping it in a public place? There's far too much of that sort of thing. Only yesterday I saw an old mattress rotting on the grass verge just outside the Close. People are so thoughtless. I blame the working classes — such as yourselves — who really have no regard for the environment. It simply reinforces my opinion that you don't belong in a decent residential area. You really must go back where you came from, then we'll all be happier."

With that she walked to the door. "And if I see any coal dumped in the vicinity, I shall know where it originated. So you'd better make proper arrangements for its disposal."

She opened the door. "I hope you feel better soon, Mrs Potts, and I shall contact you further regarding our earlier conversation."

With that she stormed out.

"Get off back to bed, Sylvia," Iris said. "Take the baby with you."

"I can't sleep now," says our Sylvia. "I'm all disturbed. I shall have to sit and watch the telly for half an hour." She plonked herself on the settee and switched the TV on. It was a film about a serial killer who stabbed people and chucked them in the canal.

I looked at Iris, and then at the pram. She looked at me and then at Sylvia.

"What's all this about coal, Mam?" our Sylvia says.

"Oh nothing. We were just having her on. I wish you'd go to bed. It's not good for you stopping up all night."

But she was determined to sit there. I was sitting next to her, chewing my finger nails, worked up into a frenzy. Iris was standing in the hall guarding the pram.

"Doreen," she says, "Why don't you do a bit of cleaning. *On the landing.*"

The scene on the landing kept flashing in my mind. The blood. Oh God, the blood. It all had to be cleaned up. I jumped off the settee and got a bucket of hot water, a scrubbing brush and a bottle of bleach.

I went straight on to the landing and started scrubbing like fury. No sooner had I started than Derek emerged from our room on his way to the toilet.

"What are you doing, fettling at this time of night?" he said.

"You know I can't abide mess."

"What's that you're cleaning up? It looks like blood."

"No. No." I said. "It's pickled beetroot. I dropped a jar of pickled beetroot."

"What the hell are you doing with pickled beetroot at this hour?"

"It's your mother. She's got a craving. She sent me to get it and I dropped it."

He scratched his private parts and went to the lav shaking his head.

When I got downstairs our Sylvia was watching this film.

She'd got the baby sleeping soundly in her lap, a box of chocolates beside her, and a cup of tea on the table. There was no chance she was going to go back to bed. I went into the hall. It was starting to get light. Dam and blast these long days.

"What are we going to do now?" I whispered to Iris.

"We'll have to leave it here until tomorrow night. We'll have another go at getting rid of it in the early hours."

"No. Absolutely not. We can't leave a dead body in the hall for the whole day. It'll smell. It'll attract flies." I started to feel faint again. "I wish I'd never listened to you."

"Don't get weak now, Doreen. It's in your interests. You're the one who'll be saved from a life sentence."

By seven o'clock our Sylvia was stirring. "What a lovely spring day," she said, drawing the curtains back. "I think I'll take the baby for a walk. If I put a head scarf on and a pair of sunglasses, no-one will recognise me. I'll just get a shower, then I'll come and get the pram ready. I haven't had the chance to use it yet."

As soon as she was upstairs I said to Iris: "What now?"

"We'll take the pram down to the canal, put some stones in it and drop it in there."

She'd been watching that film with our Sylvia.

"Come on then, let's get it done. I can't stand much more of this."

She opened the door again. The Close was like Pond Street bus station, what with people going to work, the milkman delivering, the postman doing his rounds and that young lad shoving the free newspaper through the letter boxes.

"Look nonchalant," she said. "Smile and carry on as though everything's normal."

I tried but I couldn't have raised a smile to save my life.

Iris, though, was grinning as though she had a feather in her drawers, nodding greetings to everybody, saying what a nice day it was, and pushing this body along as though it were the most normal thing in the world. I, on the other hand, was just about managing to stay upright.

It seemed to take ages to get to the canal, and it was a titanic effort to get the pram down the steps to the tow-path without tipping you-know-what out. Then we sat on this bench, pretending to chat.

"Pick some stones up and drop them in the pram when nobody's looking," says Iris.

I waited till the coast was clear and then picked up a rock and put it in with the body. A man came into view, walking his dog along the canal-side. We sat back down on the bench again, all innocent, reckoning to be talking.

"Morning ladies," he said, doffing his hat, like these old chaps do.

"Morning," says Iris, all friendly. "Lovely weather for the time of year, isn't it?"

I thought: for God's sake don't encourage him, he looks very much like one of the I'll-enjoy-my-retirement-even-if-it-kills- me brigade. You know the sort — nothing to do all day except to talk about forced rhubarb to complete strangers.

"I was just saying to the missis," he says. "It'll bring the allotment on a treat will this bit of sunshine. I can see it being a bumper year for soft fruits."

He stood there, obviously parking himself to give an inventory of the state of his vegetable plot.

"Yes. We thought we'd get a bit of sun on our backs while we can," Iris was saying.

I thought: where the hell does she think she is — in a shelter on the sea-front at Morecambe?

"I think it's going to be a good year for caulis. Mine are coming on champion," the old bloke was saying.

Iris was nodding, but that little dog of his was sniffing round the pram.

"Get away," I said to it, and shooed it with my hand.

"Oh, don't worry missis, he's a friendly old thing. Just like me. He wouldn't harm the baby, would you Rex?"

The dog was getting excited by the smell, wagging it's tail and jumping up on its hind legs. It shoved its snout into the pram and barked.

"Come out!" I shouted, and gave it a kick.

"Steady on missis," the old chap said. "He's only being friendly. He's lovely with kiddies is our Rex."

"Aye, well, it might have worms," I said. "I don't want to take no risks."

He took umbrage at that. "Come on, Rex," he said. "We'll find somebody a bit friendlier to talk to."

He gave a tug at the dogs lead, but it was reluctant to leave the pram. In the end he had to drag it away. He strolled off muttering to himself.

"Calm down, Doreen," Iris whispers to me. "You'll have him suspicious. If they appeal for information on Crimewatch, we'll be the first thing he thinks of."

We sat there a couple more minutes. There was nobody else on the tow-path at that point so Iris said. "OK. Now."

With a great heave, she launched the pram over the edge of the canal and into the water.

I expected it to sink straight to the bottom, but no, somehow it managed to stay upright and afloat like a little boat.

"It's not heavy enough. You should have put more bricks in," Iris said.

The pram started drifting along with the slow canal current, away from the side, out of reach.

"Get some stones," said Iris. "We'll try and sink it."

I looked round and saw another boulder. It was quite a big one and it took both of us to pick it up together. We swung it between us and chucked it as hard as we could at the pram.

Fortunately it landed smack in the middle of it. The pram sank lower but the water was still only trickling in.

The trouble was that the stone had dislodged the cover and layette, and now there was a hand sticking out of the pram in plain view. *His* hand. His dead hand.

"Another one, quick," says Iris, who was starting to get worked up, too.

156

I looked round desperately for another big stone, but what I saw was two young lads on their bikes coming along the path towards us.

"Crack on you're feeding the ducks," said Iris, even though she knows the canal is too polluted to support any form of life.

We stood there reckoning to chuck bread into the water.

The lads rode up, passed us by, and didn't seem to notice the pram, delicately drifting along with this hand sticking out. It was gently rocking from side to side and the hand seemed to be waving. I went behind a hedge and had a spew.

The pram was slowly, ever so slowly sinking. We walked along the canal bank beside it, glancing out of the corner of our eyes, until it eventually went under completely and disappeared from view.

I was that exhausted I had to sit on a bench for ten minutes. I couldn't get that hand out of my mind, sticking up, waving at me in such a friendly way.

"Come on, let's get back home," says Iris. "We've a lot of thinking to do. We'll have to cover our tracks. Remove as many clues as we can from the house."

But as we went up the steps back to the road I saw this notice. "Please note that the canal tow-path will be closed for three weeks commencing 10th June to allow for drainage and clearance of rubbish from the canal basin. We apologise for the inconvenience. Working for a cleaner, safer environment."

* * *

Story from the front page of The Daily Chronicle, 6th June
"CHRONICLE REPORTER FOUND MURDERED Phil Bolam stabbed while investigating the 'miracle house'
The body of one of The Daily Chronicle's most senior reporters, Philip Bolam, was found last night dumped in a canal near Rotherham, where he had been investigating events at the so-called 'miracle house'. Bolam had been stabbed several times with what police believe was a large-sized kitchen knife and then dumped in the canal.

Mr Bolam was conducting an investigation into the alleged sightings of the Virgin Mary and the attendant miracles in Evergreen Close.

Detective-Sergeant Herbert Casey of the South Yorkshire police said last night that the attack had been 'frenzied'. He said that Mr

Bolam had been killed at an unknown location and his body dumped using a baby's pram to transport it.

"Chronicle editor Mark Howard said last night: 'We are all shocked that such a thing could happen to someone who was simply doing his job. We send our sincere condolences to Phil's wife, Claire. Everyone on the paper will miss his skill as a journalist. We appeal to anyone who may have any information about this dreadful crime to come forward and contact the police as soon as possible."

* * *

Doreen's Diary 12th June 1996

It was only a matter of time before the police came to visit.

We knew it was inevitable, but all the same I was a bag of nerves when I saw them coming up the drive. It was about half-past ten that the doorbell went.

"Good morning. Mrs Potts, is it?" It was this big, lumpy looking chap in the muckiest old coat I've ever seen. Teeth too big for his mouth. Thread veins in his nose.

I nodded and tried to smile, although my legs had turned to potted meat.

"I'm Detective Sergeant Casey. Local CID. Can I come in for a minute?"

I must have gone as white a sheet because he was forced to enquire if I was OK. I led him into the sitting room and he sat down.

"Now, as you probably realise, I'm here because of the body that was discovered in the canal quite near to here. Down by the Coach and Horses public house. Do you know where I mean?"

"Canal?" I said, as though he were talking a foreign language. "Oh yes."

"That's where the body was discovered."

"Body?"

"A dead body. Murdered."

"Oh yes, that reporter. I read about it in the paper."

"Did you know him?"

"I can't say that I knew him. No. Not in the sense that I was on friendly terms or anything. Although he had been to the door, wanting to interview us about the events."

"Yes, the events. The miracles and that," says this Casey chap. "I understand that Mr Bolam was doing a story about that."

"So I gather from the papers."

"And did you talk to him?"

"Only to say go away. Or words to that effect. He was a bit insistent, you know how they are."

"Did he come into the house?"

"Oh no. We've not had any reporters here since The Sunday World News. That was quite enough."

"Yes, I've been reading that. Very entertaining. Although you know what they say — you can't believe everything you see in the papers, can you? I've had a look at your Sylvia's records, Mrs Potts. She isn't quite all they've cracked her up to be, is she?"

"She was unjustly crucified by the courts over a misunderstanding regarding a man in a car and a soliciting charge."

"Is that right? I must have missed that. I was actually referring to the shoplifting conviction," says Casey. "And them drugs charges."

"All persecution. Not a scrap of evidence to back it up.

Not to my satisfaction, anyroad."

"I see," his eyes were all over the room, taking it all in. I expect they're trained in looking at things. "Now this Mr Bolam. I believe from his editor that he was planning to do some kind of unsympathetic story about your family, Mrs Potts. Some kind of exposé."

"He would have had a job. We haven't got nothing to expose. There's no skeletons in our canal...er, I mean cupboard."

"So you think he was barking up the wrong tree?"

"You know what they are. They could make a scandal out of the Archbishop of Canterbury's vest and pants if they wanted to. I don't take no notice of them."

"Have you any idea about what could have happened to Mr Bolam, Mrs Potts? So far we've been unable to trace his movements on the night he was killed."

"How should I know anything about it? I never went anywhere that night. And my family was here to prove it. I never go nowhere any more because of the attentions of the public. I'm a known face."

"Only, you see, our forensic people have been examining a rug that the body was wrapped in. It can tell you a lot can a rug. A repository of all kinds of information. And the pram.

The body was stuffed into a pram, you see."

I tried not to have a coughing fit, but I couldn't stop myself. It was that bad I nearly had my lungs up on the carpet. He patted me on the back and fetched me a glass of water. After I'd stopped coughing, he said: "Do you have a pram in the house, Mrs Potts?"

"A pram? No. What use would we have for a pram?"

No sooner were the words out of my mouth than little Charmaine Bernadette started crying for her dinner upstairs.

"That'll be the little kiddy that was in the papers, will it?" he says, looking up at the ceiling. "Proper little celebrity, isn't she? My wife goes all gooey every time they have her picture in the paper. Has little Charmaine got a pram, by any chance? For knocking about in, like?"

"No, we haven't bought one yet. We must get round to it.

Our Sylvia has one of them like papoose efforts slung over her back for our Charmaine. Apparently it helps with bonding or summat she was saying."

I got my cigarettes out and lit one up as best I could. It took a good half a minute to hold the lighter steady enough to make contact.

"Well, the thing about this pram is that it's fairly common, not an expensive one. There are a lot of them around, but the manufacturers have ways and means of tracing them. You know, being able to say roughly what part of the country that particular specimen was sold in and even which shop it ended up at. So, you see, we'll find the pram-owner eventually, Mrs Potts, and they'll have a bit of explaining to do, won't they? And goodness knows what tale that rug is going to be able to tell. We already know that the owner smokes Rothman's."

I gulped and discreetly put my cigarettes away.

He got up. "Well, it's been very pleasant meeting you, Mrs Potts. Always a treat to deal with a celebrity. My wife will be thrilled to bits when she finds out I've been in the miracle house."

As he talked he was peering in every nook and cranny.

Nothing escaped his attention. I hurried him to the door.

"Well," he said. "If you do think of anything, please don't hesitate." He handed over one of his cards. "Our enquiries are proceeding quite nicely. Whoever did this left enough clues for us to be going on with, and it's only a matter of time." He looked me straight in the eye. "That's all, Mrs Potts, just a matter of time."

I tried to smile, but it ended up as a type of grimace. The kind of face you pull when you've got a pain in your arse.

"Good morning," I managed to say as I closed the door on him.

When I got back in the living room, Iris was there, clutching her chest. She'd been listening to the whole conversation from the top of the stairs.

"They've got nothing on you, Doreen," she said. "Detective Sergeant Buggerlugs is just trying to unnerve you."

"And he's succeeding. If he's got nothing on me, why come round here cracking on that he has? Only a matter of time, he said. Why did I ever listen to you? Why didn't I go to them in the first place?" "Don't try blaming me, Doreen. It was your own choice.

You forced me into helping you. I'm an innocent bystander."

"You're an accessory after the act. You're just as guilty as I am. Not that I'm guilty."

"No way," she says. "I'm not the one with the blood on my hands. I'm not the one who was standing over the body. And I'm not the one who's going to prison — should it come to that. This is your baby."

"Well, I'll tell you this much, Iris — if I go, you're going with me. If they find out about me, I'll make sure they know all about your part in the proceedings."

"You'll never pin nothing on me. I'm an old lady of seventy-two. As far as they're concerned I'm ninety per cent senile, far too frail to have done anything like that. Don't forget, I'm only just out of a wheel-chair."

"You old liar. You're not letting me take all the blame. If it hadn't been for you..."

Just then there was another knock on the door. It opened and in came Mrs Henshaw.

"Hello, Mesdames Potts. Hope you don't mind me calling, but I thought this was as good a time as any to get the business we spoke about recently cleared up. You promised to get back to me, but you didn't. I hope you aren't thinking of reneging on your promise."

I was hardly listening to her as I tried to recover myself.

"Put the kettle on Iris. I need a calming cuppa." I said, trying to stop my hands shaking.

Iris went into the kitchen.

"Now, then, Doreen," Mrs Henshaw was beaming. "I've taken a straw poll among the neighbours and the consensus seems to be that they're prepared to help you with your removal expenses. Mrs Banner's husband at number fifteen is an estate agent, and he can give you all the help you need.

He's promised to go out of his way."

At one time I would have told her to shove her oversized bosoms into a bucket, but now I'm warming to the idea of moving on. My dream home has become a house of horror. I want out. So we got down to the particulars.

* * *

Doreen's Diary 22nd June

So this is how things turn out. I knew we were courting disaster from the moment I agreed to Iris's hair-brained scheme. Now look where I am, sitting in a police cell, writing in an exercise book with a piece of crayon. But I want to keep a complete record of what has been happening while it's clear in my mind, so I'll struggle on. I know how memory can play tricks on you once you've forgotten things.

I was just beginning to relax about the police, when I saw that Casey chap — Buggerlugs as Iris calls him — coming trundling up the garden path again. He was with this policewoman. What a face she had, like a rat with a nettle in its gob.

"Mrs Potts. Sorry to trouble you again, but I wonder if I might have another word."

"I told you I'm unable to insist with your enquiries. I have no relevant information," I said.

But they came in anyway.

"Maybe you haven't, Mrs Potts, but we have. It's in regards to the pram we discussed on my last visit."

My heart started pounding.

"Oh yes?"

"As I told you, the forensic were pretty confident that they'd be able to track it down."

"Oh yes?"

"They went through the procedures I told you about — and guess what?" He paused, no doubt waiting for me to blurt out something regrettable. I kept my trap shut. "I'm afraid they failed dismally. The pram's a discontinued model. Hasn't been manufactured for years, and no shop has it in stock. So you see, that turned out to be a dead end. This is typical of police work."

"So, you're no nearer finding out who did it, then?"

"I didn't say that, Mrs Potts. There are other avenues of enquiry. As one door opens another closes."

I started to relax. Oh yes, I thought, the only further avenues you've got are all blind alleys.

"There's the rug."

I went tense again.

"Oh yes?" I says.

162

"Because the rug had been submerged for those few days in that filthy, polluted water much of its usefulness was washed away. Burned away, actually. I'm afraid that was a bit of a failure, too. Most unlike our forensic boys to draw a short straw like this."

"So, you're no nearer finding the murderer?"

"I can't reveal that at the moment," he coughed uncomfortably. "But rest assured, there's plenty going off behind the scenes."

They haven't a clue, I thought. They've got nothing.

At that point Iris came in from the garden where she'd been tending her begonias. She stopped in her tracks when she saw Buggerlugs and his oppoe.

"These people are from the CID," I says to her.

"Regarding the murder."

Iris's eyes glazed over. I've never seen her complexion change colour quite so dramatically, not even that time she cracked on she had the yellow-fever.

"Are you all right, madam?" this policewoman says, offering an arm to support Iris.

"What do they want?" Iris croaks to me in a blind panic. I tried to discreetly signal to her that it was all routine, but I could see that she'd got the wrong end of the stick. She thought this was it, and that the day of judgement had arrived.

She had to be helped to the settee.

"I'll get her a cup of tea," I said. "All this has been too much for her."

I rushed into the kitchen hoping that if I was sick — which was quite possible — I'd be able to do it in the sink. But Sergeant Casey followed me in and through sheer will-power I had to postpone the vomiting.

"You seem a bit distressed, Mrs Potts," he was saying. "Is anything the matter?"

"No, everything's fine," I was breathless and holding myself up on the draining board. "We had some suspect polony yesterday, that's all. And I can't help thinking about that young man's mother. Have you heard how she's taken it? It must have been a shock for her to hear that her son had been done away with like that."

"I believe she passed away some years back," Casey was saying, "so I don't suppose she was greatly concerned."

His eyes were all over the kitchen. They alighted on the knife rack.

The knife rack with a great big, empty space on it where the carver used to be.

"You're missing a knife, Mrs Potts," he says.

"Oh, it's knocking about somewhere," I said, opening drawers pretending to look for it. There was no chance of finding it, of course, it was on the tip with everything else that might have provided clues.

"Would you like a cup of tea, Sergeant?" I said, but I'd lost control of my voice — one minute contralto, the next soprano.

"No, but I'd like to know where your missing knife is, Mrs Potts. Any idea?"

"It might be on the dump. I mean, accidentally chucked away with the tater peelings."

"Recently?"

"Oh no. Weeks since. I think Iris — that's my mother-in-law — I think she accidentally put it in the dustbin. She doesn't really know what she's doing. Brain damaged, you see."

"I'll ask her," he said and went back into the living room.

I followed him in, with my hair standing on end.

"Now then, Iris," he says, talking to her really loud as though she were simple. "What do you know about this here missing knife?"

Iris's eyes were out on stalks. She was terrified. "M-m-missing knife?"

"I told them that you..." I started to say, but Casey put up his hand and stopped me.

"You told them that I what?" says Iris, sweat pouring from her forehead. "You're trying to blame me, aren't you? You're telling them that I did it."

"No," I said. "I never said..."

The bobby stopped me again.

"Go on, Iris," he said. "Why would she say that you did it? Did you?"

"No! It was her. I saw her with the knife, standing over him! It wasn't me. I couldn't have done it, I've got irritable bowel syndrome!"

Sergeant Casey turned to me.

"Well?" he said.

"She's got dementia. It's making her paranoid. Take yesterday — she thought she was receiving radio messages through her dentures."

"Did you kill him, Doreen?"

"No. No! Don't be silly. It wasn't me, it was somebody else."

"Not me," shouts Iris. "If she's trying to incriminate me she's giving you falsified untrue information. She's the one you're looking for. I'll testify. I saw it all."

164

"I think you'd better come with me to the station, love. We'll get this sorted out properly."

"It wasn't me. There was somebody else."

"Aye well, you can tell us about it in a more sensible fashion at the nick. Get your coat, love."

"Iris, tell them," I screamed.

Iris had passed out on the settee, breathing heavy, her eyes rolled up into her head.

The policewoman looked at her in a worried manner, went over and tried to rouse her, then said: "I think this is an ambulance job, Sarge."

She used her walky-talky to get the ambulance on its way, and it was there in minutes. Our Sylvia had appeared on the scene by this time, and as she realised what was happening she got herself hysterical.

"Mam, what's happening?" she shrieks, and tries to get the policewoman's hand off my arm.

"Are they having you up over the television licence?"

"No, love," I said. "It's a bit more serious than that. They're arresting me for murder."

Once more Iris was being carried away on a stretcher, totally unconscious and out of touch.

As they took her through the front door, I shouted after her: "I know what you're doing, you rotten old bitch. Leaving me to face the music on my own. Well, I'll get you. I will. I'll get you."

The policewoman had to restrain me but I said to her: "Can't you see what she's on with? There's nothing wrong with her. She's done this before by practising Indian mysticism. She's an old fakir!"

"Now then, madam, you'll do yourself no good with that type of language," this policewoman said, getting me coat and taking me to the door. Mrs Henshaw was standing on the step.

"I saw the ambulance, Doreen, and I came straight over. Is it your mother-in-law? Is she all right?" "Excuse us, madam," said the policewoman. "I'm afraid we have to be on our way."

"Doreen, what's happening?" said Mrs Henshaw, as our Sylvia clung to me, weeping copiously on my coat.

"I'm leaving," I said. "Just like you wanted me to. And I doubt if I'll be back for a long time."

* * *

Letter from Gary Potts

Dear Terry,

I've been to see Mam in prison and gave her your best wishes as requested. She asked me return them. She's a bit worried about what your Mam will think of all this, and says will you tell her that she's not to take notice of what she reads in the papers. All this is nothing but a silly mistake which will be rectified soon.

They've got her in the remand wing, where she's allowed to wear her own clothes and have a few other little privileges.

All the same, a little lump came to my throat when I saw her.

How are you supposed to cope when you see your dear old Mam banged up behind bars? She looked totally lost and bewildered, but I controlled myself so as not to upset her. We managed to have a bit of a chat and I'm writing to you to tell you what happened in case you have any suggestions about how we might start a "Doreen is Innocent" campaign.

At first she'd refused to see me because of what I'd done for that Bolam — giving him that spare key and everything. But she changed her mind after I apologised and tried to explain. The last thing she wants now is for the family to split up.

We sat at this table with the warders not too far away, but because she's still awaiting trial they weren't too strict about it.

"How is everybody?" she asked. "How's little Charmaine Bernadette?"

"Who's that?" I said.

"You know who it is," she said.

"Oh you mean the Monkey? She'll be swinging through the trees soon, when her arms have got a bit longer."

"You are cruel, Gary. She's a bonny babby. Whatever you might think of our Sylvia, don't take it out on an innocent child. And your Dad, how's he?"

"No better. We've had to have him admitted to St. Joseph's with clinical depression. They're trying to sort out a drug that's strong enough to penetrate his mood. He just sits on the ward, staring into space. I don't know what we're going to do with him."

"If only we could get back to being a normal family, he'd be better in a flash. We all would." She paused, then said. "And your grandma Iris?"

"Still in a coma. No change."

"Coma!" she said. "That woman uses comas like other people use airline tickets to South America. It's her mode of escape."

I hesitated for a moment, then I said: "Mam, I've got to ask you..."

"Have you, Gary? I'm sorry about that because I thought you above all would have known I was innocent. I'm your Mam. You've known me for many years now. You must realise I couldn't kill nobody, with the possible exception of your grandma Iris. It's just not in my nature, son."

"I shouldn't have said anything," I said, and held her hand. I felt ashamed of myself for even suggesting it. "So what *did* happen, then? I've got to know if I'm going to do anything about getting you out of here."

"You've heard it all, Gary. I haven't got nothing more to add. There was somebody climbing out of the window when I got on the landing. Then I found that Bolam chap dead at my feet."

"But why did you hide the body? Why didn't you just call the police? This is what's mystifying everybody."

"It's a long story, but basically it was your granny Iris's idea. She persuaded me to shift him and pretend we knew nothing about it. Yes, I know it sounds pathetic, but I wasn't in my right mind. She could have told me black was white and I would have believed her at that moment. You see, Gary, love, you tend to go a bit senseless when you stumble across a blood-stained corpse on your front landing. But I'll never listen to her again. Never."

"Have you any idea who might have done it?"

"Whoever was climbing out of the window, that's who did it."

"You made such a good job of cleaning the scene of the crime afterwards that the police had nothing to go on. If there was any evidence of anyone else being in the house, you bleached it off the face of the earth."

"So where do we go from here?"

"I don't know. The police seem to think that it's all over bar the shouting. They're making a case against you. And all the papers seem to be convinced that you did it, too. They stick by their own. It would have to be a lousy reporter that you did in."

"I didn't do him in!" she shouted. "You don't believe me, do you? Nobody believes me!"

She got up and ran back through the door to the cells, crying.

It was only a slip of the tongue. I don't really believe that she did it. But everybody else does. Any suggestions?

Your friend Gary

* * *

167

Doreen's Diary 17th September

I've been in this remand wing for nearly two months now, and it's taken me all this time to persuade them to let me have my diary. The police have been studying it, but now they've given it back. I get the impression they think everything I've written in it is made up just in order to mislead them. They've got very suspicious minds, but I don't care. I know what really happened, and I'm sure that when the time comes for the trial it will all come right. I have utter faith in the British system of justice (the Cleckheaton Seven notwithstanding).

But here I am, in prison. If they weren't already dead, all this carry on would have killed my old Mam and Dad. My mother would rather have put her head in the gas oven than face the neighbours with a daughter in prison. In them days it only cost a shilling to do away with yourself. These days you have to have tablets, and the prescription charges are crippling.

Apparently, when I was first brought here, word went round among the other inmates like wildfire. It's been in all the papers and on the telly, everybody knows who I am.

They've turned me into a cause celebrated. Apparently I'm a hero to the convicted because they think I murdered a journalist. In the main prison wings they were cheering and chanting "We want Doreen".

Actually it isn't all that bad in here once you get used to it.

On the quiet I think prison life suits me. No decisions to make, no bills to pay, no adding up to do and no shopping.

Not only that, but they give you lots of cleaning jobs to keep you busy. There's nothing more satisfying than scrubbing a really mucky floor, and believe me, you could fry chips with the amount of grease on the floor here.

I'm sharing with a young girl called Brenda Callaghan.

Nice lass, used to work on the buses, red hair, scrawny. She brained her husband with a knobkerrie he brought back from South Africa when he was in the navy. Mind you, you can't hold that against her — she was only giving him a taste of his own medicine. The difference was that when he used to beat her up, the police would say it was a domestic disturbance and nothing to do with them, but as soon as she attempted to return the favour, the bobbies chucked her straight in the nick on a charge of grievious bodily harm. Where's the so-called justice in that? The day-to-day routine is not as strict as it is in the proper prison. After all, why should it be? I haven't done nothing to be put on bread and water for. I manage to keep up with Coronation Street and our Gary comes to see me every other day and our Sylvia pops in when she can — she's busy with the kiddy. I just wish she'd bring little Charmaine Bernadette to see me, but she says that the corrupted atmosphere of a prison is no place for an impressionable child.

The only thing I worry about is Derek, sitting in that mental hospital. I just wish I could be there for him. I blame it all on Iris. If it hadn't been for her, none of this would have happened. The Vaughan Williams Towers seems like heaven compared to what we're having to endure now.

The food here, as you'd expect, is awful. I don't know who cooks it but they want a few lessons in making steak and kidney pie. The crust is like plasticine and there's that much gristle in it that denture-wearing prisoners are more or less reduced to a vegetarian diet.

I'm glad I've got you, though, dear diary, because sometimes you're the only one who really listens to me. Not that there's a lot to write about. My solicitor comes in from time to time to tell me of the progress being made towards my trial. Not much as far as I can make out. All the same, I'm looking forward to being reunited with my family when the judge hears all the details. He'll give me a fair hearing and realise I'm not lying.

* * *

Letter from Gary Potts
Dear Terry,
As you know, I've moved back into Evergreen Close. It seemed only sensible if we're going to conduct an effective campaign. Our Sylvia and Bill had the place to themselves, with our Sylvia having sole access to all that money.

I've tried to put the hatred on hold until we've got Mam out of clink, but every time I see the two of them going upstairs to bed I feel sick with jealousy.

Not that Bill has got himself a bargain. Our Sylvia makes his life a misery — fetch this, fetch that, do as you're told.

Worst of all, she makes him do the cooking and insists on meat with every meal. It's something he would never do for me. If he protests, she demands sirloin steak. She binned his "Meat is Murder" apron and cancelled the subscription to Greenpeace.

I can see him cringing as she undertakes her one-woman crusade to personally destroy the planet. She's got this cheap hair spray off the market, made in China. I think it's the last hair spray ever to use CFCs to propel it. God knows how they get it into the country. She also uses that perfume that was exposed in the paper as being tested in rabbits' eyes. Bill tries to get her to stop using it but she says *she* likes it and *he* can lump it. She won't let him recycle nothing, either. She says the place for rubbish is in the dustbin, so all the newspapers and the cans and the bottles all get chucked away before he can get them to the recycling dump.

He's not allowed to talk about work because she says it makes her feel sick; she hates vegetables and says beans and pulses make her fart too much. She won't let him play his Mozart discs when she's in the room, it's got to be *her* choice of music — generally Cliff Richard, whom I know he detests.

The other night we watched that environmental series *Disappearing World* on the telly, all about the hardwood of the rain forests being cut down to make daft furniture. They showed this teak table as an example of the profligate use of disappearing resources. As soon as she saw it, she said she liked it and wanted one and next day there it was in the front room.

I said: "Don't you realise that table represents the habitat of fifty-five animal species that are now extinct?" In reply she went out and bought a fur coat. Ocelot I think.

All Bill's principles have been sacrificed to her selfishness.

I tut every time she commits some new environmental atrocity. He looks at the carpet shame-faced.

You could cut the atmosphere with a knife when me and Bill are in the same room, I despise him. But I'm going to have to put up with it for the time being. We only speak when it's absolutely necessary in order to keep going.

Most of the rest of my day is spent going between St Joseph's to see Dad and the District General to see Gran. Then over to the prison to support Mam.

Our Sylvia then announced that she was thinking of having a séance to see if she could find out who the real murderer was.

That was it as far as I was concerned, the straw that broke the camel's back.

"You're an absolute idiot," I said to her with all the contempt I could manage. And then I said to Bill, "And you're tarred with the same brush. I'm surprised at you."

Our Sylvia threw her chair at me, but it missed.

"I'm going out to the pub," I said. "And don't wait up for me. I've a feeling I'm going to score tonight."

None of this has helped Mam very much, so it's back to the drawing board.

But I'll keep you posted.

Gary

* * *

Report from The Daily Chronicle
Miracle House Murder Case Opens Doreen Potts denies killing Chronicle reporter

Doreen Potts, the woman accused of murdering Daily Chronicle journalist Phil Bolam, pleaded not guilty today, as the trial opened at Sheffield Crown Court. Mrs Potts is charged with stabbing Bolam as he investigated the notorious 'miracle' claims of Mrs Potts' daughter, Sylvia.

Detective Sergeant Herbert Casey told the packed court how he had led the investigation into Phil Bolam's death.

Forensic evidence was thin, he said, because the body had been dumped in a local canal which was unusually polluted.

Chemical reactions to the body and the rug in which it was wrapped, had rendered both almost unrecognisable. However, on a routine visit to the Potts' residence, D.S. Casey told how Doreen Potts had accidentally incriminated herself. His evidence was reiterated by WPC Helen MacIntosh who accompanied him to the home of Mrs Potts on the day of her arrest.

Mrs Potts claims that on the day of the murder she discovered the body on the landing of her house in Evergreen Close. At the same time she alleges she saw a man making an escape through the landing window.

The prosecution asked Mrs Potts how she imagined that this unknown intruder had managed to jump from the first floor window to the outside patio without serious injury, given that it was a drop of almost twenty feet on to concrete.

Mrs Potts could provide no answer, but stuck by her story.

The case continues.

* * *

Letter from Gary Potts
Dear Terry,

171

As you've probably read in the paper, the trial has started.

And it doesn't look good. Everything Mam says sounds feeble. They're all convinced she's lying. And the fact that Gran is still unconscious makes it very difficult to get any confirmation of the story at all.

The papers are supposed not to speculate about the guilt or otherwise of people on trial, but they're making it pretty clear who they think did it, and why.

We tried to start our "Doreen Is Innocent" campaign, but the local paper refused to touch it. The national press just laughed when I called round and asked if they would support such a campaign. "What do you think we are — idiots?" said one of them. "Yes," I said. "That's exactly what I think you are."

Even the Sunday World News has turned against us.

They've now carried the full story of our Sylvia and her criminal record, and they're all back banging on the door and shouting through the letter box. This time the police aren't so enthusiastic about restraining them. "They're just doing their job," says the desk Sergeant at the station when I ring up and complain. The Chronicle organised a phone-in vote for it's readers asking whether hanging should be brought back for women murderers — 90% said it should.

I've been grateful for your support, but I wouldn't blame you if you didn't want to keep in touch any more. Everybody else has lost faith in us. Even Darryl has stopped talking to me. Says he doesn't want to be friends with a murderer's son.

I still don't care what they say, my mother *is* innocent. I know she is.

Your distressed friend,
Gary

* * *

Report from Daily Chronicle
Doreen Potts' story 'a ludicrous pack of lies'.
... Summing up the prosecution case, Mr. Dennis Fishguard said that Mrs Potts' story was 'a fantastic fairy tale, a stupendously ludicrous pack of lies'. He said her contention that a mystery intruder had done the deed was unbelievable.

He went on to say that her assertion that she had concealed the body at the suggestion of a senile woman — presently in a coma — was 'pathetic in the literal sense'.

'The jury really has little to weigh in this case. They have only the word of Mrs Potts — a woman who was only recently involved in a series of pseudo-religious events that defied credulity. Her record is that of a bare-faced liar and a confidence trickster on an epic scale. Now she expects us to believe some hare-brained tale of mystery intruders with the ability to jump twenty feet on to a concrete patio and disappear into the night unseen. There is not a shred of evidence that such a person exists anywhere but in Mrs Potts's rather limited imagination. Her motivation for killing Mr Bolam, though, is clear. The editor of Mr Bolam's newspaper, Mr Mark Howard, has told you that Mr Bolam was working on exposing the Potts family for the fraudsters they are. Given the large amounts of money that the Potts's were raking in during their supposedly supernatural experiences, it was obvious that Mr Bolam's story would be very inconvenient. When Mrs Potts discovered him on the landing that night — admittedly he was there illegally, but that is not the point — she must have thought it an excellent opportunity to silence him once and for all. It is clear that no third party was involved.

We must also consider the missing carving knife. Mrs Potts maintains that the knife was thrown away on to the council rubbish tip in a clean up operation the day after the murder. Despite efforts by the police to unearth that implement, it remains missing. Can it be coincidence that Mr Bolam appears also to have been stabbed with a domestic knife of similar dimensions to the one that once resided in Mrs Potts's kitchen?

The conclusion to be drawn from all this couldn't be clearer: Mrs Potts killed Philip Bolam, and her motives were purely mercenary — making this crime particularly repugnant'.

For the defence, Mr George Hawthorne said that Mrs Potts' record as a citizen was one of uprightness and, until recently, honesty. She had simply been the victim of other people's greed. He said: 'She is a woman fiercely protective of her family, but easily led. The religious events which occurred at her home cannot be quite so easily dismissed, as they were by my learned friend, as a mere confidence trick. There are people in authority within the established churches who are still not convinced that what happened in Evergreen Close during the summer months was necessarily a scam. Respected clergy have said that they still believe something unusual, and maybe even supernatural, occurred in that quiet suburban Close.

'The strangeness of what happened not only fascinated theologians but also, unfortunately, the morbidly curious and, in some cases, the downright lunatic. The family was under siege for many days as the events in their home were unfolding. They were the subject of intense national, nay international, scrutiny. The police who were assigned to duties at Evergreen Close at the time of these events have testified that it attracted many questionable people to Rotherham — some of dubious mental stability. Religion for such people is a psychiatric condition. Under the circumstances, is it really so incredible that one of these disturbed individuals should attempt to enter the house?

'We have heard already the reason for Mr Bolam's presence that night. Mrs Potts' own son, Gary, has told you that Mr Bolam was constructing for his newspaper an exposé of the Potts family. Gary has told you that he colluded with Mr Bolam in order that the journalist could gain entry to his parents' home. Mr Bolam entered surreptitiously through the front door, using the key supplied to him by Gary Potts. The reporter was anxious to lay hands on an exercise book which he believed would confirm his own theories beyond doubt, and expose Miss Sylvia Potts, someone he held in the utmost contempt, as a cheat and a liar.

'Is it really so fantastical to suppose that another intruder found his way into the house that night, through the window leading on to the landing? Bear in mind, this was the first night that the police had adjudged it unnecessary for them to keep a presence at Evergreen Close in order to ensure the Potts family's safety. And is it so impossible that these two intruders met on the landing? And what is so unimaginable about Mr Bolam meeting his death at the hands of some deranged religious fanatic intent on harming the Potts family?

'Mrs Potts' story is not so silly when you consider it in those terms. And if there is any doubt in your mind, any doubt at all, then you must not convict this woman.'

It is expected that the judge will complete his summing up on Monday, after which the jury will retire to consider it's verdict."

* * *

Letter from Gary Pott
Dear Terry,

It was looking bad for Mam. Everybody you talked to was convinced she'd done it. We were at our wits' end trying to come up with some new angle, but there was nothing.

Then, the other evening, our Sylvia was opening some of the letters that had arrived at the house during the controversy. There are thousands of them, great sacks of them, a lot with cheques and postal orders included. She's making sure they all get paid into the account before they go out of date.

Since Mam was arrested another great mountain of mail has arrived. I don't think this latest batch is going to be quite so sympathetic, judging by the first one I opened. It was from somebody who said he was "writing as a true Christian", and went into great detail about what murderous things he would like to do to Mam if he could get his hands on her. He said that the Bible quite clearly supported capital punishment, with its eye-for-an-eye passage, and therefore, if there was any justice, Mam should be strung up, preferably in a public place to serve as a moral lesson to the nation's children.

As she sat there opening her letters, Sylvia suddenly came across one that made her jump.

"Here, Gary, have a look at this," she said, and handed me this letter scrawled on lurid orange paper. It said: "The holy child will be reclaimed. You have no right to keep it. We will be getting it back at the first chance."

"Another crank," I said. "There's no shortage of them."

"Yes, but this one's different. It's from Guru Unsworth. I'd recognise that scrawl anywhere."

"Unsworth?" I looked at it again. "You've had letters from him before, haven't you?"

"Yes, and phone calls. Loads of them. But this one reminds me of what he always says: coming to reclaim the child. He always said he'd have her off me."

"Kidnap her, you mean?"

"I wouldn't put it past him," she said with a shudder. "Here, Bill, check that the chain's on the door. It's frightening."

"When's it dated?" I said.

She picked up the envelope. The postmark was the 1st June.

"Three days before the murder," Bill says.

"You don't think it could have been him, do you? The one climbing out of the window?" our Sylvia said.

"Of course it could!" I said. "It all makes sense now. He was here that night, planning to abduct the Monkey-child. Meanwhile, that

175

Bolam chap had beaten him to it, and when they met on the landing, Guru's your uncle! Just like Mr Hawthorne said. It's only natural that a man of peace like Unsworth should be going equipped with a carving knife."

"So me Mam was telling the truth all the time," says our Sylvia.

"Of course she was. This is just what we need."

I rushed to get my coat. "I'm going to the show this to Mam's barrister. He'll know what to do."

Bill was all excited, too. "I'm coming with you," he said. "You'll need some support."

He got his coat, too, and we drove to Mr Hawthorne's house. On the way he kept reaching over and squeezing my hand and saying: "You've made a real breakthrough with this. It could be just what your Mam needs."

Mr Hawthorne thought so, too. "This is sensational," he said. "It'll make all the papers — at last, I'll have a case worth writing about in my memoirs. We'll get Unsworth on the stand on Monday. I shall need all the information you can give me about him."

"You'd better see our Sylvia about that," I said. "She knows everything there is to know about Bernard Unsworth and his crew. She lived with him for months at the so-called ashram."

There's a lot to be done before Monday.

"Let's go out and celebrate," says Bill as we walked down Mr Hawthorne's drive.

"Celebrate? I'm happy for me Mam, that's all. Not for you. Have you forgotten that I hate your guts?" We drove home in silence, but my mind was all over the place. I'll keep you informed of what happens.

all the best
Gary

* * *

Letter from Gary Potts
Dear Terry,
I expect you've read most of it in the paper, but I'll let you know what happened from our point of view. After all, we're the ones who were caught up in it all, and the press never quite get it right, do they? A subpoena was issued for Unsworth to appear in court.

When he didn't turn up, the police went down to the ashram to arrest him, but the creep had hopped it.

I say hopped it in the literal sense, because Unsworth was still wearing a full length plaster cast on his left leg.

According to the hospital, he'd had it set three times and it still wasn't healed.

The trial was adjourned to give the police time to track Unsworth down. The papers went mad about the 'hunt for Unsworth'. His picture was on all the front pages and it didn't take long to find him — he was spotted by a Mrs Pearl Bainbridge, a Sun reader, at a service station on the M1.

Unsworth was trying to go incognito, but it's difficult when you're wearing a plaster cast of that size. He was accompanied by one of those gorillas that looks after him.

The other one had left the country when he saw what was coming.

Of course the great guru denied everything, and several of his deluded 'followers' came forward to give him an alibi for the night of the murder, so the police weren't able to proceed with charges directly. They had to release him pending further investigations, but they kept him under surveillance to make sure he was in court on Monday.

It all rested now on what Mr Hawthorne could get out of him on the witness stand.

I'm copying a transcript of the cross-examination for your records, because I know Mam has been in touch with you about doing a book telling the true story, and you'll need this.

Transcript of final day of proceedings at Sheffield Crown Court. Bernard Unsworth is on the stand being cross-examined by Mr Hawthorne.

Mr Hawthorne (defence): Mr Unsworth, you are some kind of religious leader, are you?

Unsworth: I am Guru to the Universal End-Time Charismatics. Our ashram is on Pitt Street, Rotherham. We have followers internationally throughout the world.

Hawthorne: Now Mr Unsworth, Miss Sylvia Potts, daughter of the defendant in this trial, has claimed that you are the father of her child. Do you dispute this?

Unsworth: No. I am the father of Charmaine Bernadette.

Hawthorne: And is it true that on several occasions you have contacted Miss Potts by telephone and letter, intimating that you wish to have custody of the child?

"Yes, I don't deny it."

"Would you say that your letters could be interpreted as being threatening in any way?"

"I would not."

"What about this one." (Hands witness exhibit 14.) "Did you write this letter to Miss Potts? For the benefit of the jury, it reads: 'The holy child will be reclaimed. You have no right to keep it. We will be getting it back first chance.'"

"No I did not."

"Did you authorise anyone else to write it on your behalf?"

"No I did not."

"What do you think the letter means, Mr Unsworth?"

"I don't know."

"Now, perhaps you can tell us something about your...your organisation. For instance, what are its tenets?"

"Y'what?"

"What exactly is it that you and your followers believe?"

Mr Fishguard (prosecution): I really must object, Your Honour. This is nothing but a crude attempt to ridicule Mr Unsworth's sincerely held beliefs.

Mr Justice Arnott: Mr Fishguard has a point, Mr Hawthorne. Is there some relevance in this line of questioning?

Mr Hawthorne: I believe so, Your Honour. If I may continue for a few more minutes?

Mr Justice Arnott: I will permit you to continue so long as I am assured that it is relevant.

Mr Hawthorne: Now, Mr Unsworth, as I was saying. Your beliefs...

Mr Unsworth: We believe that all religions have an element of truth, but none of them have got it completely right. So we take the truthful bits from each one and incorporate them into our own religion.

Mr Hawthorne: In other words you pick and choose the bits that suit you?

"It is an amalgamation of all that is true from all philosophies of faith."

"From what you say, it seems that you are prepared to believe just about anything."

"We have faith. That's all that is required."

"But faith in what?"

"Faith in what we feel is true."

"And who decides what is true?"

"I do, of course. I'm the guru. They have faith in what I tell them to have faith in. I lead, they follow."

"So if you told your flock, for instance, that Dr Who really existed, they would believe you?"

"Of course they would. That's what faith is all about. It's unquestioning."

"Even if it were patently untrue?"

"Nobody has yet proved that Dr Who does not exist.

There could well be Time Lords in another dimension for all we know. It is arrogant to say something isn't true when you don't know. It is blasphemous to deny revealed truth. Everybody knows that."

(Disturbance from the public gallery)

Mr Justice Arnott: Silence. Silence in the public gallery. I will not have such hysterical displays in my court. If anyone else shouts Hallelujah or shrieks in that manner, I shall have them removed. Continue, Mr Hawthorne.

Hawthorne: Well, I hesitate to lay myself open to charges of blasphemy, Mr Unsworth, and so we will move on. Now tell me, where do you find your recruits? The sort of people who are prepared to believe what you tell them?

Unsworth: They volunteer.

Hawthorne: Is there any truth in newspaper reports that you pick up homeless people from street corners? Is it true that young people in difficulties are particularly targeted by your organisation for recruitment?

"We don't shy away from helping the socially disadvantaged. If they're homeless, we give them somewhere to sleep."

"And the charges that once they are in your 'ashram' you proceed to brainwash them with various techniques that were developed in Moscow during the 1950s. Is there any basis of fact in such reports?"

"Of course not. We simply reveal the truth of our message to those who are interested. There is nothing sinister about our methods."

"And where does the money come from to finance your impressive international operation, Mr Unsworth."

"Donations."

"Donations from whom?"

"Supporters."

"Is it true that you send your followers out with collecting boxes? Are they told to mislead the public by asking for donations for unspecified 'charity work'."

"We do undertake charitable work."

"Such as?" "We have innumerable projects on the go at all times."

"Can you name one?"

"There are too many to go into. Our funds are spread around the globe."

"Including Switzerland?"

"Eh?"

"Miss Sylvia Potts has told us that when you send your followers out collecting, you tell them not to bother coming back if they have amassed less than fifty pounds in a day?"

"That is not true."

"Is it true that you have a personal collection of vintage motor cars valued at over a million pounds?"

Mr Fishguard (prosecution): Objection. What has this to do with the matter in hand, your Honour?

Mr Justice Arnott: I agree with you Mr Fishguard. Objection sustained. Fascinating though it is, please desist from this line of questioning, Mr Hawthorne, and keep your questions relevant to the case we are trying.

Mr Hawthorne: Yes, your Honour. Now, Mr Unsworth, may we ask how you came to have the broken leg you are so unfortunately nursing at the moment?

Unsworth: I fell off the stage of our church during a blessing ceremony.

Hawthorne: You have witnesses to this accident?

Unsworth: Yes, the congregation saw me take this tumble. It was during a Toronto blessing, I got carried away by the occasion, was slain in the spirit and went arse over tit.

Hawthorne: And you say that on the night of the murder of Philip Bolam you were 'meditating' in your room at the ashram? And you never left your room the whole evening?

"That is correct."

"Did anyone see you that night?"

"My personal assistant, the Reverend Eric Crawshaw was with me during that time."

"You refer to Mr Crawshaw as 'Reverend'. May I ask from whom this gentleman received his ordination?"

"I ordained him. The holy spirit passed through me unto him. He thus became a minister of the Universal End-Time Charismatics. The spirit moves within him."

"Is this the same Mr Crawshaw who has subsequently left the country for an unknown destination?"

"I believe he's gone off evangelising."

"Other than Mr Crawshaw, did anyone else see you that night?"

"Several of my flock came to my room that evening for my special blessing. The Stoke Newington blessing, as we call it."

"For the benefit of those of us who are slightly out of touch with modern religious practices and beliefs, could you explain to us exactly what the 'Stoke Newington blessing' is, Mr Unsworth."

"Its aim is to brings people closer to the Great Spirit."

"The Great Spirit?"

"Some call it God, others have no name. As a result of passing into this elevated state, many are slain in the spirit."

"Is it at this point that they fall to the floor howling, screaming and barking like dogs?"

"No, you're confusing it with the Toronto blessing. It's during the Toronto that the congregation can be took in ways that alarm the unsaved. Some speak in tongues, others simply laugh and dance. With these signs and wonders they express their love of the Great Spirit. It can be awesome to behold such total surrender. It's His last great work before the End- Time comes."

"And the Stoke Newington blessing. How does this differ?"

"I introduced the Stoke Newington blessing to my followers after a vision I received while preaching to my flock in the London area. The Stoke Newington is more intimate than the Toronto. It allows me to introduce the Great Spirit into my followers personally on an individual one-to-one basis. The spirit can then go deeper — it is transforming and healing."

"Do you give this blessing to men and women alike?"

"Oh no, only the female members can receive the blessing from me. We do have ministers who can give the blessing to our male members, but there's not a lot of call for it."

"Have you ever given this blessing to a Miss Sandra Baldock?"

"Oh, her."

"Yes, Mr Unsworth — 'her'. Miss Baldock, has told the police that she was one of those privileged to receive your 'Stoke Newington blessing' on the fateful evening when Mr Bolam met his end. In the circumstances, I feel that we need not enquire too closely into the details of this particular benediction, but perhaps, Mr Unsworth, you can confirm that Miss Baldock is also pregnant with your child?"

"I make no secret of the fact that my seed is precious and to receive it is regarded by many women as an honour."

"I see. It may interest you to know, Mr Unsworth, that Miss Baldock told the police that after you had 'anointed' her that evening, the two of you went 'out to the pictures'. Afterwards, she says, you 'went for an Indian' together and did not return until after one-thirty a.m. How do you explain this inconsistency?"

"She's confused. She's got mixed up. I've never been to the pictures with her."

"It might also interest you to know that another lady follower of yours, a Miss Cindy Dewhurst has come forward to tell us that she was also with you on the night of the murder. According to Miss Dewhurst, you were in Manchester together at a night club. Is she mistaken, too?"

"Of course she is mistaken. A lot of these people are three sheets to the wind."

"Your followers you mean?"

"It's misguided loyalty. They just want to help me."

"And are they prepared to perjure themselves to do it? It seems that many of the ladies whom you have invited into your cult are prepared to go to enormous lengths to protect you. Unfortunately, not one of them remembers you falling from a stage. None of them could explain your broken leg, and when they enquired about it, they say that you told them to 'mind their own effing business'."

"They're a lot of stupid women. I told them not to say anything. I told them they'd only make it worse."

"I'm afraid, Mr Unsworth, that I have to go back to the topic of Miss Baldock. Now, you say that she visited you in your room on the night of the 3rd June. You say you — well, let's not beat about the bush, Mr Unsworth — you had intercourse with her — because that is what the Stoke Newington blessing amounts to, isn't it? — and then she left you so that you could continue 'meditating'. Miss Baldock says that after you had — well — you had had sex together, you went to the cinema and then for a meal at an Indian restaurant. Now which of you is telling the truth?"

"I am."

"I put it to you Mr Unsworth, that you were not at the so-called ashram for the whole night on the 3rd June. I put it to you that you were not at the cinema, restaurant or night-club, either. I put it to you, Mr Unsworth that you went to number eleven Evergreen Close that night, with the intention of stealing Miss Sylvia Potts's new-born baby because you felt it belonged to you. I put it to you that you and an accomplice — possibly someone who has now left the country — arranged to break into the Potts' home through a landing window. Unfortunately, when you got on to the landing you were confronted by Mr Philip Bolam, who had gained entrance through the front door. In a panic, the two of you fought, and during this contretemps, you stabbed Mr Bolam."

"No. It was that Potts woman. Everybody knows that."

182

"I suggest, Mr Unsworth, that you then panicked and instead of using the ladder you had brought with you for the purpose, you jumped from the window, injuring your leg as you did so. Your accomplice then assisted you to the waiting car. He then collected the ladder and you drove off."

"No. No, it's not true. I was at the ashram. You can ask anybody."

"We have asked anybody, Mr Unsworth — anybody and everybody, and none of your followers seems capable of coming up with a consistent story. Your brainwashing techniques may work on impressionable young people, but you didn't do a very good job of briefing them, did you?"

"It's all lies. I was nowhere near Evergreen Close that night."

"Mr Unsworth, yesterday I went to the Rotherham District General Hospital and there asked the Casualty Department to check their records for the early hours of 4th June. At approximately four-thirty a.m. a young man calling himself Ronnie Heppenstall was admitted with a broken leg. Mr Heppenstall said that his injuries had been sustained in a road accident. The leg was set, but the young man refused to be admitted to the hospital for observation, although the doctor on duty had explained to him that there could be complications. Are you Ronnie Heppenstall by any chance, Mr Unsworth?" "No."

"It would be a very simple thing to bring the doctor from the hospital to see whether he remembers you, Mr Unsworth. And we could easily check to see when you actually did have your leg first set."

"Yes, all right. I did say I was Ronnie Heppenstall. I didn't want to be recognised. My security person insisted on me having a nom de plume. There's a lot of jealousy in the millenarian movement."

"And you broke your leg that evening while meditating, did you? Or was it as you left the Indian restaurant? Or perhaps you did it dancing in the night-club in Manchester? Come, come, Mr Unsworth. First you tell us that you never left the ashram on the night we are referring to, and now you tell us that you went for hospital treatment. What is the truth, Mr Unsworth?"

"I'm special. I'm a holy person and have a unique dispensation. Truth is relative to a person such as myself."

"And do you feel, Guru, that you have dispensation to murder people?"

"No. No. It was an accident. I didn't murder him. He set about me. I was just protecting myself."

183

Well, that was it — there was uproar in the court, as you can imagine. The reporters thought it was Christmas, New Year and their birthdays all come at once. It was just like you see on the telly when they all go rushing out to phone their editors.

The judge said it was the most extraordinary experience of his career, and he had pleasure in discharging Mam. But no sooner was she out of the court than she was re-arrested on a charge of concealing a body and wilfully impeding a police enquiry.

However, given everything that has gone before, it isn't clear whether the Director of Public Prosecutions is going to proceed with that, and Mam is home again.

You can hardly believe it, but Unsworth's 'flock' have set up a camp outside the prison where their 'master' is being held, pending his own trial. They say he's being persecuted for his religious beliefs. It's just what they needed, a martyr.

Is there no end to people's gullibility? Never mind, we had a fab home-coming celebration. We laid on the Babycham for Mam because we know she loves it.

Dad came out of the hospital — just for the evening — and even managed a smile.

For the first time in my life, I saw Mam and Dad kiss.

That old friend of Mam's, Beryl, who lives next door came, too, just to let everyone know that she had never thought the murder charges were true. Mrs O'Boyle put in an appearance, too, just to reassure Mam that the neighbours weren't all disapproving, and some of them were quite happy that she'd got off with it.

No sign of Mrs Henshaw, though. Mam put the Birdy Song on as loud as she could and then opened the windows in the hope of keeping her up all night. And Mam instructed everybody to slam their car doors as loud as they could as they went home in the early hours.

And there's more. Just as the party was finishing, Bill says to me: "Can we go for a walk, Gary?" I wasn't happy with the idea, but I nodded and we strolled along the road for a bit.

"You've no need to think you'll talk me round, because you won't," I said. "You've hurt me and I'm not going to forgive you. Once all this is over, I'm going to leave Rotherham and go to London and forget all about you."

Go to London! Me! I was talking big, but I'd sooner go to the North Pole than go to London. "That hell-hole" as Mam calls it, and she's not wrong.

He didn't say anything, and we walked along in silence for a few minutes. We were just strolling aimlessly through the deserted industrial estate.

"I know I've behaved badly, Gary," he said. "I've got no excuses for what I've done to you. I'm ashamed. Especially after everything we've shared."

"And now I suppose you think we can still be friends?"

"Can we?"

"No. You can eff off."

We walked a bit longer without saying anything. Then he murmurs: "I was very confused after all that business with the Hindley court case and the eviction. I was at my wit's end."

"So your answer was to turn straight. Ex-gay. Very nice. Bog off."

"I thought that if I made a fresh start things would be better."

"And they weren't?"

"No."

"What a surprise. Particularly when our Sylvia's involved — the woman who gets her children from the planet of the apes."

"I miss you."

"I'll bet you do. If I was shacked up with our Sylvia I think I'd miss a brain tumour."

"I made a mistake."

"And you want to come back to me? Is that it?"

He nodded.

"After you've been with the whore of Babylon herself? You're not shagging me after you've shagged her."

"I haven't shagged her."

"She says different."

"She's lying. I couldn't get it up."

"Eh?"

"I tried, but I just couldn't. It wouldn't rise to the occasion. I just felt sick at the idea. And what that tells me is that I'm not straight. I'm not bisexual. And I hope not to be ex-gay for much longer."

I started to laugh. He started to laugh. We laughed into each other's arms, and he kissed me. It was so good I just stood there and let him. Then I put my arms round his neck and snogged him as though he were a glass of water in the Sahara. I couldn't stop myself.

Terry, I want to thank you for sticking by us through all this. You can't imagine what a comfort it has been to be able to confide in somebody who wasn't involved in it all. Writing them letters to you

185

helped me get a grip on events. I'll keep writing, and I hope you'll keep being my friend.

Your pal,

Gary

* * *

Doreen's Diary 21st July

I'm writing this while sitting on my outdoor patio seating area. The sun is blazing down and I've got a sun frock on with factor eight sloshed all up my arms.

It's many months since I last wrote in my diary, so there's a lot of catching up to do.

It took a long time to get over the drama of the trial last year, but I had the support of my family, and we eventually returned to some resemblance of normality. Derek completed his course of treatment at the hospital — electric shocks through his head. Now he's back home and there are more tablets in the bathroom cabinet than they've got at Boots.

I said to him: "What was this ECT treatment they gave you? It seems to have done you a power of good."

He said: "Oh, they just put these wires to your forehead and electrocute you for five minutes, and when you come round you feel champion."

I said: "Well next time you're feeling miserable, I'll chuck the electric fire in the bath with you and see if that cheers you up."

He's not the jolliest of people, I don't think he ever will be, he just isn't made to be happy. But he's patched it up with his pals at the Trades. They had a whip round for him while he was in the hospital, and sent a message saying that his skills in the darts team were sadly missed. That perked him up.

Our Gary and Bill have also settled their differences (or perhaps I should say their sameness) and have got together again. They've moved into another flat, this time they're buying it and not depending on no landlords for their security.

Our Sylvia is still enthralled by little Charmaine Bernadette, just like I am. She's a child in a million is that babby, but I don't mean that in any supernatural way. I don't think she is in any way specially touched by the hand of God.

It's just that I see her through a grandmother's eyes, which are biased.

And talking of grandmothers — Iris made another miraculous recovery from her coma after the result of the verdict came through.

However, I turned her away at the door when she came back expecting to resume her place here. I said: "No way, Iris, are you getting back on to these premises. I will negotiate visiting rights so that you can have contact with Derek from time to time, but you are not living under this roof again."

She tried to argue, but I think she saw it was fruitless. I just can't trust myself when she's around. Derek reluctantly agreed that she was a bad influence on me, and so she threw herself on the mercy of the council, who have fixed her up with a warden-controlled flat of her own. I said to Derek, I said: "I don't know about a warden, what she needs is an armed guard."

The icing on the cake came when news reached me that Mrs Henshaw had given up her campaign of evicting me from Evergreen Close. There was no part of the law that says a person can be slung out of a house and home that is bought and paid for. So she decided that if you can't take the mountain to Mohammed, then Mohammed has to take the mountain somewhere else. And that is what she's done. She's upped sticks and buggered off. Hopefully to some place where her nasty ideas will be appreciated — Iran or somewhere like that. There's been a much more relaxed atmosphere in the Close since she moved out, almost as though it's been liberated.

We occasionally still get visitors who want to see our Sylvia, who continue to think she's miraculous. I bring them into the front room and let them have half an hour with her.

They soon change their mind.

So, all is going swimmingly. And what I have learned from this is that our Gary has got a point. I'm going to become an Atheist like him. The trouble is, I don't know which church you have to approach for the particulars.

And I want to make a new start. I want to do something that will permit me to put this behind me. I'm sure I can find something.

If you enjoyed *The Potts Papers,*

you will also enjoy its sequel

THE CHIP SHOP WAR

which features Doreen Potts and her family in a new adventure.

Also available from Amazon.

Printed in Great Britain
by Amazon